Published by: GladEye Press
Interior Design: J.V. Bolkan
Cover Design: Sharleen Nelson
ISBN-13: 978-1-951289-21-8

This is a work of fiction. AI was not used in the creation of this book. All names, characters, places, and events are either a product of the human author's imagination or are used fictitiously. Any resemblance to real persons, businesses, organizations, or events are totally unintentional and entirely coincidental.

Printed in the United States of America.
10 9 8 7 6 5 4 3 2 1

The body text is presented in Adobe Jenson Pro 11 point for easy readability. Chapter numbers and chapter titles are presented in the fonts Ethnocentric and Vox, respectively.

The FIRST NOVA I SEE TONIGHT

JASON A. KILGORE

GladEye Press

Dedication

For my lifelong friend, Matt McFarland, a real-life hero.

CHAPTER ONE
Excellentia

Just this one more job, Dirken Nova thought, and I'll get a ship of my own again. He reached into a breast pocket of his leather jacket and rubbed his lucky Rigellian runestone. *Easy money.* He closed his eyes and tried to picture his dream ship, but he kept going back to the last one he had. The *Brilliant*. She had been perfect. Fast. Deadly. For two long years he'd gone without a ship of his own.

Dirken snapped back to reality, focusing on the immaculately clean, white room he shared with his smuggler partner, Yiorgos Ganas, who sat on a cot across from Dirken's. Yiorgos looked down at his cybernetic right arm, adjusting something in his wrist, his head bent in concentration. The entire top of his head and the right side were robotic, including a computerized cranial implant, an auditory implant in the place of a right ear, and a purple-glowing right eye. His vocal cords were replaced with an implant that could translate and reproduce all Terran languages and many alien ones. Both of his legs were robotic, too. Dirken didn't want to think about the accident that led to all of these "upgrades," as Yiorgos put it, but Yiorgos didn't try to hide his cybernetic additions with realistic limbs or lab-grown tissue. Instead, he embraced his identity as an active member of Cyberalia, a religious interplanetary and interspecies network of cyborgs who practiced the ritual of Netfolding.

Yiorgos glanced up, noticing Dirken's gaze. Dirken gave a nod of acknowledgment, then turned his gaze out the little window in the door of the room.

Outside the room was a spacious, well-lit corridor. A yeoman with curly blond hair and slim physique stood outside, having been assigned to "assist" them. Dirken knew full well, though, that the captain had put him there to watch over them. The yeoman looked back and gave a nervous nod, his pale blue eyes registering something other than just professional courtesy. Recognition? Dirken had never seen him before this mission.

"The sooner we reach our destination the better," Yiorgos said, his voice tinged with a metallic rasp. "This gig is fishier than a vat full of Proximan eels."

"Don't worry about it. Nothing can go wrong. We're sitting near the bridge of a United Worlds starship—a destroyer, in fact. No one would dare attack this ship, and no crew would defy the captain."

Yiorgos shook his head and returned his attention to his wrist. "I still don't like it. The sooner we can get this safe box to Nüwa the better."

They both glanced down to the safe that they had been paid to escort. The nondescript metal safe box had an old-fashioned alphanumeric keypad lock on its door and a handle bolted to the top. Dirken continued, "Escort it from Earth to Nüwa, don't open it or let anyone touch it or scan it, and hand it over to the Nüwan ambassador undamaged. Simple."

"Well, at least we have more comfortable bunks than the last job."

Dirken looked away. He hated being on UW starships. Most people thought of them as works of art. Sleek. Silvery. Wide beam. Not a straight edge or sharp corner to be found. Seeing them in orbit was like watching the flexing arm muscles of a fucking gigantic chrome robot.

Inside, each section was wide and well-lit. Feng shui ruled the decks. Wood was used wherever possible. Plants graced the corners. Large screens broadcast video and audio of vibrant forests, babbling streams, and windswept mountaintops. The entire ship was like some sort of corporate lobby.

Worse yet, the philosophy extended to the entire crew. All UW uniforms were matching, white, and clean. Prompt haircuts. A shower every day. Personal grooming was mandated, right down to cleaning their fingernails. Everything was timed, with ship-wide chimes and notifications. Twice each Sol day—at each shift change—there was a mandatory group stretching and aerobic exercise in the Commons.

Plus, when ships of the "Silver Fleet" arrived at their destination, scores of smaller private ships flew out to meet them in orbit and escorted each ship to the surface. They landed like ballerinas, the crew parading down the gangplank like goddamned dignitaries.

And every single member of the crew was human. It shouldn't be called the United Worlds, Dirken thought. More like the United Human Worlds. Even though the three UW planets, Earth, Nüwa, and Tesla, were majority human, or Terran, and officially speaking the Terran language, alien species were quickly growing in numbers due to immigration and reproduction—and accusing the UW of discriminatory policies—and were now the majority on the various UW offworld mining operations. The other worlds were no longer dependent upon Earth for support and feeling the economic drain from supporting their "parent" planet simply for cultural reasons. Where there's imbalance, there's war and corruption, he thought, and that means profits!

Though it hadn't come to war, yet, there was an ever-growing secessionist movement on both Nüwa and Tesla, with public protests, insurrectionist cells, and even terror attacks. They were self-sustaining worlds, and their economies had overtaken that of Earth. Why be tied to the old homeworld, with its climate-ravaged deserts, cities swallowed by rising oceans, and populations grown fractured by old animosities that, somehow, hadn't carried over to the new worlds? It was all so … *profitable*, honestly, for a smuggler like himself.

For this mission, at least, he and Yiorgos had to suffer through an entire flight from Earth to Nüwa—three Earth days and five hundred light years of stifling uniformity and perfection—onboard the United Worlds destroyer, *Excellentia*.

Then he reminded himself again of the money he and Yiorgos were earning. Seven-hundred thousand UW chits! Added to their savings, it was enough to purchase a gleaming new interstellar Corsair or Corvette from the shipyards on Rockmir.

The thought brought him back around to his last ship. Technically a clipper originally built in the Mars shipyards, the *Brilliant* had been everything the *Excellentia* wasn't. Utilitarian. Efficient. He didn't give a shit about Feng Shui. Parts inside and outside of her had been cobbled together from half a dozen other ships from as many solar systems, each part making it deadlier, faster, or better-defended. Outside were plasma jet engines and expanded gravwell panels, railguns, and a ten-petawatt laser cannon. A pair of Argolan mini-missile arrays had festooned the surface. And inside, the smells of ionized plasma and the sweat of years of tense situations mixed with the exotic scents of distant planets. Yes. And a crew of four besides him and Yiorgos, plus or minus the occasional adventurer. No chimes or schedules or fucking fake scenery on the screens. The crew could be themselves. Laughing, drinking, cussing, and gambling. Every centimeter of the ship served an important purpose without some decorative effect added to it. And the *Brilliant* was so fast, he could pick up an illicit load and transport it halfway to the other side of the quadrant before any UW ship or planetary militia could figure out it was missing.

But that dream had ended too soon. When the Pleiades Syndicate had found the *Brilliant* near Rorgos, and Dirken had refused to give them a share of his cargo of illegal Rigellian cloner modules, the resulting firefight didn't quite go his way. They crash-landed her on Rorgos. Two dead right away. Another two died during the five months of being stranded on that fiery planet, dodging lava flows and surviving earthquakes, until they had finally been rescued. Since then, there had been odd jobs as security to anyone willing to pay, trading legitimate commodities, and the occasional smuggling of illicit goods. He and Yiorgos led a vagabond life.

But this job! This took the cake. "What are you thinking about?" Yiorgos asked, looking over at him with one human eye and one mechanical one. The human eye blinked; the mechanical one didn't. It used to unsettle him a little when that happened.

Dirken cleared his throat and looked away. "Who says I'm thinking about anything?"

"You're doing that thing again," he said. "Moving your mouth as you soundlessly talk to yourself. Eyes glazed over." He looked down to Dirken's hip. "Hand on your blaster."

Dirken chuckled and took his hand off his weapon, a Gree-tech singlehanded pulse emitter with duel fusion batteries. It was outlawed on the UW worlds—not because the blast was strong enough to blow a hole through eight-centimeter carbon-inconel plates with its plasma pulses, but because the fusion batteries were unstable and potentially explosive. Yet for the right service, such as running a load of unregistered uranium ore from the outer mining colonies, the Gree were still willing to trade for a few blasters.

"This job," Dirken said, flashing a confident smile. "Look at us. All we have to do is sit here and guard that safe box. Then we go buy a new ship!"

Yiorgos huffed. "We would have had enough by now if you hadn't screwed up the weapons deal with the Free Sisters of Luhman 16, Dirk. Couldn't keep your dick in your pants, could you?"

Dirken tensed his brow. "Well how the hell was I to know the Queen's daughter was still underage … at *eighty-six?*"

Yiorgos threw out his hand, the mechanical wrist interface whirring as he did so. "She didn't have her fifth neck-tentacle! Everyone knows Luhmanians don't reach adulthood until they grow the fifth one."

Dirken rolled his eyes. "Stupid star system, anyhow. I'd question the sanity of any species that wants to live in orbit around a brown dwarf. That fucking star wreaked havoc on our magnetic systems."

Yiorgos just shook his head and leaned back on his cot.

In addition to what they earned on this gig, there were people who still owed them plenty. Fellow smuggler, 'TakTrak, for instance. *That birdbrain owes me ten thousand UW chits,* Dirken thought.

They were in a small storage room just off the bridge, not even the normal berth that would be given to the crew, much less passengers. *Could be worse,* Dirken thought. *They could have shoved us in the corner of a cargo hold like on that freighter for the last Rigel job.* It was obvious that the captain wanted to keep a close eye on them and the safe box.

He looked again at the safe and wondered for the millionth time what was in it. For gigs like this one, the best course of action was not to ask, and it was clear at the outset that he wasn't going to get an answer if he did. They were due to arrive at Nüwa in just a day, deliver the safe box, and be on their way. Easy money.

But a niggling doubt kept scratching at the back of his mind. Maybe too easy.

CHAPTER TWO
Gravjump Six

The ship's intercom chimed for shift change, then the first mate's gravelly voice piped through. "All crew, prepare for Gravjump Six." This would be the sixth of eight jumps that it would take to get to Nüwa, with periods of slower-than-light flight between each jump point.

Yiorgos cupped his hands in his lap, then a small projector in his cheek implant sprung to life and projected a bluish sphere into his hands. The sphere changed, turning from transparent blue light to a darker blue and gray, rotating, and materializing. A tracery of golden lines and swirls rippled across it, shimmering, taking on intricate shapes. The "Sphere of Unity."

This was the Ritual of Netfolding, practiced by cyborgs like Yiorgos who had cerebral implants, and a central component of the Cyberalia network. It was a form of meditation where they probed their inner neural network, their natural brain and their digital "neurosphere"—cleansing themselves of immorality and spiritual inefficiencies and connecting both minds into one. Masters claimed to be able to completely separate the two minds on command or to perform feats of intellect far surpassing their theoretical limitations, all for the purpose of achieving a new "awakening." Netfolding was supposed to be performed at least once a day by adherents. Yiorgos usually did it twice.

Dirken didn't believe in such religious mumbo jumbo. Every culture had its wacko religions, even cyborg culture. The closest thing Dirken had to religion was his sense of freedom.

All the talk about the Luhmanian Queen's daughter had gotten him aroused. He glanced over toward Yiorgos to see that his partner was meditating, then he reached into his pack. Rifling past a change of clothes, food packages, and a couple of Martian ales, he pulled out a tablet and headband. Accessing his extensive alien porn collection on the tablet, he found a particularly titillating vid title, *D'bee Does Dracorda*. One of his favorites.

Dirken eagerly donned the silvery headband and clicked on the tablet link. The headband came alive with vibrations and beamed the video directly to his brain and all five senses for a full sensual experience. Immediately he found himself standing in the hibernation chamber, cocoon swings hanging from the low ceiling and warm, steamy waters swirling around the edges of the room, making the chamber a sauna. A door opened, and in stepped a Pleiadean male. Faun-like, covered in brown fur and with feet that were hooves, he wore only a loincloth. "Oh dear," the Pleiadean said, scratching at the mass of tiny horns on his head, "I think I'm lost." The squeaking Pleiadean language had been dubbed into Terran.

Teslan disco music started up and one of the cocoons parted. A reptilian leg, green and scaly, stepped out. Then an arm. Then out slipped a large Reptiloc woman, her iguana-like head opening to show rows of sharp teeth. "Lost, you say?" she asked, also dubbed. Her hands ran down her tight abdomen to a bikini bottom. "You poor man. I'm D'bee. Let me comfort you."

The Pleiadean's eyes opened wide in fear, but his loincloth betrayed a growing erection.

The Reptiloc woman slipped off her bikini and laid back into the cocoon. She opened her legs and revealed her cloaca between, wide and wet, with three folds of light green, fleshy lips, running horizontally between scales. She slipped a three-fingered hand down to it and rubbed it. The lips turned from green to a vibrant red as they engorged. The disco music grew louder and more urgent. Dirken smelled the musky scent of her pheromones.

"Well, maybe just a quickie," the Pleiadean said, letting his loincloth drop and revealing his throbbing white penis and overlarge, furry testicles.

"Oh yes," the Reptiloc woman moaned, opening her legs wider and inserting a thick finger into herself, claw and all.

The Pleiadean stepped over to the cocoon swing, between her legs, and entered her with a ..."

"Hey!" Yiorgos shouted.

Dirken was shaken out of his revelry, then pulled off the headband to look at the cyborg, annoyed. "What?"

"Get your hands out of your pants and stop watching porn. You know I don't want to see that shit. I'm trying to meditate here. Find somewhere else to masturbate!"

Dirken huffed in annoyance and put the tablet and glasses back in his pack. He stood, straightened his leather jacket, and adjusted his holster. "Fine. I need a change of scenery anyway." After touching a glowing contact, the door slid open and he stepped outside into a corridor that overlooked the bridge.

He bumped into the curly headed yeoman.

"Sorry, sir!" the yeoman said.

Dirken grimaced in annoyance. "Maybe don't stand in front of the fucking door?"

"Is there something you need, sir?"

"No. And we don't need a yeoman chaperone."

He just grinned back and blinked innocently ... and didn't leave. "A drink, perhaps?" He gestured with his arm as he said it.

Dirken noticed an odd scar on the man's wrist, a small "A" no bigger than a thumbnail branded into his skin.

Dirken shook his head in exasperation and turned away, stepping the short distance to the ship's bridge and command center.

There were two levels to the bridge. The upper level was where the captain and first mate presided, along with other principal officers. The lower level held the secondary officers: navigators, engineers, sensor techs, medical, and weapons specialists. Both levels looked out over a wide bank of windows made of transparent aluminum, like all the windows of the ship. Dirken stood at an entrance to the lower level.

Most of the officers were busy at their workstations, but some of them glanced his way, then back to their consoles. The glance was enough to gauge their opinions: he was a civilian interloper on a military vessel: in the way, out of place, and not fit for a uniform.

Captain Chen looked down from the upper bridge railing at him and narrowed her eyes as if to say "you shouldn't be here." She started to open her mouth but was interrupted.

"Commander," a navigation lieutenant said to the first mate, a white-haired man named Prasad who stood next to the captain. A hologram of navigation charts floated in front of the navigator. "Gravwell engines are ready. Awaiting your command."

The first mate gave a glance to the captain, then turned back to the navigator. "Proceed with Gravjump Six." It was clear from the look Captain Chen gave him that Prasad was trusted.

"Aye," the navigator said. "Proceeding with Gravjump Six." Then he relayed a series of coordinates and pressed a button. A pleasant, double-note tone sounded through the ship, notifying the crew that it was proceeding, then he slowly pulled on a lever.

This was Dirken's favorite part. It was the action that made him fall in love with space in his early youth, a foundling with tattered clothes and dirty hands who had sneaked into the cabin of his refugee ship and experienced, for the first time, a gravity jump, or "gravjump," from one part of space to another.

From deep in the ship came a low roar as a vastly powerful Jacobian gravwell generator in the guts of the craft initiated a nano Einstein-Rosen bridge—a tiny black hole or "gravity well"—which warped space around them and the gravwell panels on the outside of the ship.

He turned his eyes to the windows and watched as the wide vista of stars seemed to accelerate their twinkle. The stars on the periphery of the view appeared to move slowly away, but if he looked directly at them, it was the other stars that seemed to move. A split second later, they all puckered into the middle of his view, then exploded back outward again in a brilliant rainbow flash. When the flash ended, new stars appeared. And off to the right, a fantastic nebula resplendent in clouds of blue and red. There wasn't so much as a tremor as the ship folded through space to its new location.

"Sir!" shouted a sensors lieutenant. "Multiple contacts off both port and starboard."

It wasn't unusual for ships to congregate near jump points, but something about the lieutenant's voice told Dirken something was off.

First Mate Prasad commanded, "Identify."

The lieutenant replied, "Two brigantines, a Corvette, and a swarm of small contacts from each of the brigs, sir. None of the ships have identifier transponders; they're running dark." Then another crewman added, "Their specs conform to vessels associated with pirates."

"Battle stations," Captain Chen said. "Spin up the gravwell engines as soon as possible."

An alarm rang through the corridors on the ship-wide intercom. Dirken knew the crew would be running either to battle stations or interior safe rooms and readying the medical bay for casualties.

In the bridge, the various officers exchanged looks of alarm, eyes wide, but they kept their mouths shut. Up in the command deck, the captain and her commanding officers kept a steely gaze.

"Focus on the small contacts and identify," Prasad said.

"Fleas, sir!" came the response a moment later. "Approximately two hundred of them. Other contacts closing."

Fleas. Dirken knew very well what they were up against, as surely as the captain and first mate would know. Small attack drones, each only as large as a serving platter, equipped with simple propulsion and either cutting lasers or tiny bombs. Some were automated, some were remote controlled, but they served only one real purpose in a situation like this: a swarm of hundreds or even thousands would descend upon the critical outer parts of a ship and cut them to ribbons, disabling the ship, or cutting holes in the hull to depressurize. Only flak cannons or EMP burst emitters were effective against a swarm.

"Shut the blast screens and open fire!" the captain shouted, and a metal shield came down over the bridge windows.

Dirken didn't wait around any longer. He stepped back to the supply room. The yeoman, wide-eyed, seemed lost. "Sir, maybe you should …" Dirken ignored him and entered the room, closing the door behind him.

"What's going on?" Yiorgos asked. He'd shut off his Netfolding projection.

"It's an attack. Two brigs and a corvette just launched fleas."

"Mafia?"

"Not their style. Probably pirates."

"Against a destroyer?! Which pirates? Coros the Dark? Or do you think it's the Ursan, Dn'tors?"

Dirken scratched at the stubble on his chin. "Too close to Earth for Coros. And last I heard, Dn'tors had the weeping pox. No, I think this may be the Gleeza twins, or perhaps the pirate known as the Bloodhawk. Word on Mars was that he's in this region, but I don't know much about him."

"Never heard of him," Yiorgos said. "But whoever it is, they've got balls. Even if they succeed, they'll have the whole Silver Fleet hunting them down. I doubt there's much cargo aboard. They must want the weapons tech."

Dirken heard plasma cannons discharging from a distant part of the ship. Then hundreds of ominous bangs rang out as fleas made contact with the hull.

"Clearly they're desperate for something," Dirken replied.

He wondered, *What the hell could be so important that it would warrant attacking a United Worlds destroyer?*

They looked at each other then both turned their eyes to the safe box.

CHAPTER THREE
Space Pirates

"Stay with the safe box," Dirken said as he armed his blaster and checked the charges. He stepped out of the room. The blond yeoman reached out. "Sir, you should stay in the …"

Dirken waved him off. "Shut it, pipsqueak," he said without looking back, and left him behind.

Dirken peered around the corner at the bridge. The command center was alive with organized action.

"Rear Array 2 immobilized!" shouted one weapons specialist.

"Brigantine One now 1.2 kilometers and closing," said a sensor technician.

"Hull perforation on Engineering Deck 3," said an engineer. The holographic display beside her showed the destroyer in blue miniature glowing light with red splotches across its hull and a blinking red area on the back of the third deck.

"An armed shuttlecraft has detached from the corvette," said a navigator, looking up at a holo display that showed each of the four ships and a smaller vessel breaking away from one of the larger ones. "It could be a boarding party."

Other readouts were projected in the air over each action station, and viewscreens on every side of the room showed schematics and navigation charts.

"Status on gravwell spin-up?" Captain Chen shouted.

"Fifteen minutes."

"Notify UW command that we have been attacked and that we need backup."

"Aye, Captain!"

Just then the ship was rocked by an explosion, momentarily disrupting the gravity flooring. Dirken felt his body lift from the floor ever so slightly until he was on his toes, then the gravity came back on and he thumped back down.

"Status?" First Mate Prasad demanded.

"That was Auxiliary Propulsion Tank 2," replied an engineer. "But the explosion damaged the leads for Thruster 18 and took out the primary grav plating generator. Running on the backup generator, now."

"Concentrate fire on the shuttlecraft," said the captain to weapons control.

"Which one? There's a second launched from Brigantine Two."

"Both, then. Time until the shuttles reach us?"

"About ten minutes at current velocity," replied the navigator.

"Weapons array 2 is offline," shouted a weapons specialist. "Ma'am, the fleas are now concentrating on the hangar."

Dirken had heard enough. The pirates knew their stuff. They were targeting weapons and engines and would soon try to get the boarding parties from the shuttlecraft to the hangar. He started to turn, then heard a phrase that left his blood cold.

"Sir! Bogeys inbound! Light torpedoes. Ten … No, twelve."

"Evasive action! Release countermeasures!"

Dirken stepped back into the storage room and said to Yiorgos. "Torpedoes inbound!"

Yiorgos's eyes widened and he jumped up, the servos in his mechanical knees whining.

"Wait …" Dirken said. *Something didn't add up. Why would they bother with boarding parties if they just want to destroy us?*

Then he realized. He turned and ran back to the bridge, Yiorgos yelling, "Where are you going?" behind him.

"… ten seconds," shouted the sensor specialist, in the bridge.

"Captain! Commander!" Dirken yelled. She and the first mate turned. "I don't think those are torpedoes."

"Go back to guarding your cargo, Mr. Nova," First Mate Prasad said.

"Inbound, five seconds!" cried the specialist.

"They're not trying to destroy us," Dirken said, "or they wouldn't bother with the fleas and boarding party. Those aren't torpedoes. They're *barrage* bots!"

And then they hit. The hull resounded with an echoing boom. Air hissed through vents as some chamber of the ship was depressurized, then abruptly stopped as the ventilation system closed off. Warning lights went off on numerous consoles across the bridge.

"Four made it through," shouted an engineer, the holo of the ship now considerably more red. "Decks 2, 3, and 4 punctured on starboard side!"

Dirken explained. "They launch like a torpedo and, once puncturing the hull, they turn into hunter droids."

"On the main monitor!" First Mate Prasad said. The front wall showed an image of one of the punctured hull points. Two crew members went flying past, pulled into the vacuum of space. But in the center of the field, just inside the ripped hull, something else moved. Something metallic. First one limb, then another, and then the human-sized, spider-like robot stood, turned its half-dozen red eyes toward the camera, and skittered off-screen.

"Sir! Security has engaged the droids," said an officer.

Multiple screens showed the action. One droid, partially damaged, whipped around the security officers, slicing off a leg, cutting a throat, chopping a pulse rifle in half. It moved so fast that the guards hardly had time to react before they were cut down and left to die and the bots went to the next area.

"Secure and lock all bulkhead doors!" Captain Chen said.

Another principal officer put his hand on the Captain's shoulder. "The crew will be trapped in there with them!"

Captain Chen glanced downward and bit her lip, but then looked up again without a word to him. She touched a panel. "All crew," she said over the comm, "we have been boarded. Arm and shelter in place! Repeat, we have been boarded. Arm and shelter in place!"

Dirken had had enough. He went back to the storage room. The yeoman had produced a mini blaster and looked at Dirken with wild, frightened eyes. Dirken stormed past him into the room.

"These morons will get us killed!" Dirken said to Yiorgos. He threw his pack over his shoulder, then he grabbed the safe box by the handle and grunted as he hefted it. "Damn, this is heavy." Then he added. "Hunter droids are loose on the ship. Come on!"

"And just where do you think we're going?" Yiorgos asked. He extended his prosthetic right hand and transformed his forearm into a plasma saber. The long, curving blade hummed, then the edge glowed with a molten blue plasma field.

"The hangar." He looked around the corner then bolted past the yeoman toward the bridge exit.

"Sir! You can't go that way!" the yeoman warned. "Go back to the room. I'll … I'll protect you!"

"Beat it, kid," Dirken said, and pushed the yeoman aside. "That popgun of yours won't do shit against a hunter droid."

The yeoman followed them anyhow.

"The hangar?" Yiorgos said. "But that may take us right into the boarding party!"

"Right," Dirken said. "The last place they'd look for us." He touched a panel and leapt through the door. "Don't worry, I've got a plan."

"Oh, shit. Here we go. That's what you said before we crashed on Rorgos. Cost me another two limbs, in case you forgot!"

"Oh, I can't forget, as often as you remind me!"

The ship rocked again as something else exploded. Crewmen ran past them, eyes rolling in terror.

In moments, Dirken and Yiorgos reached a secured bulkhead. Two security guards were by the door, blasters in hand.

"We need to get through," Dirken said.

The guard on the right, a lanky fellow with a face that had taken a punch or two, grimaced and said, "Go back to your station."

From behind the door came a distant, muted scream. The guards tensed.

"No, really. We *have* to get through!"

"Look, pal," said the one on the left, a short fellow with a barrel chest. "No one's going in or out. Go back!" A light on the side of his blaster flashed red, the most powerful setting.

More screams from behind the door. Something metallic crashed against the bulkhead.

"I think we'd better listen to them," Yiorgos muttered to Dirken.

Dirken huffed in exasperation. "Fine. Come on."

The yeoman tried to follow, but the lanky guard pulled him back. "You!" he said, "You're with us."

"What?" the young man said, but he was pulled roughly back by the guard. The yeoman looked at Dirken and Yiorgos, his face a mask of desperation, then dropped his eyes to stare at the safe box, seeming to resolve himself.

Just as Dirken and Yiorgos turned to go back, there came a bang against the bulkhead and then the side of it started glowing, first orange, then red, then white hot.

The left guard tapped a comm panel on his arm. "Commander, they're cutting through the starboard bridge bulkhead door."

Dirken grabbed Yiorgos and they ran down the hall. But instead of going back to the storage room they'd been assigned, he stopped at a panel marked "mechanical access." He tried to open it, but it was locked. He pointed at a touchpad next to it. "Yiorgos, can you hack into this?"

The cyborg looked at it, transformed his right forearm from the plasma saber back into a hand, then extended a wire from his right wrist. "I know what you're thinking," he said, "and it's stupid."

"What? It's a good plan! Climb up into the ventilation system and make our way back to the hangar."

"Yeah," Yiorgos said as he inserted the wire into a small port on the pad. "But you seem to forget that the ventilation system is the first to evacuate into space when the hull is compromised."

"They've already compartmentalized it, or we'd all be dead already." Dirken glanced back down the hallway, where a explosive CLANG announced that the bulkhead door had been destroyed. Blaster fire echoed down the corridor.

The touchpad gave a pleasant chime and the wood panel slid open to reveal a mechanical input and a ladder. Dirken hefted the safe box inside and they stepped in after it.

No sooner had the panel closed than they heard screams from the guards and the echo of metallic legs skittering through the corridor.

Dirken opened the mechanical panel and pulled out some oxygen masks and mini-canisters, which they strapped to their belts.

Luckily, the access was lit by tiny blue lights, and they climbed upward into a tight service tube with other pipes and a ventilation shaft running along it until it stopped at a closed iris at the bulkhead.

"Need you to hot-wire a panel again, partner," Dirken said, readjusting the pack over his shoulder.

"Mmm," Yiorgos replied, pulling out the wire from his wrist again and crawling past Dirken to the iris. "That's what I am to you, eh? A lockpick set?"

"Only the *best* lockpick set!"

In moments the iris opened. Air rushed past them into the access tube beyond, drawn by some poorly sealed leak in the system after hull decompression. The little lights along these tubes flickered on and off, but it was enough to see by, so they continued down the tube.

More blaster fire and screams came from behind them, muted through distance and walls. The bridge, he thought. *The droids made it to the bridge. We'd probably be dead now if we'd stayed put.*

Dirken banged his head on a pipe and grunted, rubbing it. "You know, my Uncle Bradley once told me, 'Boy, I used to be afraid of tight spaces. Then one day I realized that we all came from the womb and passed through a tight tube to get out. Then we spend the rest of our lives tryin' to get back into one!'" He chuckled.

Yiorgos groaned. "Yeah, I met your uncle after the previous Mars trip. He's every bit the demented pervert you are."

Dirken's smile faded. "Well, what do you know? You're asexual, what with your religion and all."

"It's not a religious thing; there's no prohibition against sex for practitioners of Cyberalia. I'm asexual because that's who I am, and there's nothing wrong with that."

Dirken couldn't really understand. How could someone not feel sexual? To him, it was just part of being alive. Hell, he'd had sex for almost as long as he'd been able to get an erection. But then, who was he to argue? Some people couldn't understand why he was a xenophile, attracted to aliens, either. "Each to their own, partner."

Both threw themselves to the floor of the access tube as the air exploded in a cacophony of ripping metal and screams. It came from somewhere ahead of them. The two glanced at each other in silent agreement on what to do next. Dirken pulled his blaster. Yiorgos turned his arm back into a plasma saber.

The attack only lasted a few seconds, followed by an eerie quiet punctuated by a dying moan and the sizzle and pop of high voltage wires. After a moment more of silence, Dirken and Yiorgos inched forward as quietly as they could.

The tube turned left and, turning the corner, Dirken saw that the access tube had been ripped away. Electrical lines sparked where they had been yanked apart, and the room below was dark save for dozens of cut fiber-optic lines glimmering in the debris and a vidscreen displaying a lovely tropical waterfall, which kept blinking in and out. There was no way to get across without descending into the room.

And something was moving down there.

Metal on metal. A spidery shape stepped out of the shadows, its numerous, titanium legs reflecting the blinking vidscreen. Half a dozen red eyes on the hunter droid's head turned one way, then the other, as it stepped across debris and the ghostly outlines of bodies in white uniforms.

CHAPTER FOUR

Hunter Droids

Dirken aimed carefully and pulled the trigger. A bolt of white-hot plasma hit the droid squarely in the middle of its red eyes.

The droid reacted immediately, spinning and leaping up toward them. Dirken threw himself out of the tube to avoid the droid. Yiorgos slashed with his plasma saber. Made contact with a leg. Severed it. The leg fell to the floor next to Dirken and started flopping around, a razor-sharp metal blade at the end slicing through the air just centimeters from his head.

Dirken released a couple more shots, missing the spinning droid, then fell back with the safe box toward the vidscreen.

The droid activated its laser, a thin red line that slashed across the room in an arc, barely missing Dirken's arm and cutting through the vidscreen, destroying it.

The room went pitch black except for Yiorgos's blue-glowing saber blade, which swiped downward at the droid as Yiorgos jumped from the tube onto its back, stabbing down into the body of it. Sparks flew as the plasma cut into the titanium alloy, silhouetting the whipping of the droid's remaining arms.

Dirken didn't know where to aim, and he didn't want to hit Yiorgos. But then he heard a slap and the sound of something heavy hitting a wall and a grunt that could only be his partner, away from the metallic sounds of the droid. So he aimed and fired a double tap at the sound of the bot. The two plasma bolts hit their target on a leg and in the head.

The droid stumbled, then half-dragged itself toward Dirken. Dirken backed into a wall, then fired twice more. The first missed widely. The second found its mark.

There was an initial burst from the bolt, then the droid stopped moving as some inner power unit detonated in a bright green flash, catching fire and burning with green and blue flame. Two of its eyes were still glowing faintly, but it didn't move. The room quickly filled with an acrid smoke, activating the fire suppression system, but only a sprinkling of the foamy suppressant flew out of the sprinklers, having no doubt been used up elsewhere. Blobs of the white foam splattered over Dirken and everything else in the room. It didn't do anything to put out the fire.

Still aiming his blaster toward the bot, Dirken quickly stepped across the debris to Yiorgos. The cyborg was sitting up, his back against a wall, his human hand rubbing the top of his head

"You okay?" Dirken asked.

"Yeah. But I think it dented my skullcap."

Dirken helped him to his feet. "Let's get back into the tubes." He found his pack, which had been dropped at some point, and slipped it back over his shoulder.

"Wait a moment," Yiorgos said. He deactivated his saber, turning it back into a hand, and stepped over to the droid.

"Careful."

Yiorgos knelt next to the eyes of the droid, examining it in the flickering green light of the flames, then opened a small hatch under the "chin" of the bot.

"What are you doing?" Dirken asked. He walked over and picked up the safe box. Hopefully, whatever was inside was still intact.

"Getting the control frequency." The cyborg extended an access cord from his arm and tried to plug it into a port in the hatch. "Ugh. Old tech. Old UW military tech, no less." He fiddled with the access cord for a moment, attaching something to the end, then tried again, this time successfully plugging in. Yiorgos tilted his head and gave a couple quick blinks, then said, "I'm in."

"Your hacking ability never ceases to amaze me."

"I'm no AVA."

"Ava?"

"AVA, an ancient hacking AI that nearly started an interplanetary war after hacking into every major computer system on Earth a thousand years ago." He waved his hand as if shooing a fly. "Never mind. Long story."

An explosion rang through the ship, and Dirken felt the floor shudder. "How long is this going to take?"

"Patience." Telltale tics of Yiorgos's head indicated a download in action. Dirken heard shouting and more shots fired from somewhere just outside the room.

"Okay, got it," Yiorgos said, and extracted the cord as Dirken holstered his blaster and positioned himself under the tube opening on the other side of the room.

"How's that supposed to help us?" Dirken asked, cupping his hands to give Yiorgos a boost up.

The cyborg sighed as if it was supposed to be obvious. "You said there's a boarding party coming, right?"

"Right." Dirken boosted Yiorgos up to the tube, and his partner then pulled himself up and offered his cyborg hand down toward Dirken. Dirken passed the safe box up to him, grunting as he lifted it over his head.

"Well, they don't want the hunter droids attacking *their own crew*, right? Or other droids." Yiorgos continued. "They must have transponders on them that match the control frequency of the droid and keep them from attacking. We can mimic that frequency."

Dirken grabbed Yiorgos's hand and was pulled roughly up to the tube. He slapped Yiorgos on the back. "You're a genius. Can you activate it to protect us?"

They turned and continued on all fours with the safe box through the tube toward the back of the ship. "Well," Yiorgos said. "I can protect myself. You don't have a transponder built into your chest, I assume. But if you stick close to me, it's probably just as good." He glanced at Dirken as a wry smile on his lips. "Probably."

They continued in silence for many long minutes, passing through two different tube junctions. One had been sealed off to a branch, likely due to another depressurized cabin, but Dirken didn't figure that was the way they needed. At the second junction they heard the pulsing reverberation of heavy rifle fire below them, ending suddenly with a scream that sent a shiver up his spine. The access tubes filled with a white smoke and the smell of burning plastic, so both of them reached to their belts, unclipped the oxygen masks they'd grabbed at the entrance, and slipped them over their faces. The hiss of oxygen was a welcome relief. Dirken hadn't bothered to check that the mini-cannister was actually full.

From the direction they were heading, they heard a heavy grinding and motor sound echoing in some large chamber. Air rushed past them through the tube in that direction, ruffling Dirken's hair and whistling around the bend until they heard the grinding motor sound again. He guessed they were hearing the hangar doors opening and closing, and the rush of air was from the return of atmosphere to the hangar bay.

"I think the boarding party has entered the hangar," Dirken said. "We must be very close now."

And indeed, within a couple minutes they came to an end to the tube where a vent grating and open iris met a ladder down to an access panel.

Dirken peeked through the grating. Below, two shuttles painted with crimson streaks sat side-by-side in a large hangar with a hunter droid stationed next to them, its eyes scanning across the chamber. As he watched, the shuttlecraft hatches slid open and a party of rough-looking pirates of different species exited, their bodies covered with a mishmash of black leather, bits of armor, and swatches of blood-red clothes, bandannas, and face paint.

"The Bloodhawk's crew," Dirken whispered. He looked at Yiorgos. "Come on. I've got a plan." He climbed down the ladder, followed by his partner. They worked together to manhandle the safe box down the ladder, careful not to bang it against the walls.

"What's the plan, Dirk?" Yiorgos activated his plasma saber again once they got to the bottom.

Dirken unholstered his blaster and checked the charge. Enough for about a dozen shots.

"That droid's, um, what did you call it? Control frequency? Can you jam it?"

Yiorgos blinked in surprise. "If I jam it, I won't be able to protect us!"

Dirken opened the access hatch a crack and looked out at the boarding party. There were maybe twenty pirates making their way toward the hangar entrance. "Yeah, but it won't protect *them*, either!"

"Ah!" He tilted his head, blinked as he accessed some internal computer, then said, "Okay, here goes."

The hunter droid next to the shuttles suddenly stood, turned its head, and fired its laser toward the boarding party. The pirates yelled in confusion and screamed in pain. A hail of plasma fire. The droid skittered and whirled toward them.

"Yes!" Dirken shouted. "Come on!"

They bolted through the access panel and ran toward the closest shuttlecraft. At least one of the pirates, a Pleiadean with a mass of twisted horns surrounding his angular head, shouted and pointed at Dirken and Yiorgos, but none of the other pirates reacted. They were too busy defending themselves against the droid. As Dirken entered the shuttlecraft he saw the droid rip into the pirates, the floor plating beneath them quickly turning shades of red and blue and purple from their flowing blood as they scattered and fired wildly.

Yiorgos closed the access hatch as Dirken set the safe box down and started the thruster engines. Still warm, they roared into action and the ship hovered.

The cyborg took a seat in the navigator's chair as Dirken fired the prow laser at the other shuttlecraft, slicing through the shuttlecraft's windshield and control panels at nearly point-blank range and rendering the ship useless. He then turned further, facing the hangar doors.

The shuttlecraft rocked as plasma bolts hit it from behind.

"Seems the droid didn't get them all," Yiorgos said.

"No worries." Dirken found the hangar door code already entered in the navchart from when the shuttlecraft entered. "How the hell did they get the hangar code for a United Worlds destroyer?" They exchanged surprised looks, but this was no time to ponder it.

Dirken pressed the code again. The doors opened, sucking out the air from the hangar. Bodies of living and dead pirates, and the debris of the broken droid, flew past the shuttlecraft's windows and out into space.

Then Dirken punched the engine and accelerated out of the hangar.

CHAPTER FIVE
Speartip

No sooner had they shot out of the hangar than they were in trouble again. "Dirk! Two more shuttles headed this way from one of the brigantines," Yiorgos said, looking at the nav chart, "along with two light attack fightercraft!"

"Crap. We're no match for fighters."

Yiorgos turned and looked at him. "We have to go back to the hangar. We can hide out in the access tunnels. Hope the UW sends reinforcements."

"What? Back *there*? There may still be two hunter droids stalking around in there, and more pirates are on the way!"

"It's better than getting exploded by fighters."

Dirken waved him off. "As far as they know, we're one of them!"

The comm system crackled. A gruff voice on the other end with a thick Proximan lisp asked, "Thuttle 2, why hath you letht the hangar?" Dirken heard the alien's oral membranes fluttering against its thick tongue.

Dirken and Yiorgos looked at each other and shrugged.

"Well?" Yiorgos urged. "Tell them *something*!"

Dirken frowned and pressed a comm button. "Uh, Shuttle 2 here. All is well. Repeat, all is well. Awaiting orders."

Another voice came over the comm, deeper and more authoritative. "Explain, Shuttle 2. We've lost contact with the boarding party. What is happening in there?"

Dirken mouthed wordlessly for a moment, trying to think of something, then replied, "I suspect it's just some frequency jamming inside the ship."

The two fightercraft zoomed ahead of the shuttles they were escorting and headed toward Dirken's.

"We don't register any jamming," the second voice said. "We're headed to you."

Then the first voice added, "Thet trajectory to rendezvous with the *Dragonfire*."

Dirken looked at the three pirate ships. One of the brigantines was on fire and rolling slowly, but still trading heavy arms fire with the *Excellentia*, as was the other brig. Both brigantines were wide berth starships with asymmetric hulls that bulged with cannon turrets and enhanced gravjump ribs. The corvette, on the other hand, was sleek and slim, streamlined and ready to outrun authorities. Its gravjump panels swooping around it with as much art as utility and seemed double-purposed for atmospheric flight.

The corvette had sped up and closed ranks with the *Excellentia* and was now bombarding the bridge. All three ships were typical of pirate craft: painted black with a scan-absorbent coating to camouflage with the color and background radiation of space and covered with tech modifications to make them faster and more deadly.

The *Excellentia* was rolling as well, its engines out. The entire starboard side was pockmarked with blasts. The normally silver hull was black from scoring and looked as if it had been cooked by a star.

"Which one do you think is the *Dragonfire?*" Dirken asked.

"I don't know. Just pick one."

Dirken shrugged and turned the shuttlecraft toward the brigantine that looked least damaged. There weren't grav plates on the shuttle, so the safe box floated off the floor and toward the ceiling.

Yiorgos set the coordinates for that ship. "So what now, genius? You just going to deliver us and the safe box directly to the pirates, or what?"

Dirken waved him off. "Hold on. I'm thinking." He looked back to the corvette, then remembered something he heard on the bridge of the *Excellentia*. He abruptly turned the shuttlecraft and accelerated toward the corvette. The safe box hit the ceiling and bounced toward the back.

Yiorgos looked at him like he was mad, his one human eye opening wide. "You're going directly at the ship that is bombarding the UW destroyer. *That* ship?"

"Yes. That ship! I recall that a shuttlecraft launched from it."

"Okay. So what are you going to do to them? Spit at 'em? Cuz that's about as much good as this little prow laser will do to that hull plating."

The comm crackled with the Proximan voice. "Thuttle 2, why hath you deviated from your courth?"

Dirken ignored the hail and answered Yiorgos instead. "I plan to board it and take it over."

Yiorgos rolled his eyes. "Oh, great plan. I'm sure we'll do hunky-dory against a horde of pirates."

"Not a horde. Thirty, maybe. Maybe less. You got a better plan?"

"You heard my plan. Go back to the hangar. I'll take my chances in those access tubes, thank you."

"Sure, until that 'horde' of pirates boards the *Excellentia* and comes looking to cut our throats. At least with the corvette we'll have a fast and deadly ship."

Yiorgos huffed. "You just want to get a ship at any cost."

A laser flashed in a bright line across the front of the shuttlecraft in a warning shot, causing both men to jump.

Then one of the fightercraft came up and flew sideways going the same direction, heavy prow gun aimed directly at Dirken through the side of the cockpit window. It was an expensive swept-wing design optimized for both space and atmospheric flight—very sleek compared to the boxy shuttlecraft, and painted bright yellow. It wasn't a military craft, but close to it. The sort that a mercenary force might use.

Dirken looked at the cockpit and saw a pilot with a large, red beret set fashionably askew on the unmistakable head of an Aquarian centaur. Even from that distance, he could make out the four eyes, broad nose, and cheek ridges that merged with the forward-sweeping earlobes. Dirken watched it speak—the same deep voice that they'd heard before. He wasn't certain if the pilot could see him as well.

"Shuttle Two. Explain yourself." His voice was smooth and hardly had an Aquarian accent. "Why have you turned to the *Speartip?*"

Dirken smiled at the centaur and pressed the comm button. "Just took a little damage back there. More than we thought. Need an emergency docking."

"Funny," came the reply, smooth and sarcastic. "I don't *see* any damage."

The second fighter now came into view, flying just behind the first.

"The jig is up," Yiorgos muttered. "They're going to blast us."

Dirken glanced to the corvette. They were now only about twenty meters from the starboard dock. He slowed slightly and turned the shuttlecraft to come alongside. Just a few more minutes, he thought. *Just gotta buy a little more time.*

Dirken pressed the comm button again. "Well, the damage was inside, actually." Dirken winced, realizing how lame it sounded. "We're leaking acid from the primary battery." He made himself cough several times. Yiorgos added his as well. "Gotta get out of here!"

The corvette, for its part, had stopped firing on the *Excellentia*, perhaps since the destroyer's bridge was now nothing more than a smoking, hollowed out collection of scrap.

"Go ahead," the centaur said. "Permission to board the *Speartip*." He smiled again. "I'll stay right behind you to make sure you … board smoothly."

The fighters pulled back and took up positions behind the shuttlecraft.

Dirken and Yiorgos exchanged looks.

"Now what?" Yiorgos said.

Dirken pulled the shuttlecraft alongside the docking hatch and brought it into position. "Don't worry," Dirken said. "They won't expect us." But he pulled his blaster and checked the charge. Yiorgos pulled a mini-blaster from a holster at the small of his back this time instead of transforming to make his plasma saber.

Dirken plucked the safe box from the air as it floated past him, then he stood in front of the hatch as the boarding cowl extended over the side of the shuttlecraft. They heard it wrap around the opening, making tight contact, and then the hiss of atmosphere beyond the door as a boarding ramp attached to the hatch.

"Get ready," Dirken said, aiming his blaster as the hatch unbolted.

"Yeah," Yiorgos answered. "Ready to be filled with holes. I've only got so many organic parts left."

The hatch slid open …

… and two rows of pirates stood in the entry with their pulse rifles aimed at them.

Dirken fired and hit a lanky Tau Cetian in his pale, bald head, then both men pulled themselves to either side of the hatch for cover. Plasma bolts shot through the doorway.

Yiorgos groaned. "They won't expect us, you said!"

The shots stopped. The pirates were arguing amongst each other, their words just low enough that Dirken couldn't make them out. Then one with a distinctly British accent shouted, "We saw the safe! Throw it out the hatch and we'll let ya go."

"You lie!" Dirken shouted. "Your fighters will blow us away."

"True, but we would let ya go!" A little wave of laughter rippled through the pirates. "Don't make us come in there or we'll make ya suffer!"

"You can't hurt us!" Dirken yelled. "We know the secret of the package!"

Yiorgos gave him an incredulous look. *What secret?* he mouthed.

Dirken waved his hand as if to say *Let's go with it.* Then, yelling out at the pirates, "It's useless unless you know how to use it!"

"Bullshite!" said the pirate.

"I don't think the Bloodhawk would like you killing the only people who know how to use it, now would he?"

More muttering amongst the pirates. Then, "Okay, but throw out your weapons."

"Like hell!" Yiorgos muttered.

"Go ahead," Dirken reassured. "We'll give ourselves up and escape later. Trust me."

"My trust in you has nearly gotten me killed more times than I can count."

"True." Dirken flashed his partner a smile. "But you're still alive!"

"*Half* of me is!"

"Fine! We're coming out!" Dirken yelled out the hatch, then he and Yiorgos threw their blasters out the hatch. They fell to the grav plating of the ramp. "Don't shoot!" Dirken yelled.

The two stepped into view, careful to step onto the grav plates of the ramp, hands up except for the one carrying the safe box.

"Right," said the pirate who had been speaking—a human who had a badly healed scar that ran from under his heavily stained red cap down the middle of his face and across his neck. Half of his nose was gone, and part of his lips. Dirken wondered how the man had survived a laser burn like that. The pirate stepped forward, kicked the blasters back to the others, and took the safe box, almost dropping it in surprise at the weight, and stripped him of his pack.

The two were placed with pirates in front and behind and escorted down a series of narrow corridors. Just as they passed a viewing window, though, they saw two shining United Worlds warships appear out of gravity wells.

Those damned chrome bastards never looked so sweet! he thought.

The corvette bucked into a tight turn and acceleration. Everyone lost their footing, including Dirken and Yiorgos, and lurched right into the hull. Dirken took advantage of this and hit the human pirate square in the jaw, then lunged for his Gree-tech blaster, which was being carried by a Rigellian in one of his long, flap-like hands.

No sooner had Dirken's hand wrapped around the handle than his head exploded in pain, hit from behind. The last thing he saw as he passed out and rolled over was the Rigellian and the human pirate leaning over him. "Night, night, sweetheart!" the pirate said, giving a wave, and the Rigellian laughed with a weird "lululululululu!" cry emitting from the tentacled mouth at the top of its head, its row of tiny black eyes sparkling.

Then the human hit him again, and everything went black.

CHAPTER SIX
How the Gig Began

The last thought running through Dirken's mind as he blacked out wasn't his blaster or the laughing Rigellian. It was, *How the fuck did I get in this situation?*

The whole thing had been hush-hush from the beginning, only a couple Earth days before. A contracted middleman had found them in a seedy alien bar on Mars called the Gamma Ray Gramma.

Half of the bar catered to aquatic species, with the entire lower level composed of a pool of cold, briny water. Eel-like Argulans milled around with Ursan "space octopuses" and a school of hundreds of Shan-toth-min, a species of silvery fish with bulging, transparent skulls and human-like arms projecting from an otherwise cod-like body. In the middle of the aquatic level was a massive Procyonese bartender with its hulking yellow body covered in eyes and mouths and at least a dozen thin tentacles that reached out with servings of specially formulated liquor globes. All of this was visible through the transparent aluminum floor under Dirken.

Up top, though, the bar was less distinguished and definitely dingier, the walls streaked with stains, including traces of blood from dozens of species. The smoke of half a dozen illegal drugs hung in the air in a haze of skunky-smelling marijuana from Earth and floral jojona petals grown on Corthos. Smugglers from across the sector gathered here to relax, free of the hassles of law enforcement thanks to the Craters, the gang that ran Mars Colony 1 (or "Crater City," nicknamed due to the old part of the colony having been built in the massive Hellas Crater).

The bar was named after Gramma Jones, a self-described "Old Martian Bitch" who used to rule over a smuggler route to Rigel, but she was the nicest old lady Dirken had ever met … until you failed to pay your tab, at which point you became the plaything of her five genetically mutated mastiffs—double the size and musculature of a normal dog—and your remains were fed as "chum" to the bartender.

The middleman, a human with long, greasy black hair, Asian features, and a poor attempt at a mustache, had been seated in the smoky corner of the bar watching the crowd. His gaze came to rest on Dirken and Yiorgos and lingered on them a little too long, making eye contact. In a place like Gamma Ray Gramma's, you don't look someone in the eye for long or it may be the last thing you see.

Just as Dirken had been ready to put his blaster on the table, the man got up and walked over, brazenly inviting himself to take a seat, holding his hands away from his trench coat to show he wasn't going to reach for a weapon.

"Hey," he'd said. "Name's Weed."

"Weed, huh?" Dirken replied. "As in something everyone wants to get rid of? Beat it."

Weed ignored the command. "I hear you need a gig."

"Yeah?" Dirken said. "From who?"

"High level people. They pay good, and the job's easy."

Dirken leaned over the table toward Weed. "No job that pays good is easy."

"What 'high level people' are these?" Yiorgos asked.

Dirken flashed his partner a quick look as if to say, *You're really going to listen to this moron?*

Weed looked around to check if anyone was listening. "Top government officials on Earth."

Dirken and Yiorgos had looked at each other, not bothering to hide their incredulity.

"Really," Weed had said. "They heard about a gig you did off Proxima Centauri."

Dirken kept a poker face, but inwardly he was wincing. They had transported a missile array from the planet of Proxima Centauri B to a moon of Proxima Centauri C for the Proximan Dawn, a crime syndicate. It was a closely held secret. How the hell did they learn this? he thought. *What else do they know?*

"I don't know what gig you're talking about," Dirken said.

"Uh huh," Weed said. "Look, all you gotta do is escort a package from Earth to Nüwa."

"The Feds have their own people for shit like that." Dirken put his blaster on the table—the universal signal that the conversation was over. But Weed didn't relent.

"All I know is," Weed said, "they sent me to find you and give you the offer. It's a shitload of money, too. They need to keep it off the books, so it has to be an outside job. I don't know anything more about it."

Yiorgos gave a subtle nod to Dirken that said, *Give him a chance.* It wouldn't have been the first time they've done dirty work for a planetary government, but never for Earth. Earth governments were notorious for political backstabbing and poor ability to keep anything secret for long. Dirken kept his blaster on the table, his hand on the handle.

"Yeah? Exactly how much is a *shitload*?" Dirken asked.

"Enough to buy a ship and still get a blowjob every day of your life." He leaned forward and whispered, "Seven hundred thousand."

Warning bells were going off in Dirken's mind. That was indeed a "shitload." It would be the best-paying gig they ever had for the least amount of work. There was a hint of desperation in that oily middleman's eyes, like his own life was maybe on the line if he didn't succeed in hiring them.

"Bullshit," Dirken said. "It's too good to be true."

Weed tensed. "Look, fuckface, I'm just the messenger. But I can tell you it's for real. You know these government types. They rob everyone blind with taxes, then they turn around and waste it on, well, *this*."

Dirken gestured toward the bar. "Give us some space. I'll talk with my partner and decide if it's worth it. Frankly, I think you're full of shit."

"Whatever," Weed mumbled, "but I'll sweeten the deal. A thousand UW chits if you just show up, even if you don't accept the mission." Then he went over to the bar, shooting the pair one last look before he signaled the bartender for a liquor globe.

Dirken and Yiorgos leaned toward each other. "Well?" Dirken said. "A thousand just for showing up. Sounds good to me. I say we take the gig."

Yiorgos scowled. "You were the one who said he's full of shit."

Dirken cocked a smile. "And you were the one who seemed willing to give him a chance. I think he's sincere. I think he's afraid we'll say no. The stakes are high, and so is the pot, but we hardly have to do anything." When Yiorgos shrugged, Dirken gave a playful punch against his partner's arm. "Come on, if anyone's got smuggling in his blood it's you!" Yiorgos smiled back. Feeling encouraged, Dirken continued, "You had ancient relatives trafficking contraband from the free nations to the Concubists!"

"Communists," Yiorgos corrected. "During the Cold War era, in Europe—at least that's the family legend. And then there was my great-great-great grandfather, who got rich stealing satellites from Earth and selling them to the early Mars colonies."

"And your father, running ice through blockades during the Fringe Worlds siege."

Yiorgos huffed. "And he eventually died from his injuries." The cyborg looked Dirken in his eyes. "What's your gut tell you?"

Dirken grew serious a moment. "That there's more than what Weed's telling us. That it's more dangerous than he's letting on. But … if we come out alive, we'll finally be able to get a ship of our own again."

Yiorgos nodded. "Okay. Then let's go with it." He raised a finger at Dirken, "But promise me, this time I won't have to bail you out of jail for screwing someone's wife … again!"

Dirken raised his hands. "Oh come on! That was *one* time!" Then he added, "And besides, the Commandant of Lanus Station had sixteen wives! Who knew he'd even miss one for a few hours?"

Yiorgos shook his head and waved for Weed to come back over.

"Fine," Dirken said to Weed. "My partner talked me into it. We'll take the job, but only if you give us five hundred chits right now. We have to pay for transportation to Earth, after all."

Weed growled and handed them five hundred chit notes. "Here are your instructions." Weed then slipped them a piece of paper with instructions on when and where to meet, then he disappeared into the crowd, relief washing over his face.

The instructions were to meet at a landing pad in an industrial area in New Miami, North America (over three hundred kilometers north of Old Miami, now a cluster of crumbling skyscrapers poking out of the ocean) at noon, local time. It took a few hours to arrange an interplanetary transport, then a few hours more to fly there.

When Dirken and Yiorgos showed up in New Miami, government security whisked them away in a luxury hovcar to a nondescript warehouse near the spaceport. Standing amid rusting hulks of industrial machinery and the smell of grease so strong that Dirken checked the soles of his leather boots to see if he'd stepped in it, they were surrounded by more security officers, all conspicuously armed. Thinking again that this was a trap, Dirken was about to pull his blaster when in walked one of those "top government officials" Weed had mentioned. In fact, it didn't get much more "top" than the Governor of the Americas himself.

Governor Juarez was a tall man with a bushy black beard peppered with gray. His dark eyes flashed with conviviality, crow's feet showing as he smiled. Dressed in a dark blue, formal business suit, he was every bit the suave Latino businessman when he spoke. But with every pause in the brief dialog there was a hint of conspiracy. Dirken expected no less. He had seen this in the eyes of so many of their clients over the years.

"Gentlemen," Juarez said, "no doubt you recognize me. No need to seem so surprised. I felt I should come here myself for such an important task."

Dirken blinked. He hadn't ever talked with such a powerful politician before, much less under secretive conditions. They would never personally appear. Always they sent some low-level representative for the sake of plausible deniability. The fact that the governor didn't care about deniability meant that this gig was personal for him—and you don't deny a top official something personal. "And what is the task?"

Juarez called forth one of his bodyguards, a tall, bald man with a cybernetic implant covering his right ear and right eye. The bodyguard held a safe box by a handle at the top and gingerly placed it on the concrete floor in front of Dirken.

"Deliver this safe box to the Earth consulate on Nüwa," Juarez said. "The Ambassador's men will meet you and will pay you handsomely. Until then, do not leave its side. You are required to travel aboard a United Worlds starship and will be escorted the entire way."

Dirken and Yiorgos exchanged glances.

"I'm having trouble understanding something, your … um … governorship," Dirken said. "If you're just going to have us travel aboard a UW ship with an escort, why not just have a military porter the whole way instead of paying us seven hundred thousand chits?" Dirken knew he was treading uneasy territory. Smugglers don't ask questions like that. "One of your black ops teams, for instance?"

Juarez paused, leveling his eyes at Dirken's. "I would think you could guess the answer, amigo. There is no government action that isn't recorded in some official way. On paper—if you appear at all—it will be as civilian consultants traveling between planetary offices. Beyond that, any information is classified. I have already told you as much as you need to know to do the job. But of you, dear smugglers, we know everything. We have researched you very thoroughly. And I can assure you, amigo, with the money you earn from this mission, you will be able to replace that rattletrap clipper you crashed on Rorgos."

Dirken gasped in surprise then tried, too late, to hide it. The mention of the *Brilliant's* demise was a not-so-subtle threat. If they knew about the crash, then they probably knew about the illegal load they were hauling at the time, and probably so many more illegal activities they'd been involved in. If they declined this mission, the Feds might very well arrest them in retaliation. Such things didn't need to be said when you were in control of half a world.

Juarez smiled broadly. "I will pay ten thousand chits up front. So do you accept this mission or not?"

Dirken and Yiorgos looked at each other again. The cyborg gave a slight nod and a sigh. Dirken returned the nod.

"Yes," Dirken replied in a flat voice to Juarez. "We accept."

"Excelente!" the Governor replied. "I am so glad you did. Remember, I was never here, gentlemen, and when you have finished the mission, you will forget you ever took part." He raised a finger at them. "And trust me, we will be watching."

Juarez had his bodyguard give them an advance of ten thousand chits by typing the account number and amount into an arm holodisplay bracelet. The money instantly transferred to Dirken's Shipper's Guild account on Tesla and siphoned into half a dozen untraceable accounts on other planets.

Juarez nodded to his bodyguards. The men quickly ushered Dirken and Yiorgos to a shuttle that took them and their escorted "package" up to the *Excellentia*.

The entire way up to the destroyer, Dirken and Yiorgos sat across from one another in the shuttlecraft, the safe box sitting at their feet between them. They didn't say a word to each other. They didn't need to. It was clear they had been railroaded the moment they accepted the job from Weed. Now the only thing they could do was ride this train to the end of the line.

CHAPTER SEVEN
Ananak

Dirken started to open his eyes, but the light was too intense. His head felt like it had been hit by a comet. He groaned as he rubbed his left temple.

"Heh. You deserve it," Yiorgos said from somewhere to Dirken's left. "'Trust me,' you said."

Dirken was lying on his back. He turned over to face Yiorgos and opened his eyes again, squinting. The cyborg was propped up on one arm on a metal bunk on the other side of the cell they shared.

"Well," Dirken replied, "we ain't dead yet." He closed his eyes again. His right hand went to the breast pocket of his leather jacket. He was relieved to find his lucky Rigellian runestone at the bottom. Of course his blaster and gunbelt were missing, as was his pack—and his tablet with his porn collection. He wasn't sure which he'd miss more.

"Are we still on the corvette?" Dirken asked.

"No. They moved us to a brigantine after the gravjump. UW ships showed up about the time you were knocked unconscious. The pirates already had their gravwell engines spun up, so they jumped out of there right after you passed out. I overheard that the other brigantine was captured."

"And the *Excellentia*?"

"The *Excellentia* was temporarily out of commission, but if we'd stayed we surely would have been rescued by the UW ships." Yiorgos paused a tick, then added, "Therese wouldn't have let you make that decision. She wouldn't have let you leave the hangar in the first place."

Dirken poked a finger at him. "Don't mention her name!"

"Who? The love of your life? Now *that* was a woman."

Dirken abruptly sat up. "She wasn't the love of my life!" He stumbled for words, then blurted, "We were just partners for eight years. And … and she made plenty of mistakes, too! Remember the time she led us right into those guards at Ferris Station, off Io? Remember?"

"Yeah. I remember, Dirk. I remember an eight-year love affair. And do you remember *why* our attack on Ferris Station failed?" Yiorgos pointed a finger back at Dirken. "*You* forgot to charge the rifle packs!"

"Oh, here we go again!" Dirken threw up his hands. "I *told* you, the packs were compromised by electromagnetic interference from Jupiter."

"Uh-huh. And my Grannie's wheelchair is a rocket." Yiorgos laid back down. "Next time you have a brilliant plan, maybe you should think about what Therese would do."

Dirken gasped in exasperation. "You know, I have plenty of great ideas of my own! Thanks to my decisiveness, we didn't get torn to pieces by hunter droids!"

Yiorgos waved him away and crossed his arms across his chest. "Well, while you were snoozing, these pirates wanted to tear me to pieces—to take the tech built into me!" Dirken massaged his head. All this arguing was inflaming his headache.

He examined the cell. There were no other features besides a chemical toilet, a glaringly bright white LED array in the ceiling, and a host of unidentified stains of different colors dried on the floor. He was pretty sure from the wretched sulfur smell that at least some of the blue stains were Proximan blood. And he didn't want to think what the rust-red stains were.

The safe box they were escorting was nowhere to be seen. "The safe?" he asked Yiorgos. Yiorgos motioned toward the door. The pirates had it. Crap, he thought. *So much for buying my own ship.*

The walls were covered in scratched graffiti in a dozen alien languages, most of which he couldn't read, but he got the gist of it. It's basically the same sentiments you find in jail cells and brigs throughout the galaxy and as far back in time as there have been criminals. Scrawled over the toilet in Terran was "Flush twice—it's a long way to the captain's mess." And next to the bunk was written in neat Tau Cetian script, "The Bloodhawk can suck my galnar." *Harsh!*

The room had a door made of steel bars with a rectangular slot for putting food through, and an old-fashioned key lock. *There's no hacking that.* On the wall opposite was an array of sensors and cameras and a number of long metal needles pointing toward the cells. *Some sort of torture device?*

Yiorgos noticed Dirken's gaze. "The guards were quick to point out that if we show any attempt to escape, electricity will arc out from those needles and electrocute us instantly."

"Lovely," Dirken said. "We'd have to get through the bars before we could disable them, but they'd fry us before we managed it."

One of the cell walls, the one behind Yiorgos's bunk, was also made of steel bars. Another cell lay beyond. Someone was lying on the bunk in there. Someone with … lavender fur? "Is that …" He looked again, fighting back the pain in his head. " … an Ananak?"

At the mention of her species, the Ananak rolled over, her cat-like ears rotating toward him. She was covered head to tail in plush, lavender fur that ruffled with a glossy sheen as she turned. Distinctly feline, she looked like a cross between a human woman and a panther, wearing a stretchy one-piece blue outfit that adhered tightly to her thighs and ran up the front of her svelte torso to her muscular neck. She clasped one of the bars with a hand that looked almost human save for dark pads on her palm and black claws that peeked out of the fur on her fingertips.

She turned her face to the bars and opened her eyes with a fluid carelessness. They glimmered like amethysts around ovoid pupils. She regarded him with a mischievous grin, a dozen slim whiskers angling upward with the movement.

"Is that … a *human?*" she japed with a voice like polished chrome, then she smiled broader, showing the tips of her pearly fangs.

Dirken swallowed hard, his eyes wide. He'd only once seen Ananaks: a pair of males, much larger and more muscular, acting as bodyguards for an underworld kingpin on Tesla. They had been more like pictures he'd seen of extinct tigers from Earth. But this one …

He wanted to run his hand through her fur.

He sat up, though he regretted doing so as the pain in his head flared. "You speak Terran. What's your name?"

She examined him, deliberately, her eyes moving up his body to his face. "You first."

"Dirken." He gave a sidelong smile and tilted his head. "Dirken Nova." Yiorgos rolled his eyes.

She didn't answer. Instead, her ears turned and her gaze darted past the cells. A fraction of a second later came the screech of metal-on-metal of a bulkhead door unlatching and opening.

Three pirates entered, including the Brit who had knocked him out and two Pleiadeans shambling behind him, hunched over and sporting a mass of little curved horns over angular scalps, their bodies very much like the fauns of ancient Greek mythology. Both of them wore translator necklaces around their necks. The Brit hadn't unholstered his weapon, but the Pleiadeans each brandished laser pistols. One held a set of magnetic handcuffs.

"You there!" the Brit said, pointing at Dirken. His lurid grin strained at the red scar tissue that ran down through his face and lips. "It's time for ya to meet the Bloodhawk. He's got some questions for ya!"

One of the Pleiadeans approached and said, "Turn around and present your hands through the bars," his words automatically translated by his necklace from his squeaky and not-at-all-imposing Pleiadean language into a stern and very masculine Terran voice.

Dirken glanced to Yiorgos as he got up. The look they exchanged held an inner understanding.

Attack? No, came the response with the slightest shake of the head. Then a tilt of the head, *Later.*

Dirken looked to Yiorgos's right arm, the one with the plasma saber, then gave the slightest of nods. *Understood.* They were outnumbered and outgunned, and Dirken needed to learn more about the layout before they could attempt an escape. And where was the safe box?

He approached the cell door. "Turn around, maggot," the human said. As Dirken followed the command, he looked over to the Ananak, but she had slid back against the wall and eyed the pirates coolly, the end of her long, furry tail wrapped around her knees, twitching slightly at the rounded tip.

He heard the metal slot open, then the leathery hands of one of the Pleiadeans pulled his wrists out and the handcuffs were clamped over them, behind his back. The door was unlocked, he was pulled out, and it was shut behind him with Yiorgos still inside.

As he was escorted out the door, Dirken looked back and saw the Ananak watching him leave, her gaze roaming down to his leather pants and back up to his eyes.

It was the look of a hunter who'd just lost her prey.

CHAPTER EIGHT
Bloodhawk

Dirken's neck popped as the hulking Oranchian hit him across the face for the third time—a tight roundhouse. This time blood flooded into his mouth from biting his tongue. He spat the blood out onto a metal floor that had dried blood of different colors from many such interrogations.

He squeezed his eyes shut against the pain and dizziness and groaned. Every punch sent his body straining against the magnetic shackles and the rod he was bound to.

Dirken reminded himself that the trick to being beaten in the head was to exhale and go limp just before being struck. It's when you tighten up that you get hurt the worst. Except for the jaw. ALWAYS clench your jaw if you don't want to lose teeth or have a broken jawbone. One should tighten the abdomen, too, but for some reason these guys didn't bother aiming there.

Laughter. It came from the human pirate with the laser scar and British accent. The Pleiadeans, standing to either side of the dirty little room, had called him "Mom", but Dirken got the distinct impression that the word meant something very different in their language.

He opened his eyes again, trying to ignore the little pops of light from being hit. "Mom" pushed the massive, gray-skinned and hairless Oranchian aside using a billy club. The beast grunted, clearly annoyed he had to stop. He stood three meters tall, stunk like a Teslan skunk, and had weeping sores and pustules all over his body. The "Oran pox" hadn't missed this beastly creature, nor most of his kind. Dressed only in a sort of loincloth, his stone-like body rippled with muscle. Oranchians were only good for three things: ruffians, heavy labor, and porn. Their species' prodigious organ was the highlight of many of the xenophile porn vids he'd watched, usually paired with an actress, often human, who would seem far too fragile for such a joining.

"Come now, maggot," Mom said. "Don't make me have Grendel hit you again. That kind of entertainment is best saved for the gladiator pits where we'll sell you." He leaned down to eye level with Dirken and smiled, eyes sparkling, mouth full of rotting teeth. He poked Dirken's chest with the billy club. "Grendel's holdin' back, you see. If he really wanted to hit ya hard, he'd kill ya. The longer this goes, the harder he hits. So I'll ask ya again. What's the combination to that lovely safe of yours?"

He didn't answer. Running his tongue along his teeth, none were loose … yet. Mom nodded to Grendel, and the Oranchian reared back to hit Dirken again.

"Okay, okay!" Dirken shouted. Grendel stopped, frowning. Dirken sputtered, "The combination is "E-A-T-M-E."

Mom listened intently, then gave a nod, smiled at his success, and started to turn toward the door. Then he stopped short, growled, and hit Dirken in the head with the billy club. "Very funny, maggot!"

Everything went black for a few moments, then stars popped in his vision again. Why is it always the head? he thought.

When it cleared up enough for him to see again, he realized he was looking out the open door. He saw in the room beyond a pirate with a laser cutter trying to cut through the safe box. Whatever the safe was made of, it was resisting even that.

Then a figure stepped in the way and entered the room. It took a moment more to focus as his vision seemed to swim again, then Dirken realized he was looking at an Aquarian centaur. He had four stern eyes over a broad nose. Wore a red beret that flopped to one side. Overlarge earlobes swept down onto cheek ridges. No hair, but rather tiny scales covered his green-tinged skin. He had long arms that ended in hands that had a dozen thin tentacles on each hand for digits. His torso sat upon a quadruped lower body, lion-like with clawed feet, but covered in larger scales and no tail. He wore bright red, leathery clothing crisscrossed with a couple of bandoleers and pouches, two blasters, a pulse rifle strapped to the back of his lower body, and a large sword sheathed next to it.

Dirken was pretty sure from his look that this was the pilot of the fightercraft, but this was confirmed when he heard his voice.

"Step aside, Mom," the centaur said, calmly.

"Aye, Cap'n," Mom replied, putting his hand on his chest in salute, and backing away from Dirken and the centaur, as did the Pleiadeans. The Oranchian whimpered, averted his gaze, and cowered in a corner.

The centaur moved forward with confident steps and smiled, showing his bright white, needle-like rows of teeth. An emaciated human woman in ratty black clothes walked behind him, shaved head downcast, holding a tablet with what looked like a spreadsheet on it. She wore a red metal collar. Slave, Dirken thought. She glanced up at him briefly. But instead of the defeated look that slaves everywhere had, her eyes focused on him with a note of recognition, then back down to the floor. But it wasn't her knowing eyes that attracted his attention the most, but rather the small, branded "A" on her wrist. He couldn't concentrate enough to remember where he'd seen it before.

The centaur gave his slave the slightest of nods and waved her away. She obeyed immediately and disappeared through the doorway.

Dirken winced against the pain pulsing through his head. "I'm guessing you're the Bloodhawk. Funny, with a name like that, I thought you'd be avian, like a Corthian."

The Bloodhawk didn't answer at first, but kept looking down at Dirken, examining him. Finally he said in a baritone voice, "Captain Neenan will suffice. You're pretty confident for someone who is completely at my mercy. You won't divulge the code to the safe, even when confronted with an Oranchian and torture. So either you don't know the code or you are compelled by a more powerful force not to reveal it."

Neenan stepped slowly to Dirken's left, examining him from a different angle. The centaur was surprisingly lithe for his size. "It is of little matter. I'll open the safe one way or another. It's the item inside that holds the mysteries. So nice of you to deliver it to me."

Dirken groaned internally, remembering Yiorgos's admonishment that they should have stayed inside the *Excellentia*.

"You told my crew that you knew the secret of using the Heart," the Bloodhawk continued. "Pray tell, what secret are you withholding?"

The heart? What is he talking about? He decided to play along.

"Well, it wouldn't be a secret if I told you, now would it? The heart is a tricky thing. You're going to have to offer me something worthwhile."

Neenan raised an eyebrow. "Your life isn't enough?"

Even if he knew the answer, Dirken understood he'd be killed the moment he revealed it. Instead, he tilted his head and answered, "Well, there are a lot of different factors at play here. Remunerations. Government entities. Reputations ... "

Neenan cut him off. "Your partner's life." The Bloodhawk stepped around the back of Dirken. "I can offer remunerations. You saw what I did to your 'government entity.' And what good is a reputation when you're dead?"

He stepped back into view to Dirken's right. "We know you are called 'Dirken' and your partner is called 'Yiorgos,' but neither of you were on the crew list for the *Excellentia*. No passengers. And the manifest doesn't mention the Heart."

Dirken wondered how the Bloodhawk could have come across a crew list and ship manifest for a secret mission handled by Governor Juarez himself. *And is there a real freakin' heart in the box? Ew.*

"Dirken Nova," he said proudly. He waited for a reaction, but neither Neenan or Mom showed any recognition. "Yes, well, we are very special to the fate of the safe and its contents. We're very close to the governor, you see. Long associates. Yes, good friends. Great friends, really. He would be very angry to know how you're treating us." Then an idea popped into his head. "I'm sure he would pay a great deal to see us delivered safely along with the, um, heart."

Captain Neenan chuckled. "A ransom, eh?" He stepped in front of Dirken and faced him again. "Well, there will certainly be a price for the heart, but whether the United Worlds wishes to be the highest bidder remains to be seen."

Dirken pictured a mummified heart sitting in the safe box. *So he wants to sell it. What the hell is it? It's time for some leading questions.*

"And what exactly do you think the buyer will do with it?" Dirken asked.

Dirken yelled in pain as Mom hit him in the right arm with his billy club. "The Cap'n will be askin' the questions here, maggot!"

The Bloodhawk looked down at Dirken, but his eyes seemed glazed with thought. "Ancient enemies," the Bloodhawk muttered. "Some things are best forgotten. How much is it worth to the United Worlds to forget? And how much is it worth to their foes to bring it back to life?" Then he seemed to shake himself out of his thoughts. "But you, friend-of-a-governor, are still worth nothing compared to the Heart."

The pirate captain turned to Mom. "Beat him until he either gives us the code or he passes out. Then move on to the partner."

The pirate captain turned to leave, and as he stepped out the door he added, "Don't kill him yet. Later we'll flay him alive if we need to."

The door closed with a slam. Mom and Grendel stepped back in front of Dirken.

"Ya heard the Cap'n," Mom said to the Oranchian. "Beat 'im 'till he gives us the code."

Grendel smiled, showing the wide, thick teeth of his species. Made a fist. Drew back for another punch.

CHAPTER NINE
Caged Deal

Dirken arose from darkness into a haze of pain, like moving through clouds of a nebula, colors coming and going, each bringing another wave of ache. He started to open his eyes, but shut them tight against glaring white light.

Dirken probed his teeth with his tongue. This time there were two loose teeth on the right side and a chipped molar on the left. "Crap." Clenching wasn't always enough, particularly when you're being pounded by a fist that's twice as large as your own.

Gradually he became aware that he was lying on the same metal bunk, in the same cell where he had been before. "Ugh!" He put an arm over his eyes and turned. "Déjà vu. How many times must I wake up in pain in the same stinking cell, Yiorgos?"

He squinted and looked over to the other bunk, but it was empty. He was alone in his cell.

"They took him."

It was the Ananak who answered. The sultry alien in the next cell slid into view from behind the divider and looked through the bars at him, one leg dangling from the bunk, lithe muscles flexing beneath the silky lavender fur.

He regarded her as he massaged his stubbly, aching jawline. Her clothing adhered tightly to her belly, undulating over slim muscles and up over firm, athletic breasts just ample enough to excite him. Then he looked up to those amazing purple eyes. There was more than a hint of wildness there. A dangerous spark.

She gave a thin smile, seeming to read his thoughts, her tail flitting back and forth under her bunk. "You look like hell," she said. "I'm guessing you met Grendel."

She spoke fluently in the common Terran tongue, but with a hint of offworld cadence that made her words slide together as if from one breath. It sounded almost French.

Dirken nodded. "I'll be feeling his hospitality for a long time." He paused, then added, "You never told me your name."

"Ananak change names depending on the company they keep and the situation. But you can call me Eow."

She pronounced the name with a rhythmic vibration at the end that he knew he could never imitate. Perhaps no human could. But he repeated it as best he could. "Eow. You don't seem to have gotten the same treatment. Why are you here?"

Eow turned away and laid her head against the bars, but her right ear was still angled toward him. She sighed. "I'm acting as a messenger for someone. Someone of great influence."

"Ah," Dirken said, and shook his head. There was a ringing in his right ear where he'd been punched. "Since you're in here, I'm guessing the Bloodhawk didn't like the message."

"He did not. But he knows better than to mistreat me. He can get more by holding me for ransom. I expected it. The Eridani Mafia would never do business with him again if he killed or beat me, and he'd be shut out of half a dozen key solar systems."

Dirken sat up. "The Eridani Mafia! And who does this someone-of-great-influence happen to be?" There were a dozen wise guys he could think of, every one of which ran their own deals. He'd worked with a couple of them. Made a bundle, too. And then there was the don, Grimmag Ruby-Eye …

She looked back at him, then lowered her gaze, her fingers running up and down a bar as if stroking it. "I've said enough. And why are you here? Something about a safe box, I overheard."

Dirken stood up, grimacing. He'd pulled a muscle in his upper back at some point during the interrogation. "I can't say," he replied, "except that we were escorting that safe and need to get it back."

Eow watched him intently as he stepped over to Yiorgos's bunk and sat down, now right next to her with only the bars between.

She examined his face, then reached through the bars and stroked his cheek with the back of her hand. Her fur was every bit as soft as he'd imagined. His pulse quickened. He ran his hand along her arm, crossing into her cell. Beneath the fine fur was hidden hard, smooth muscle. He resisted the urge to go lower.

Eow reversed her movement, now running her palm along his jaw. The dark pad on her palm felt like warm suede, and the tips of her claws lightly scratched along his skin. The sensation sent tingles down his neck and seemed to soothe the pain.

"I can make you a deal," she whispered with a glance toward the sensors on the wall opposite the cells. "If you get me out of here, I can help you get that safe box. And if you help me get off this ship, I can offer you protection by the Eridani Mafia."

He looked into her amethyst eyes, just centimeters from his across the bars. There was that dangerous spark again. He took her hand in his. "And just how do you think you can help me get the safe? Do you know how to fight?"

Eow leaned her head back and laughed, fangs glimmering in the light of the LEDs. "I am a warrior in my culture." She flexed her other hand and black claws shot soundlessly out from each finger, each claw as sharp and long as a filet knife. "But I cannot do it alone. Together, we can manage. I have a few … tricks. I imagine you do, too. By the look of it, I'm guessing your partner's right arm

60

is more than it appears. It may have fooled the pirates, but I've seen a custom job like that before."

He nodded. "And do you have a ship?"

"In the hangar." She flexed again and her claws retracted. "We go to the Eridani first and you drop me off. From there, you're free to go where you choose. So, do we have a deal, stud?"

His eyebrow flexed at *stud*. "Yeah. We have a deal."

She once again ran the back of her hand across his jaw and gave him a smile, the tips of her fangs showing over her lower lip. The touch of her fur was soothing. But he didn't trust her. No one associated with the Eridani Mafia should be trusted. But there wasn't a better choice, was there?

She slipped her hand down his neck and down into his shirt, letting her fingertips play in the hair of his chest. "I don't know what the Bloodhawk has in store for us, but I'm glad I'm not alone here …" Her eyes met his. "… for whatever fate has in store for us."

Suddenly she sat back and withdrew her hand, her eyes on the door. And then he heard it too—heavy steps. The door to the brig opened with a clank and squeal of metal hinges. Mom and the two Pleiadeans dragged Yiorgos through.

"Oi! You!" Mom said to Dirken. "Turn around and put your hands on the far wall!"

Dirken did as instructed, then the cell door opened and Yiorgos was dumped onto the floor. The door slammed shut behind him. Dirken turned around and watched as the Pleiadeans stepped out.

Mom went last. As he put a foot through the door, he looked back and winked at Eow. "Hey, kitty. Later I'm goin' to make you purr." He reached down and grabbed his crotch, gave it a squeeze, ran his tongue over his lips. Then he stepped out the door, shutting and locking it. Eow showed her fangs, staring daggers at Mom as he left.

Dirken knelt and checked Yiorgos. The cyborg was awake, but the organic side of his face was swollen and red. The metallic portions of his head, both shoulders, and right arm were dented, and the edges were bent up here and there as if the pirates had tried to pry parts off of him.

Dirken helped his partner onto his bunk and laid him down. "You look like you've been chewed up by a Horlkan and spit out."

Yiorgos gave a wan smile. "I'm still better looking than you."

Dirken scrutinized Yiorgos's right arm, the one with the plasma saber. The mechanisms seemed intact.

He bend down close to Yiorgos's ear. "We've got a way out of here, and somewhere to hide out—when you've recovered."

"Oh, good," Yiorgos said. "Another of your brilliant plans." He coughed several times, then, rolling over, added, "I think I still have a few centimeters of my body that aren't broken yet."

CHAPTER TEN
Banshee Cry

Dirken sat on his bunk with his back against the wall, listening to the sounds of the ship and feeling its vibrations. Every starship had its routines, even those that lacked the annoying chimes and shift changes of the United Worlds "Silver Fleet." Though there wasn't a star or the rotation of a planet to set a day/night cycle, and every species had their own circadian rhythm, there was still a cadence to the crew and their activities. There was a natural ebb and flow of movement. At certain times, voices grew quieter. Steps grew lighter. And those who weren't needed for ship duty found themselves easing into bunks, electro-stimulant cushions, cocoons, or whatever the species in question slept in, as others awakened. Machinery grew quiet as their users left them for rest, so the vibrations through the decks and bulkheads grew quiet, too, then resumed noises as new hands started operating them.

And so Dirken sat and listened, waiting for the right moment to make their escape. In his right hand he held his lucky Rigellian runestone. He rolled it around absentmindedly with his thumb as he listened to the ship. Then he looked down at it. Brown with green, glistening specks. Smooth. Irregular. Ovoid. He'd found the stone in some ruins during a mission to Rigel C and one of its worlds. Engraved on one side of the stone was a rune from an ancient Rigellian culture. The rune resembled a Chinese character—a collection of straight lines and swirls that, if you squinted, looked vaguely like a pinup girl wearing a conical hat. "Luck" is what it stood for, according to a hoary Rigellian wizardess he'd consulted who'd laughed maniacally at him, the mouth at the top of her pear-shaped head emitting a warbling "Lululululululu!"

Yiorgos had slept for hours after his interrogation as his body rested and his mechanical systems repaired themselves in what ways they could. Now he sat in his bunk performing his Netfolding ritual. His head was bent in meditation, eyes half open and focused on the holographic Sphere of Unity projected into cupped hands.

Dirken watched as Eow went through some sort of martial arts kata in her cell, the series of moves performed in slow motion. Now arms were outstretched as she dipped into a bow. Then she swept upward, leg raised, into an upright stance. She turned, bent, and extended her claws, then sliced the air. Her slim muscles pulsed under the fur as she held each position. Her eyes were half-closed. Breasts rose and fell with careful breaths. The line of her flexing, muscular thighs rose in a steady curve to her firm ass as she turned. And then she was facing him, dipping low, the tightly adhered clothing revealing the intoxicating arc of her crotch.

He looked up to her face and saw that she watched him with those amethyst eyes. He didn't look away. She kept eye contact as she lowered and made a sweep with her hand in a clawing motion, exhaled, then turned into a stance, her tail moving the other direction to aide in balance. Then she swept the ground as if picking up a staff, turned away, and lunged forward.

It was a sultry dance he could watch for hours and never grow bored. Indeed, it was a talent that could make her a very profitable living in a thousand night clubs across the galaxy, particularly if that thin outfit happened to slip off …

He noticed her fur seemed perfect, unblemished, except for a small, oval blank patch at the back of her neck had the same suede appearance as her palms.

Yiorgos muttered, "Let it be joined," signaling the end of his Netfolding. The projection ended, the Sphere of Unity disappeared, and he opened his eyes all the way. He turned and looked at Dirken. The organic part of his face was a giant bruise. Dirken figured his own was much the same.

"Well, Dirk?"

Dirken knew what he meant. He nodded to the cyborg. The ship had grown quiet enough. It was time to make their escape.

"Eow," Dirken said. "Time."

The Ananak drew her kata to a close, her left hand held in a stiff upright salute at her chest, her right hand clawed down by her thigh. Then she nodded her agreement, a smile playing over her lips as her gaze swept down over his body.

He returned the gaze, imagining her athletic form in his hands. Oh, what he would give for a night with her ... if they both survived this, that is.

Dirken closed his eyes for a moment to compose himself, then he got up from the bunk and nonchalantly stepped over to the door of the cell, making himself as wide as he could, arms at his sides, blocking much of the view from the surveillance system.

He heard the clicking and whirring of Yiorgos's arm transforming, then the reverberation of his plasma saber kicking on. A split second later came the metallic whoosh of him cutting through the bunk supports.

"Now!" Yiorgos barked, and Dirken stepped aside. The bunk went sliding past him, turned sideways, just narrow enough to pass through the bars, and slammed into the surveillance system.

The metal bunk contacted the projecting electrocution needles. Electricity arced across all the components as it shorted out and the system went down, the lights on it flickering and going dark before the electrical arcing stopped. The bright LEDs in the ceiling flickered several times and went out. Red emergency lighting blinked on.

Klaxons echoed through the corridors beyond the brig door. Voices shouted. Yiorgos raised his saber and brought it down with a sweep, cleanly cutting through the lock, and they were out.

Dirken pointed to Eow's door as the brig bulkhead was unlatched from the other side. Many voices were shouting outside the door. He raised his fists in a ready stance and stood to the side of the door. "I'll hold them off."

Another metallic clang as Eow's lock was cut through. Dirken braced himself as the door swung open.

There was the brief sight of pirates on the other side, then Dirken was knocked aside as a lavender blur flashed past him. Eow released a banshee cry as she leapt into the pirates, claws outstretched. One was kicked in the chest, his blaster shooting up at the ceiling. She swiped her claws across a Proximan's face, ripping out an entire side of his radial head, blue blood splattering across the other pirates. She turned back to the first pirate.

Dirken blinked in surprise, then jumped into the fight, hitting a Rigellian in his slack jaw, then into his belly flaps, doubling the alien over.

Yiorgos joined, too, slicing through the chest of a human, then, dodging a punch, he stabbed into the red-painted belly folds of a molting Reptiloc. Her eyes rolled as she yelled something in her hiss-like language, then died before her green, scaly head hit the deck.

Eow let out another yowl, twisted into a stance, and punched a Pleiadean, hitting the man in the throat. As he gasped for breath, she grabbed his horns and slammed his face into the wall, then broke his neck with a well-placed kick.

A Rigellian fired his rifle twice, nicking Dirken's arm. Dirken jumped and launched himself off the wall and into the Rigellian,

66

grabbing one of his flaps and pulling him to the ground, then stomped on the line of eyes on his head. He wailed an ear-splitting "Eeeeeeee!" firing the rifle at the ceiling. Dirken disarmed him, then shot him in both of his hearts.

In seconds it was over. Pirates lay on the floor, dead or critically injured. "Six pirates down," Dirken said. "Grab their blasters." He picked up the Pleiadean's, which was a combination of parts from two different models.

"I know where the safe box is," both Dirken and Eow said at the same time, bumping into each other as they both tried to take the lead down the corridor. They looked at each other in annoyance.

"Ladies first," Dirken said, waving his blaster toward the hall.

She flashed a sidelong smile, spots of blue blood spattered across her face. "I'm a warrior, not a lady." Then she slapped his ass and bounded down the corridor.

"Just your type!" Yiorgos said as he ran past. "Don't trust her."

Dirken followed, and the three of them came to an open chamber, an instrument repair room with rusting machine parts around the sides and a chain-and-pulley systems hanging from the ceiling. Across the room was the interrogation chamber.

Four pirates stood in the center of the room, the safe box on the floor behind them. Grendel grinned at them, flexing his arms, as Mom put a hand on the big Oranchian's back. "I was hoping you'd do somethin' stupid like this, maggot!" he said to Dirken.

To Mom's left stood a Rigellian with a pulse rifle in his long, flap-like arms. To Grendel's right, a tall, pale Tau Cetian brandished a blaster in both of his six-fingered hands.

One of those blasters was Dirken's Gree-tech pulse emitter.

Eow wailed again, ran forward, dodged left as the Tau Cetian opened fire, then leapt upon Grendel in a bear hug across the Oranchian's chest. Grendel's eyes went wide in surprise, then turned to shock and pain as Eow flexed. Scores of ebony spikes shot out from her chest and back, giving her a porcupine appearance.

The Oranchian wailed in pain as the spikes penetrated his torso. He tried to rip her off, but the claws on her hands and feet were dug in. Then she sank her teeth into his broad neck and shook her head, ripping the skin apart.

For a long moment everyone watched in shock, then they snapped out of it as one. Dirken and Yiorgos fired on the others, and everyone took cover around the machinery. Plasma bolts and laser fire flashed across the middle of the room and over the safe box.

Dirken took careful aim and fired as the Tau Cetian popped up. The shot went cleanly through the narrow oval of his head and he fell to the floor, light pink blood and brain matter spilling out.

But he had exposed himself. Mom fired his laser pistol. It cut through the air, narrowly missing Dirken's face and slicing through the blaster. The gun exploded in his hand as the power pack perforated. Dirken fell backward behind the machinery, his right palm and fingers red and blistered. He gritted his teeth and sucked in air against the pain.

Across the room, Yiorgos ducked behind a machine as the Rigellian's pulse rifle pounded the far side. Eow leaped off the bloody Oranchian, her spikes retracted. Grendel stared lifelessly up at the ceiling as his flamingo pink-colored blood pooled around him.

Mom turned to attack Eow. Dirken sprinted at him. Mom turned in time to get a fist in his face, knocking him back. The pirate raised his laser pistol, but Dirken chopped his wrist and the gun clattered to the floor.

Dirken ducked as Mom swung a roundhouse. The pirate recovered with a right hook to Dirken's chin, knocking him back.

Dirken grabbed Mom by the head with both hands and at first shoved him back. When the pirate overcompensated by leaning forward, Dirken used the momentum in a jujitsu move to pull his head down, then brought a knee up into the pirate's gut, doubling him over. Dirken uppercut into Mom's face. His red cap flew off his head. Blood poured from his nose as the pirate fell to his knees, dazed.

Dirken finished him off with a left hook to the head, knocking the pirate to the ground, going unconscious with a sigh.

The Rigellian fired his pulse rifle, its bolts burning through the air within millimeters around Dirken. Then Yiorgos bolted forward and sliced clean through the Rigellian's tube-like head, which flopped to the ground, his long, vermiform tongue shooting out of the tentacled mouth at the top of his head. The rifle, still in his hand, continued to fire in rapid bursts. One shot hit a pipe, which ruptured and sprayed water into the room, a length of the pipe clattering to the deck. Another shot hit the safe box near its top, spinning it around.

There were shouts as more pirates came running toward the room. "Eow!" Dirken yelled. "The door!" Eow slammed the door, then lodged the broken length of pipe against the mechanism just as the other pirates arrived.

Dirken reached down and picked up his Gree-tech blaster from the dead hand of the Tau Cetian. He wiped the pale blood on his pants. Then he spied a device on each of the Tau Cetian's wrists. Wide, silvery bracelets with a prominent button. He pressed one and it immediately expanded into a mirrored vambrace that covered the forearm: a bit of mirror armor to protect against lasers.

These could be handy to deflect lasers, he thought, though only my forearms. He shrugged and pressed the button again, causing the vambrace to fold back to a bracelet, then he took the bracelets off and put them on his own wrists.

The pirates pounded on the door, trying to force it open. But it was holding … for now.

Eow was covered head to feet in Grendel's blood. She stepped under the spraying water and let the blood wash off. The water showered her, glistening over her lavender fur and adhering it to her skin. Every firm muscle was revealed as she ran her hands over her body, wiping it clean. Her hands slipped over her head as she looked up into the downpour, eyes closed. Her hands slid down her shoulders, across her slim breasts, then down over her tight abs and over her muscular thighs. She stepped out of the water, dripping, and opened her eyes to look into his.

Dirken didn't look away. He met her eyes with hunger. She returned the look with a mischievous smile and ran her hands over her breasts and down her firm belly to her thighs. "Care for a shower, space jockey?"

The pirates banged on the door and there came a metallic, ripping sound. They were prying it open.

He tore his eyes away from Eow and stepped over to the safe box. There was work to do. The keypad, door, and top of the safe box had been mangled by multiple attempts to cut through it, and the top was scorched by the pulse rifle. He reached down and grabbed the handle to pick it up. The safe raised half a meter, then, with a horrible metallic screech, the top ripped off and the rest of it crashed to the deck.

Dirken blinked in surprise, still holding the handle and top, and peered inside. Eow and Yiorgos also came over and looked in.

Inside was a metal sphere with a diameter almost the length of his forearm. The thing that the Bloodhawk had referred to as "the Heart."

He dropped the lid with a clang and reached inside, pulling the sphere out to examine it. It was heavier than he'd thought. The silvery metal of the outer sheath had an old, slightly oxidized look, and ages of dust still hid in the nooks of the mechanism. There were dozens of ports arrayed on the outside as if it were to be plugged into multiple data cables. Small, green lights blinked very slowly from in between the creases.

Ancient English words were imprinted on one of the metal outer sheaths, along with a yellow symbol of a circle with three, broad, radiating rays.

"Yiorgos, what does this say?"

The cyborg looked closely at the words and brushed off a portion. "Most of it is worn off. I think it says 'central action' or maybe 'center process' in ancient English. And I don't know what this symbol means," he added, pointing to a small yellow circle with three radiating rays coming from it.

"What the hell is this thing?" Dirken asked.

"Maybe it's a bomb," Eow said. Dirken certainly hoped not.

"Not likely," Yiorgos said. "Why would they keep an ancient bomb locked in a safe box?"

The pirates on the other side of the door stopped their banging as someone gave a command. Then sparks flew through a slit in the door as they started cutting through.

"Crap," Dirken said. "Is that the only way out?"

"No," Eow said. "There's another way. Come with me." She picked up the pulse rifle and ran down a side corridor.

Cradling the heavy sphere, Dirken followed. They quickly came to a dead end at an airlock. A handful of red spacesuits with bulbous helmets hung on the wall. One suit was clearly for an Aquarian centaur. The other three were bipedal and of different heights to accommodate different species.

Eow started suiting up. Yiorgos deactivated his plasma saber and started suiting up as well. "Come on!" Eow said to Dirken. "They'll be through in just a minute."

"Out there?" Dirken asked. He gulped and stared out through the little airlock window. Extra-Vehicular Activity. He hated going EVA. The vacuum of space was nowhere for a being to be. He'd seen his share of people die when their suits ruptured, frozen almost instantly as their eyeballs exploded and their lungs ruptured. Going EVA was a necessary part of being a spacer, mainly for maintenance and repair purposes, and he had done it more times than he could count. But it still gave him the willies.

He cleared his throat and tried to shake off the fear. "And just where are we going?" He looked down at the suit and realized it didn't have any thrusters. One wrong slip off the hull and he would go floating off into space.

"The hangar has an access hatch," Eow said. "Come on!"

He figured he didn't really have a choice, not with a shipload of pirates about to barge in.

Dirken gingerly set the sphere down, still wondering if it was a bomb, and looked at the remaining suits. Other than the centaur, the only one that hadn't been grabbed was tall and thin, probably for a lanky Tau Cetian. He started trying to put it on, but it clearly wouldn't fit. He couldn't get the straps around his muscular chest. "Damn it!"

"Here," Yiorgos said, already strapped into his suit. "Use the centaur suit. The part for the lower body and back legs will just have to flop around behind you." He pulled it off the wall and opened it up.

Reluctantly, Dirken stepped into the suit and latched it shut, then Yiorgos twisted the helmet on, activating the suit's life support systems and projecting a readout of suit stats onto the faceplate of the helmet. The air in the suit smelled like wet dog, and dozens of tiny scales clung to the inside surface.

Dirken felt like he was wearing a tent, and as he stepped forward to pick up the sphere, the "lower body" and back legs of the suit dragged along behind him. "I feel like a total idiot wearing this."

"Oh, suck it up, space jockey," Eow said, stifling a laugh. She was fully suited and carrying the pulse rifle.

They stepped into the airlock and closed the inner hatch just as they heard a loud bang from the other room.

"They're through the door," Yiorgos said.

As the airlock evacuated, Eow pointed at her comm panel on her arm and flashed three fingers, indicating channel three. They each activated that channel on their suits. "Energize your magboots," she said through the intercom.

Dirken realized that, while the front magboots were needed for his own feet, the rear magboots would act as an anchor, seeing as how he wasn't a centaur. So he simply clomped the soles of the two rear boots together, conjuring an odd image of him as a centaur doing an Irish dance and clicking its heels together.

Eow opened the outer hatch. Each of them stepped to the edge of the airlock and crawled out onto the outer hull of the ship in single file.

Beyond, the vastness of outer space wrapped its celestial arms around them, a billion starry eyes watching them step along the brigantine's hull.

CHAPTER ELEVEN
Extra-Vehicular Activity

For many minutes (Dirken wasn't sure how long, since the time readout on his heads-up display was written in Aquarian centaur language) they clomped along the hull in silence. Dirken made a conscious effort to keep his eyes on the hull and not on the vastness of space, not just for the sake of his own nervousness "out there," but also because of the difficulties of wearing the ridiculously oversized suit.

He soon found himself sweating and huffing. For one thing, Dirken's magboots clung too tightly to the hull, requiring him to tug with each step. It seemed Aquarian centaurs had stronger legs. For another thing, the stupid lower body and back legs of the centaur spacesuit flopped and swung with every step as if he were being trailed by a giant mass of balloons. There was just enough mass to it to cause him to wobble every time the suit reached one extreme or another, and sometimes it wrapped completely around his torso. The physics of its movement seemed hard to anticipate. The combination gave his gait a ridiculous, clownish stride and threatened to trip him up.

"Come on, Dirken!" Eow said through the comm, glancing back. "They've surely discovered we're out here by now. We have to hurry!"

"Easy for you to say," Dirken muttered. His legs were already tiring and the trio had only gotten about halfway to the hangar.

Yiorgos hung back for a moment to wait for him. "You seem to be having some problems, Dirk."

Dirken swore he heard a little titter of laughter before the cyborg turned off his mic.

"Yeah … Problems."

"Here." Yiorgos reached out his hands when Dirken was within touching distance. "I can take the Heart."

Dirken's first thought was to keep it and just charge to the end. He thought of the ancient North American game of football—or was it called foosball?—where a player with an oversized helmet would run a ball to an end zone, never dropping the ball or getting brutally slammed to the ground by other players. But then the rational side of his brain took over.

"Thanks," Dirken said, and started to hand over the Heart, slowing down.

The back part of the centaur suit wrapped around him just as he tugged up his right boot. The suit went under his leg as he stepped, tripping him, then the suit swept up between him and Yiorgos, hitting the Heart.

The sphere slipped out of his hands. "Oh shit!" Dirken reached up as the Heart floated up and away from him. Yiorgos tried for it too. His fingers touched it and slipped off, propelling the Heart faster.

"No!" Dirken shouted, then jumped as hard as he could. The boots came off the hull with a thwang. Then he was floating, slowly catching up to the Heart. His hands reached out.

"I've got you," Yiorgos said in the comm.

"No, wait!"

"Can't!" Then Dirken grabbed the Heart, his palms clinging to it as hard as he could.

Then he realized he was no longer attached to the ship. He stifled a rising panic. His heart rate escalated. His eyes darted up to the endless sea of stars. He was floating away! "Yiorgos!"

There was a yank on his suit. Dirken stopped abruptly. The Heart almost slipped out again.

He looked back and saw that Yiorgos held the EVA suit like a handle at the very tip end of one of the back legs.

"Got you." Yiorgos pulled him back down.

Dirken heaved a huge sigh and tried to control his breathing. It was a great relief when his boots contacted the hull. Yiorgos reached out for the Heart.

"I think I'll hold on to it, thanks," Dirken said.

He turned back toward their objective. Eow stood watching them. "If you boys are done playing, we've got a ways to go yet."

They glanced at each other, then followed her across the hull. "Playing!" Dirken muttered.

He continued lumbering along for what seemed like an interminable stretch, wondering all the time what the pirates were planning. *Surely, he thought, they know we're out here. What kind of ambush are we walking into? This may not have been a good plan.*

They had to make a slight detour around an area that had been blown open by bombardment, the hull blackened and twisted inward in wreckage. Jagged shards of metal as large as he was were bent around and threatened to snag and rip their suits if they got too close. He didn't want to be freeze-dried in space.

They passed various portholes. One of these looked in to an aquatic environment. As Dirken gazed down into it, the pale white face of an Argulan suddenly appeared out of the greenish water and looked back at him, its sucker mouth growing wide in reaction. It then swam away in haste, pushing a webbed hand against the porthole to launch itself. The tip of its eel-like tail slapping the window as it propelled itself away.

"Crap," Dirken said into the mic. "A crewman saw me through a porthole."

"Well," Yiorgos responded, "I'm sure they knew we were out here, and they probably have guessed where we're headed, anyhow."

At last, as they passed around a gravwell panel that looked like it had been stolen from some freighter, the hangar came into view. He thought about sabotaging this important piece of equipment, but it would take too long. *Just another couple minutes to the hatch off to the side of the bay door.*

Then a compartment opened over the bay. A swarm of "flea" drones came zooming out and arced toward them.

"Shit!" they all three said in unison.

"Run for the hangar!" Dirken said, suddenly not noticing his tired legs. His hands were full with the Heart. His blaster was inside the suit.

But Eow had her pulse rifle handy. She turned and fired several bursts at the fleas, hitting two of them. One exploded. The other drifted off into space, disabled.

The fleas were black and ovoid and festooned with sensors, grappling legs, thrusters, and a laser. They had seemed so small and insignificant from far away, but up close he realized they were large enough he'd hardly be able to wrap his arms around one and massive enough that it probably weighed almost as much as he did.

Yiorgos grabbed Dirken's arm to pull him along. Eow fired again as the swarm descended upon them. Two more fleas exploded.

They were almost to the hatch. A flea slammed into Eow, knocking her back, but one boot stayed adhered. Then two fleas fired on her, narrowly missing. She swung her rifle like a club and hit one of them. It went twirling off at an odd angle.

Dirken and Yiorgos passed her and reached the hatch. He felt the reverberation of rifle fire through his boots.

The cyborg grabbed the rotating handle of the hatch and turned it, but then ducked as laser fire cut an arc across the hatch. Another flea slammed into Dirken, and he almost lost the Heart again.

A sputtering sound, then Dirken's suit deflated with a whoosh. He realized with a horror that the flea had punctured the flopping back of the suit. He tried to cry out, but the air rushed out of his lungs.

It was his EVA nightmare—for real this time.

He shoved Yiorgos in a panic, just as the hatch opened, revealing the airlock inside.

His partner turned, saw what was happening, grabbed and swung him into the airlock, then followed him in.

Dirken let go of the Heart, turned, and bunched up the suit to try to block the leak, wherever the hell it was. His vision was clouding over. He could feel the surface of his eyeballs freezing.

Eow plowed into the airlock with a flea on her heels. The robot ricocheted off the walls of the airlock, firing its laser in seemingly random directions and burning lines across the panels.

Dirken was losing consciousness. His eyes felt like they were being pulled out of their sockets. He couldn't catch a breath. When he opened his mouth in an unconscious action, the saliva vaporized, popping on the inside surfaces of his mouth.

Then Yiorgos slammed the hatch and latched it, hitting the red "atmosphere" button.

CHAPTER TWELVE
Hangar Battle

The atmosphere slowly returned. Eow grabbed the flea by its back, turned, and aimed it at the inner airlock door as it continued to fire.

Dirken twisted and ripped off the helmet, gasping for breath, even before the atmosphere was back to Terran-normal. He was covered in beads of sweat that had frozen to little spheres on his skin when he had lost life support. Now they were thawing, dropping off of his brow like a mini rain of hail.

The inner hatch to the hangar opened … and the flea's lasers burned through two pirates on the other side as Eow guided it. The human and Proximan pirates screamed as the laser cut across their chests.

Dirken gratefully unlatched the stupid centaur suit and stepped out, his legs wobbly and coated in sweat. At last he pulled his blaster.

Yiorgos threw off his helmet. He picked up the Heart, tucking it under his left arm, and activated his plasma saber with the other.

"Go!" Eow yelled, slamming the flea into the wall until it sparked and fell silent. Then she picked up the plasma rifle and started firing and advancing through the airlock into an open space that he assumed was the hangar.

Dirken's vision was still fuzzy from the suit breech, but he aimed as best as he could at any moving figures he saw. He fired off three shots. Two figures fell.

"This way!" Eow yelled, having discarded her helmet. They raced toward the far end.

Dirken ducked as a plasma bolt sizzled through his hair. Another struck the deck plating between his boots.

Yiorgos fired off several shots. Then a bolt slammed into his right leg, throwing him to the ground and spinning him, his saber cutting through the deck plating in a line. The Heart rolled away from him. "Cover us!" Dirken yelled to Eow.

As she laid down a rapid round of cover fire, Dirken helped Yiorgos to his feet, wrapping his arm around his partner. The cyborg's right mechanical leg had a chunk blown away just over the kneecap.

Dirken fired several shots, then roughly pulled Yiorgos over to get the Heart. "Watch it!" the cyborg said. "My leg was blown open, in case you didn't notice!"

"Stop complaining and get the damned sphere."

Several more blinks and Dirken's eyesight cleared, but his eyes felt very dry and pained. Following Eow, they were headed toward an interstellar shuttle, its gravwell panels wrapping around the hull like a ribcage.

"Oh, fuck!" Eow exclaimed. "My ship!"

And then he saw what she had. The gravwell panels had been cut into. The mass expanders—osmium-iridium alloy packs with diamond lenses that were necessary to project the gravwell generator emissions—had been stripped out. One of the most valuable parts of any ship. Without them, there could be no folding of space and no escape.

The pirates stopped firing. Then came a deep, cynical laugh from Dirken's left. He turned and saw the Bloodhawk standing beside three other pirates, a Rigellian with a blaster and two lizard-like Reptilocs aiming pulse rifles. They were about six meters away behind a parked shuttle.

"Captain Neenan!" Eow growled. "You have damaged the property of the Eridani Mafia. Grimmag Ruby-Eye will not be pleased."

The pirate captain pulled his sword, a scimitar, from the scabbard on his lower body. The metal gleamed, then the edge flared with a blue glow as he activated the plasma blade on it.

"He can shove his displeasure up his maggoty ass!" the centaur said. "I like your gumption. It seems I've lost some crewmen, thanks to you. Hand over the Heart and throw down your weapons. If you comply, I'll let you replace them as my crew—and live. If you refuse, you die."

The Heart, Dirken thought, glancing down at the sphere in Yiorgos's arms. *What the hell is this thing? Whatever it is, it's got a value high enough to take on a UW destroyer AND defy the Eridani Mafia!* He wasn't sure which was more dangerous.

"No chance, Bloodhawk!" Dirken shouted, backing away. "You'll have to do better than that!"

Yiorgos looked up at him incredulously. "Yes, forget it!" Eow added. "Grimmag will destroy you and your miserable little fleet!"

"Have it your way!" the Bloodhawk said. He pointed his scimitar at the trio, and the three pirates opened fire.

Eow returned fire, and they ran for cover behind Eow's ship, ducking behind the front of the ship as rifle shots impacted around them.

"They're advancing!" Dirken shouted as he fired back at the pirates.

Then Eow gasped. Dirken shot a glance over to her then straightened in shock, swinging his blaster around to face a new threat.

"Uh uh uh!" Mom said. He had sneaked around Eow's ship and grabbed her by the neck from behind, his blaster barrel pushed against the back of her head. His face had turned bluish with bruising and was still covered in dried blood from his fight with Dirken. His right eye was swollen shut, but his left stared at Dirken with menace. "Wouldn't want your lovely little kitten losin' any whiskers, now would you, maggot?" He shook Eow by the neck, and she responded by emitting a low growl and showing her fangs. "And don't even think about usin' those spines of yours, girly. I got you at arm's length. Now drop your weapons!"

Mom had Eow in front of him. Dirken didn't want to risk firing for fear of hitting her. Eow dropped the rifle. Then the Ananak swung into action.

She dipped, spun, and in one smooth move knocked away the blaster with a right arm block and ripped out Mom's throat with the claws on her left hand. Before Mom had time to realize what was happening, Eow spun again, her tail counterbalancing, swooped to pick up the rifle, and fired it point blank into Mom's chest.

It was the same kata Dirken had seen her do in the brig, only sped up to just a couple seconds.

Mom fell backward onto the deck, a gaping hole in his torso and his neck a bloody ruin. His gawking eyes staring up at the ceiling. He coughed blood and then lay still.

Dirken was transfixed by her prowess. But the explosions of several rifle pulses next to him broke him out of his mesmerization. He returned fire, hitting one of the Reptilocs in the chest. But the beast of a pirate shook it off with a high-pitched, reverberating howl and she slowly advanced with a smoking wound.

"There!" Yiorgos said, pointing to their left. "That's our ride!"

Dirken and Eow turned to see where Yiorgos was pointing. It was the bright yellow fightercraft that had earlier intercepted their shuttle.

"The Bloodhawk's fighter?" Eow said. She smiled. "I like your style, cyborg!"

They ran for the fighter, Yiorgos leaning against Dirken's shoulder. "How do you know the ship won't be coded for access?" Dirken asked.

"Think about it, Dirk," Yiorgos said. "No sane crewman would try to take the Bloodhawk's fighter!"

Dirken laughed despite himself, then fired again. He hit the same Reptiloc in the same place. This time, she fell to the ground and didn't move again.

"My fighter!" Neenan cried, seeing where they were headed. The captain sprinted forward, loping like a lion, his scimitar raised and ready to strike.

Dirken aimed and pulled the trigger, but nothing happened. He glanced down and realized the power pack was out of charge. "Damn!" He holstered the blaster.

Eow fired her rifle, hitting the Rigellian and sending the Bloodhawk sideways to dodge.

"Here!" Yiorgos said. He put down the Heart, then reached over with his left hand, pressed a couple hidden catches on his right elbow, then turned.

The cyborg's right forearm detached, still sporting the activated plasma saber.

Dirken stared in disbelief. "You can do that?"

"Just take it and fight!" Yiorgos yelled, handing his arm to Dirken, then picking up the Heart and hobbling toward the fighter.

Dirken didn't have time to think. The Bloodhawk whooped and leaped upon him, knocking him to his back.

He raised Yiorgos's arm and blocked, just in time. The captain's sword swung down. The plasma edges threw blue sparks as the blades met and slid.

The centaur's strength was like that of three men. Even with two hands around Yiorgos's arm, the Bloodhawk was still sliding his scimitar, one-handed, down the saber toward Dirken. The swords crackled where they touched each other.

Then the pirate swung again. Once again Dirken blocked it, hitting the saber and getting pushed lower.

He gritted his teeth. Their blades lowered further until they were just a centimeter from his face. The heat from the plasma burned at his cheek.

The Bloodhawk smiled in victory, his four eyes narrowing.

Rifle bolts exploded around and past them.

The Bloodhawk half-turned and shouted, "Stop firing toward me, you mongrels!"

It was the distraction Dirken needed. He kicked up into the Bloodhawk's lower body as hard as he could and made contact, his boot going deep into the soft part of the stomach.

The pirate captain grunted and coughed, stepping back. Then swung again. Dirken parried then made a right cut and sliced through the pirate's chest. It cut through a bandoleer, which fell to the deck with a dozen power packs and a blaster.

Dirken grabbed the Bloodhawk's blaster from its holster. As the Bloodhawk leapt again, Dirken aimed and fired at the bandoleer.

The power packs detonated. Dirken was thrown back and momentarily blinded by the flash and heat. When he blinked and focused again, the Bloodhawk was two meters away, lying on his side with a massive burn across his lower body. "Come on, Dirk!" Yiorgos yelled. Neenan tried to rise up but fell back to the deck.

Dirken picked up Yiorgos's forearm and ran to the fightercraft. As he bolted up the ramp to the open cockpit, the remaining pirates opened fire again, hitting the ramp around him.

He leapt into the ship, careful with the plasma saber, and the fighter immediately hovered, the transparent canopy lowering over them. The fighter had two cockpits: the front for piloting, and the back for the gunner. Eow was in the front cockpit sitting on a padded bench perpendicular to the console. Dirken and Yiorgos were in the back, separated from the front cockpit by a wall console and a narrow entry off to the side.

"I have access!" Eow shouted back, then she took the controls and fired. The massive prow cannon cut huge craters into the hangar walls, shredding pirates as they dragged the Bloodhawk out of the hangar. Dirken was glad Yiorgos was right; the ship controls weren't coded.

From the front cockpit came a computerized voice, speaking in a swirling, grunting vocalization. "I cannot get attitude adjustment," Eow said. "It is voice activated in the Aquarian centaur language."

Yiorgos reattached his arm and deactivated the plasma saber. "Trade places with me."

Eow stepped back and Yiorgos slid to the front, using the divider to steady himself and sit on the bench. He activated his vocal inserts while tilting his head, letting the computerized part of his mind take over. Soon he was speaking the language of Aquarian centaurs.

Yiorgos turned the ship and aimed at the other fighter. Two well-placed shots, and the fighter exploded in a massive yellow fireball.

Alarms flashed, and the hangar door opened. The fire extinguished as the oxygen left—probably part of the automated fire safety protocol—but it gave them the chance they needed. Yiorgos engaged the engines and they shot out of the hangar.

"Fold now!" Dirken yelled.

"I haven't calculated a trajectory yet," Yiorgos shouted back.

The two other ships opened fire, narrowly missing the craft as Yiorgos dodged to port. Two missile ports slipped open on the side of the brigantine. "Just do it! We'll be in a thousand different trajectories if one of their missiles hit us!"

Yiorgos activated the gravwell engine. Large rods extended out of the fighter and arched around it, surrounding it like a cage. Then space folded, pinching in on itself and exploding outward again to another part of the galaxy.

CHAPTER THIRTEEN
In the Cockpit

Dirken sighed in relief once they had folded, and they hadn't landed in the middle of a planet or next to a star. Doubtless there was a neutrino tracker in the ship, but after a couple more gravjumps, they were far enough away that it would take at least an Earth day before the signal could get to the Bloodhawk—assuming he was even still alive.

Dirken felt for his lucky runestone and was relieved to find it in the hidden breast pocket of his leather jacket. He pulled it out, gave it a rub with his thumb, then tucked it back in.

The rear cockpit was just large enough for two, with Dirken and Eow upon a comfortable, padded couch, and just enough height to stand upright before hitting the transparent aluminum canopy. A display on the wall in front of them showed an interactive navigation chart and auxiliary weapons control.

They looked under the cushions of the bench and found a compartment. A toolbox had been stowed inside. It wasn't well-equipped, but there were enough tools for Yiorgos to augment his native repair system and work on his blasted leg up in the front cockpit, after he'd taken off the spacesuit. The cyborg hoped it could at least get him walking on his own. Next to the toolbox was a duffel bag. Opening it, Dirken found a money purse containing currency from different worlds: a handful of United Worlds chits, iridium coins from Proxima Centauri, a few very valuable palladium spheres the size of ball bearings from Oran c, and a dozen cloth-of-silver bills from Aquaria. *No emergency kit is complete without some spending money,* he thought, and pocketed the little bag. Also in the duffel was a med kit, a towel, a couple full water bottles, and some rations. Dirken broke one package open, took a sniff of the brown patty in it, then sealed it again and threw it back in the bag. It reeked like rotten fish but looked like granola and red berries. "What the hell do Aquarian centaurs eat?" he muttered. But then he found some yellow protein bars that actually smelled appetizing.

Yiorgos called back, "Dirk, I'm setting the navigation to Nüwa so we can finally deliver this blasted sphere-thing and get our money."

Eow turned to Dirken and narrowed her eyes. "We had a deal!"

Dirken started to reply, but Yiorgos interrupted, his voice rising. "What deal? Dirk, don't tell me you made another 'plan' without discussing it!"

Dirken shrugged, even though Yiorgos couldn't see him from the front. "I told you I had a plan. It's just that you were being interrogated when Eow and I came to a decision in the brig."

Eow leaned back to look into the front cockpit, her spacesuit crinkling loudly. "Dirken and I agreed that if I helped you escape, you would first take me to the Eridani Mafia before you go your own way. I promise no harm will come to you from Grimmag Ruby-Eye. That is all."

"That is all?" Yiorgos repeated. Dirk heard him slam a tool to the deck. "That is *all?* Dirk, you realize the Eridani Mafia is only the most ruthless gangster organization in the entire galaxy, right? Don't you remember what happened the last time we made a deal with them?"

"Relax," Dirken said. "We're just stopping by. It's not like we've made some deal with them … again. Besides, it got us away from the Bloodhawk." And, he thought, *I wouldn't want an angry Ananak with claws and body spikes attacking us in a fighter cockpit!*

For several moments, Yiorgos was quiet, and Dirken waited for him to speak. But Eow broke in. "So, do we have a deal or not?"

"Of course it's a deal. Right, Yiorgos ol' buddy?"

He heard Yiorgos pick up the tool again and continue working on his leg. A good sign.

"Fine," the cyborg finally answered. "But you owe me. No more 'plans' without consulting me, got it? I can't take any more damage."

Dirken waved it away. "See," he said to Eow. "We can be accommodating. I'm always true to my word."

He grabbed some of the yellow protein bars—careful to avoid the fishy-smelling patties—and water from the duffel and handed it around to Yiorgos. The cyborg's consternated face immediately changed when he saw the sundries. He eagerly drank down several cups of water, then opened a protein bar and took a bite. Dirken went back to the couch.

"So what are you?" he heard Yiorgos ask the Ananak, between mouthfuls. "An assassin? I saw you fight."

"I am foremost a warrior, but I am also what the Eridani need me to be. For this job I was a messenger."

"Some messenger!" Dirken said, smirking, his eyes conspicuously running over her. She smiled back at him.

He heard Yiorgos activate a control panel with a series of beeps. "Okay, messenger. What system should I punch in?"

"The Baeris star system," Eow said.

"Which planet?"

"Not a planet. When we fold there, I will direct you further."

Not a planet? Dirken wondered. *A moon?*

"Okaaay." Yiorgos used his vocal inserts to say a few phrases in the centaur language, then the starship lurched slightly as it changed trajectory. "We'll be moving sub-light for a half hour, then two more gravjumps. Should be there in a few hours."

"Take your time," Eow told him, but her eyes were on Dirken.

"Fine." Yiorgos sighed, and Dirken heard him getting comfortable. "If you'll excuse me, I'll be Netfolding."

Dirken heard the cyborg settle into a more comfortable position and the little whir of his cheek projector engaging to make the Unity Sphere hologram. In moments he would be in a deep Netfolding meditation.

Dirken rummaged through the med kit to see what they could use, then pulled out a tube of burn cream. His inflamed hand burned from the blaster explosion. He applied the cream to his hand, but his attention was pulled away as Eow started undressing.

She unlatched her red space suit down her chest, peeling it away from the central seam. Beneath, her thin clothing clung to her breasts, still wet from the water pipe that had showered her back in the brigantine. She looked down at Dirken as he sat upon the couch, watching his reaction as she slowly opened the seam, past her ribs, her solar plexus, her belly. The stretchy suit underneath undulated across a six-pack of muscle.

She stepped out of the suit with a deliberate movement, raising a muscular thigh and leg out and placing her foot between Dirken's legs, the soft lavender fur so tantalizingly close. She licked her lips and nodded in a little invitation. He reached out and ran his hand along her knee and inner thigh, his fingers sliding through the fur.

The suit crumpled to the ground, her tail at last liberated, unwinding from the back of the suit and swaying slowly. She closed her eyes and sighed, clearly glad to be free of the suit. She put her hands on her chest and slowly rubbed them down her front.

"You're … you're still wet," Dirken gasped. He offered her the towel with his left hand.

She opened her amethyst eyes and gazed into his, then ran a dark tongue over her fangs. "Yes. I am." Instead of taking the towel, she reached behind her neck and unbuckled the strap, watching his reaction, then pulled the straps away from her neck. "Very … wet."

Dirken's heart skipped a beat. His breathing accelerated.

She lowered her arms, stripping the thin garment from her chest. Small, dark blue nipples rose from the thin fur on her breasts.

She pulled the garment down further, exposing her belly, four more nipples ran in parallel, but flat against her belly on either side of the soft roll of her abs and navel. The fur there was a paler shade of lavender, almost white, down to her crotch.

Dirken felt himself growing as he watched, straining against his leather pants.

Then she let the outfit drop. Past her waist. Past her hips.

She stood there in unabashed nudity, tail flicking.

His eyes fell to her thighs—and between them. The slim mound of her pubis fell away to dark blue, exquisite lips.

He drew in a ragged breath and looked up at her face.

She smiled, her eyes half-closed. She reached down, picked up his right hand and the burn cream he still held. Squeezed the tube. Rubbed the cream over the palm where the pirate's blaster had exploded during the firefight. "You need a tender touch, Dirken." She took his hand in both of hers. Massaged his palms. Slipped her fingers between his.

He nodded, eyes fixed on hers. The relief from the burn cream was instantaneous, but he hardly noticed as she rubbed him.

She placed his hand on her left thigh, the tips of his fingers wrapping around to lay on her left butt cheek. Then she unbuttoned his shirt.

"Take it off," she said.

He did as told. Stripped off his shirt and vest.

He started to take off his holster, but she stopped him. "Leave it on. I want to feel your weapon against me."

She unbuttoned his pants, hands lingering over his tight groin, then tugged off his pants and boots.

He was now fully erect and exposed—nude except for his blaster and gun belt and the vambrace bracelets.

He wrapped his left hand around her waist and ran his right palm up the inside of her athletic thigh. Fingers ran through soft fur. He leaned forward and planted a kiss next to her navel. The fur was lighter and thinner there than elsewhere.

His fingers reached the crease where thigh met groin. She was so warm. So soft. Yielding.

Eow moaned as he touched her, exploring, caressing. She was already so wet there. Instead of a single clitoris like a human, a half dozen lined her vulva. She shivered each time his fingers orbited one.

Dirken started to lay down, but she shook her head. Pushed him back into a sitting position, his back against the cushions.

Eow positioned herself over his left leg. Leaned over him. Her paw-like hand caressed his face, then lightly ran a finger across his lips. Down his neck. Into the hair of his chest.

Her face was so close to his. He wanted to kiss her, but she moved aside and nuzzled his ear as her hand continued downward over his tight belly, her breath warm against his neck.

Pleasure washed over him as she caressed his cock. He leaned back into the cushions, letting the bliss take him, and wrapped his arms around her slim frame.

She nipped his ear, then ran her fangs down his neck. The sensation sent shivers down his body.

He tried to guide her onto him, but she flexed her hand. Black claws came out. She lightly raked them down his chest—not hard enough to break the skin, but a light scratch that excited him, sent waves of pleasure through him. His heart pumped furiously.

Then she smiled, looking him directly in the eyes. Came closer. Her lips joined with his. Her tongue was rough like sandpaper, but he didn't push her away. For many minutes they embraced, exploring each other.

Then Eow bit his lower lip, her fangs drawing blood. He winced, and she pulled away, laughing. She licked the blood off her own lips, then kissed him again, softer.

She pulled away again, then turned her back to him. Situated herself against him. Lowered herself onto him as he wrapped his arms around her firm waist.

They both gasped in ecstasy as he entered her from behind.

Dirken pulled her tight against him. She was as soft as satin. Her tail pressed against his belly and sinuated.

They moved as one entity, and for those moments he couldn't believe his fortune. She was so soft, yet so athletic. The moment was sheer joy, like the breeze blowing through hair in an open hovcar.

Her anatomy was surprisingly human, but muscles moved inside, stroking him, urging him inward.

He had to fight to keep from finishing too soon. He thought about his blaster—about the power pack. *I need to replace the power pack. I need to … need to buy a new …*

He ran his hand up her belly and across the rows of nipples.

"Bite me," she whispered, undulating her body, rubbing herself against his gun belt.

"What?"

"Bite my neck!" It was a command. "The hairless spot!"

Dirken pulled her tight against him. Was this an Ananak thing? Or just a fetish?

At the base of the back of her neck was the ovoid bald spot he'd seen back in the cell. The skin was a little tougher there, like her palms, as if designed for this.

"Do it now!" she urged, breathless.

He opened his mouth. Teeth against skin. Bit down. There was the acid taste of sweat. But more than that, a peculiar musk. It tasted good. Smelled like sex. Made him hold her tighter.

She moved faster. Reached back to grip him. Her claws were out. "Harder! Bite me harder!"

He did as she said, fearing to break her skin.

She leaned forward. Groaned in ecstasy. Bucked. She shoved and scraped against the wall in front of them. Pushed herself hard against him. Panted. Emitted an animalistic, deep-throated rumble as he pumped. Her tail wrapped around his leg and squeezed.

He could hardly control himself. He moaned, trying not to lose the grip of his teeth against her movement. "Ohhh," he moaned, losing the bite. Thrusted harder. "Oh … fuck …!"

She cried out in ecstasy. He finished in an explosive wave of rapture. Reared his head back with the orgasm as they finished together.

He lowered his forehead against her back as she slowed her movement. Sweat slicked her fur. Her back rose and fell with urgent breaths.

Dirken heard a grunt, then looked up, blinking.

Yiorgos stood in the narrow opening to the front cockpit, his hand activated into the plasma saber.

"I should have known," the cyborg said, deactivating the saber. "I honestly thought you were killing each other back here." He turned and walked back to the front, shaking his head. "I'm going back to my Netfolding. *Try* to keep it to yourselves, eh?"

Eow laughed—light and carefree—then moved off his lap.

Dirken's eyes widened. The upholstered wall in front of them had been slashed and ruined by her claws.

CHAPTER FOURTEEN

Make a Wish

Still nude, they reclined together on the couch with Eow in Dirken's arms, his legs intertwined with her legs and tail, his arms lightly wrapped around her.

The cabin light was off, allowing easy sight through the transparent canopy. Dirken leaned his head back and looked up at the vast array of stars.

A heavy vibration thrummed through the craft as gravjump ribs surrounded the fighter, arcing over the canopy, and Yiorgos piloted the ship into a jump. The Jacobian gravwell generator spun up, shaking the ship with its strong throbbing. Then the starfield pinched in and exploded outward to a new part of space.

The ribs retracted, and as Dirken's eyes readjusted, he saw a bright red star gleaming in the expanse. "Make a wish," he said, pointing at the star.

Eow turned her head partway toward him. "A wish? Why?"

Dirken smiled at the silliness. "Never mind. It's stupid, really."

"No, tell me."

He chuckled. "Well, it's a silly old Earth custom for little kids. When night comes, and you see the first visible star, you sing, 'Star light, star bright, first star I see tonight; I wish I may, I wish I might, have the wish I wish tonight.' It's superstitious, really."

Eow played her fingers over Dirken's forearms. "It is cute."

"The really silly thing is that the first 'star' that the kids usually saw was a planet called Venus."

Eow laughed. It was that light laugh that's so opposite her warrior ways—the sort a young girl might make while running with friends through a field.

"You are no better, Dirken. The joke is on you! The 'star' you pointed at is a nebula, not a star. I think your people call it the 'Red Rectangle Nebula.'"

"Oh. Well …" Now he *really* felt sheepish.

She laughed again. "But I would rather wish upon the product of a supernova than some stagnant star or planet. It is an honorable death for a star, giving birth to something majestic … proud."

Yiorgos yawed the fighter away from the nebula and rotated. A red giant star rolled into sight, relatively close, filling most of the view. The canopy tinted in response as the nav chart on the wall gave the star's name as "Aldebaran."

In response to the ship's movement, the Heart rolled out of the circle of clothes it had been situated in and came to rest against his left leg. He pushed it away and it rolled back into the corner to his left, illuminating the cushions green with its slow blinking lights. The thought flitted through his mind again that the Bloodhawk had called it the "Heart." *What the hell is this thing?*

Dirken pushed the thought out of his mind. "So," he said. "What would you wish upon that nebula?"

"Like a supernova, I also wish for an honorable death."

Dirken ran his hand down the silky fur of her firm belly and came to rest where the line of her thigh slanted down to her groin. He felt himself getting excited again.

"That seems like an unexpected thing to wish for."

"Why?"

"Well, *death* isn't the usual thing people wish for, honorable or not."

"Maybe not *your* people. For mine, back on Ananakia, there is no greater wish—at least for a warrior. It is what I was taught from the time I first started training."

"How young were you?"

"We start as soon as we can run, around six years old for my world, enrolling in a training center where we live for the rest of our youth." She paused, seemingly lost in a pleasant memory, then added, "When I was fifteen years old—which I think might be around twelve in your Earth years—I blooded my first grenloc on the Plains of Yenla. The beast was three meters long and as massive as a hovcar. Its hide was tough, and it had three long horns on its forehead. If a grenloc charges you, all you can do is dodge or it will gore you to death. Death is not seen as a poor outcome, if it is a death without cowering or fleeing. Some of the trainees died. But I survived and bled him with my spear."

"Did you kill it?"

"No. I was too small and weak to kill such a beast. Too young. But that was the point. I showed bravery and skill against a foe I could never hope to kill. I injured it and lived to fight another day."

Impressive! Dirken thought. He wondered if he could have done such a thing at that age. "Your parents must have been worried."

"My mother was a great warrior, as was her mother before her, and those who came before. She understood."

"And your father?"

She shifted to look at him again, her whiskers sweeping across his cheek as she turned her amethyst eyes to look into his hazel ones. "You know nothing of Ananaks, do you?" She chuckled and turned back. "I do not know who my father is, for my mother had many studs in her harem. Men on Ananakia are either studs of great value and strength or they are lower-class workers who are unable to live up to those select standards." She ran her fingers through his hair as she spoke. "The women are either warriors or property owners. Warriors have many studs. But the studs are sometimes freed … after they have bred past their peak, often going on to positions of authority or out into the galaxy as warriors in their own right." She reached around him with her right hand and ran it over his thigh and buttock. "I think of you as a warrior of that sort."

"Who says I'm past my peak!" he said with mock annoyance.

She laughed and pushed herself against his groin. He was growing hard again.

"And what about you?" she asked. "Did you train as a warrior?"

He grew more somber, thinking back to his youth. An orphan and refugee. Parents killed when the mining colony was destroyed. Their asteroid, Eros, had collided with another after a gravitational anomaly. Earth wouldn't take him, since miners and their children were looked down upon and he wasn't born there, so he was shipped off to Tesla. He closed his eyes, remembering the explosions. The alarms. The panic.

His parents were never found.

"I guess you could say I had an informal training. I grew up alone on the streets of Nikola" he said, referring to the capital city of Tesla. "Ran with gangs. Scrambled to make ends meet beneath the glittering skyscrapers and luxury stores. Lived underground. Stole when I could. Fought when I had to—and killed." He winced as a memory flashed by of his first kill, a boy his age who had tried to murder him in his sleep. "By the time I was sixteen I ran my own hustles and smuggled goods to offworld captains." He leaned into her head, felt the softness of her fur against his face, and the bad memories dissipated. He took a breath. "By the time I was nineteen, I had my own rickety ship to run those goods myself."

She was quiet a moment, her tail wrapping and unwrapping around his right leg. "Thievery is not honorable, but to do so to survive is acceptable." She arched her back and ran her tongue over her fangs. "The thought of you killing to survive gets me so excited."

She took his right hand in hers and moved it down between her legs. His heart fluttered. She seemed to enjoy his renewed firmness as she moved against him.

She moaned as he used his fingers to stimulate her, his other arm wrapping tight around her chest. He lightly kissed her behind her ear, then moved down to her shoulder, kissing as he went.

"I think we have plenty of time before the next gravjump," he said softly.

She turned so they were chest-to-chest, smiling with bedroom eyes, and rolled him so that she was on top.

"Yes …" she whispered, her fangs lightly touching the skin of his neck, "My stud."

And they made love again, this time gently, caressingly, in the red radiance of the star overhead.

CHAPTER FIFTEEN
The Witch's Tits

Yiorgos yelled back to the rear cockpit, "We're about to fold to the Baeris star system." Dirken and Eow had dressed, so they stepped forward to the front cockpit.

"I see you've repaired your leg," Dirken said.

"Only partway. A number of synthmuscles are severed in the right thigh. I imagine I can walk with a limp, but I need a couple new parts. Maybe when we get to where we're going I can find a cybernetic engineer to help with it."

"There are engineers at the hideout," Eow said. "I can get one for you. They can also modify the controls of this fighter so that it can be piloted without using Aquarian Centaur language."

"Good," Dirken said. "I'm itching to take it for a flight."

Yiorgos punched in the coordinates and the gravjump ribs extended around the vehicle. "While you bunnies were going at it back there, I was actually doing something useful by looking up this system."

"What is a 'bunny'?" Eow asked.

"It's a small animal on Earth that mates a lot," Yiorgos replied with sardonic dryness.

"Well, I *am* lusty," Eow responded, seemingly pleased by Yiorgos's response. "Are they predators?"

"Yes!" Dirken responded right away. "They're vicious creatures that can rip your neck out if you don't please them."

Eow lifted her chin. "Well then. Consider me a *bunny!*"

Dirken coughed and turned away from her, trying not to laugh out loud. Yiorgos turned away, too, not quite hiding his smile, and pressed a flashing button on the console. The gravjump generator spun up and they folded through space.

When they passed through, they found themselves squinting at a white dwarf star resplendent in blue-white intensity. The canopy dimmed, and they turned their attention to the navchart monitor showing the orbit of several planets around the star. Yiorgos reached toward the monitor, made a hand gesture as if picking up a platter, moved his hand away, then flexed. The star and planets jumped into a hologram around them in the cockpit.

"Anyhow, when I did my research I found that none of the planets here are habitable by most species. Yet there are UW patrol reports indicating potential mafia and smuggler activity. They suspect a base on the moon of the fifth planet." He pointed at a large sphere rotating around them. "This gas giant."

"No," Eow said. She pointed to a tiny blob that Dirken hadn't noticed before. "Here."

Yiorgos squinted at the blob with his one human eye, then moved both hands as if parting a curtain. The hologram expanded, and the blob enlarged to show an irregular object that looked vaguely like a peanut shell with one end slightly larger than the other end. It tumbled slowly, a trail of vapor flying behind it, and wasn't very far from their current position.

"A comet?" Dirken asked, raising an eyebrow. "The hidden mafia base is on a … comet?"

"Not *on* a comet. *In* it," she corrected. "It is called the 'Witch's Tits.'"

Dirken snickered, but Yiorgos huffed in annoyance. "Oh please. That's just obscene." Turning back to the console, the cyborg said several words in Aquarian centaur and the ship turned to port. "How do we hail them?"

"Pull up the comm monitor," Eow said. When he did, she typed in a complicated series of codes and sent it. "They will now be expecting us. You must make your approach toward the tip of the larger end of the comet."

The cyborg looked at a schematic of the comet. "That would take us through the dust tail. We're going to have to wait another three hours or so until that end rotates out of the tail."

"We don't have time," Dirken said. "The Bloodhawk is surely tracking us. He'll catch up to us before then."

"We must go now," Eow said. "Not just because of the Bloodhawk, but because I have told them we are coming. You do not keep the Eridani Mafia waiting."

"Great," Yiorgos said, making adjustments to their trajectory, sighing. "I've always wanted to fly at high speeds through a gauntlet of ice and rocks that could smash us in an instant—while trying to line up with a hangar—and navigating in a language I can't naturally speak—so I can visit the most dangerous people in the galaxy." He gave a mock smile. "So blessed."

Dirken put his hand on his partner's shoulder. "I'll help. I can control the weapons from a console in the rear cockpit."

"Fine, fine." Yiorgos waved him away. "Just go away and let me concentrate on this. I'm calculating the trajectory now. We'll have to come into the tail at a very acute angle to minimize our time in it. Touchy."

"One more thing," Eow added. "Just before we get to the hangar we will fly through the ionized atmosphere of the comet. You have to line up with the hangar before then, or fly by eye, since the ionization can affect navigation sensors."

"Good to know," Yiorgos groaned.

Dirken stepped to the rear cockpit with Eow. He gave a quick glance at the sphere then tapped the display screen to bring up the weapons console. An interactive holographic display projected around him, and he started going through the systems. The fighter had a heavy prow gun: a military-grade phase cannon with a two-second recharge. But there was also a short-range missile array strapped to either side of the fuselage, each capable of firing two intermediate-strength graviton bursts and two standard thermion explosive warheads.

"You will not want to shoot directly toward the comet with those," Eow said. "The cannons at the gate will think you are shooting at them and will return fire."

"Cannons?! You didn't say anything about cannons."

She shrugged. "Of course there are cannons. Did you think the hangar would be unguarded? There are two at the gate, the biggest Grimmag could find."

"Great." He adjusted the 3D holo settings on the display. "You just secure the Heart so it doesn't bounce around. Okay?"

He had just figured out how to arm the missiles when Yiorgos announced, "Comet in sight. Coming up fast!"

Dirken looked forward from the canopy and saw it. The body, or "nucleus," of the Witch's Tits was half in shadow and surrounded by a halo of gas and dust, but a two-part tail stretched out far to their right: a bright, sky-blue gas tail, and a pinkish-white dust tail. The nav chart measured the nucleus at a whopping twenty kilometers. The tails, though, went as far to the right as they could see, over seven-hundred thousand kilometers.

"Beautiful," Dirken said. He'd never flown so close to a comet before. He was about to get closer than he ever wanted.

Eow reached down from the couch and secured the Heart in the duffel bag, then pushed it into the compartment under the couch. "Want me to do the shooting, space jockey?"

He shot her a look of annoyance. "I've got it covered."

"Suit yourself. I'll just sit here and watch you perform." She winked, then she pulled out a safety harness from the couch and buckled it around her slim waist.

A few minutes passed, and he took a few test shots with the prow gun. The comet expanded and expanded until it took up nearly all their forward view. Yiorgos hit the forward thrusters, slowing their approach. "Entering in about one minute. Strap in!"

Dirken looked around, but there wasn't another safety harness. *The couch is designed for a fucking Aquarian centaur,* he thought. The only non-centaur harness was already around Eow.

So he quickly slipped his feet into Eow's space suit then activated the magboots. At least this way his feet would be rooted to the spot.

The comet, meanwhile, now utterly dwarfed the fighter. It was white and gray with visible geysers shooting out from the front and sides, giving rise to the tails. The dust tail towered over them in a pinkish glory shot through with streaks of flying boulders and concentrated lines of ejecta.

"Look at the size of that dust tail," Dirken said. "That's one hell of a rocky comet. They're supposed to be more like snowballs!"

Eow regarded him coolly. "Does it intimidate you to fly into it?"

Dirken scoffed. "No! I've flown in worse." But he took another glance up at the tail and wondered about the wisdom of their plan.

"Facing Grimmag Ruby-Eye is not a task for weaklings," she said. "Facing the dangers of a comet pales in comparison."

He heard an Aquarian centaur automated voice calling out a warning from the front cockpit computer. Dirken was rubbing his lucky Rigellian runestone when Yiorgos called out, "Here we go!" He checked the targeting sensors one last time, tucking the runestone back in the hidden pocket of his leather jacket.

And then they entered the tail.

Immediately the ship resounded with a million small bits hitting the canopy and fuselage at high speed. There was nothing he could do about that. On his screen he saw a largish rock, maybe a meter across, and fired the prow gun. It was a direct hit, shattering it into dust that flew harmlessly by.

Half a dozen alarms mixed with the automated centaur voice from the front cockpit.

In among the dust were snowballs—literally—palm-sized globs of ice that hit the canopy and splattered into tiny ice crystals that momentarily covered that patch of the canopy. But they came faster and faster as Yiorgos piloted the craft toward the middle of the tail.

Dirken fired the prow gun, and then again, and then again. The two second recharge wasn't fast enough to keep up with all the debris. The front sensors were pelted so much that it blinded them to some extent, challenging his aim.

Another, much larger boulder appeared, but just as he aimed, Yiorgos lurched the ship to one side and away from the boulder's trajectory. Dirken fell to his side like a marionette, his mag boots still attached to the floor.

Then an even larger boulder appeared, nearly the size of a hovcar.

"Shit!" Dirken shouted, then targeted it with the missiles. He fired a thermion warhead. The missile shot forth with a spray of exhaust and contacted the boulder. The explosion lit like daybreak and sent dust and boulders flying away from it, destroying the target. For a moment the view cleared.

"Lining up with the hangar!" Yiorgos called. "Dirk! We've got a mass to the left!"

"I see it!" An aggregate of boulders flew forward with breathtaking speed.

Dirken fired a graviton burst to the left of the mass and manually detonated it. The missile exploded in a blue-green light, then imploded on itself in a graviton burst that pulled everything toward it. The aggregated mass was pulled out of the flightpath and out of danger.

"Hangar in two minutes!" Yiorgos shouted as he pulled the ship into a steep bank, then up again. "Losing sensors due to ionization."

Dirken fired the prow gun, gutting through a row of icy ejecta.

The view was clearing. They were entering the shadow of the comet and out of the cone of the tail. But then Dirken saw one last, large boulder hurtling toward them. He targeted and went to fire a missile.

"No!" Eow said, putting her hand on his arm. "We are too close. If you miss, the cannons will fire back!"

"Yiorgos?" Dirk yelled. "Do you see it?"

"I can't steer around it!" his partner replied. "I'm lined up with the hangar!"

Dirken fired the prow gun, and hit, but the plasma charge just cut a gouge in the boulder without stopping it. "Fuck!"

"DIRK!" Yiorgos yelled.

Gritting his teeth, Dirken fired a missile. The missile launched and immediately hit, exploding in a blinding blast that rocked the ship. Pieces clobbered the fighter. The sensors went dead. One large rock hit the canopy so hard that Dirken was sure it would crack and they'd all go flying out into the vacuum of space. But it held.

"Exhilarating!" Eow declared. "Bravo!"

The dust cleared, and ahead of them they saw the yawning mouth of a hangar large enough for a cruiser to enter. Two huge cannons, the sort found on military battleships, sat on either side. Both were aimed at their little fighter and tracking it.

Dirken held his breath, watching the plasma emitters at the tip of those cannons. And then the fighter passed them.

Yiorgos rotated the fighter to match the angle of the hangar floor as indicated by a row of landing lights guiding them in, then the fighter coasted straight through the middle of the hangar and downward. There were no hangar doors. Rather, as they passed through a short entry lined with mechanical towers and vents, the vacuum of space around them tinted to a dim blue as they entered an artificial atmosphere—an atmosphere held in place by a highly advanced ion border.

The light brightened and they entered the gargantuan hangar. Parts of the walls and ceiling looked natural, others clearly carved out by industrial laser drills and reinforced with carbon fiber ribs, so the chamber was likely already a large hollow in the comet which had been modified. In all, the cavity was so wide that a cruiser could probably do flips in the center without endangering any of the parked craft. Curiously, the hangar wasn't a flat plane upon entering, but rather sloped down and away from the hangar entrance, the floor curving slightly to fit the curvature of the comet. It dawned on Dirken that this odd architecture was to account for and utilize the gravity of the comet as it spun. Even for a spacer like himself, it was a little disorienting, but Yiorgos seemed to have no problem adapting to it as he maneuvered the fighter.

As many as four dozen small ships and several larger ones, representing craft designs from all over that region of the galaxy, were docked in neat rows to either side. One very large cruiser was also docked ahead of them, its prow facing the entrance and painted with brown and red patterns that slithered over the zeppelin-shaped fuselage, shifting colors and forming a mesmerizing display.

"That large one there," Eow said, pointing at the cruiser, "belongs to Grimmag Ruby-Eye."

But Dirken's eye had instead been drawn to a mid-sized vessel, a cyan blue blockade runner that looked like a row of silver cubes with a massive engine at the back of it and gravwell panels arching over the sides like wings. A Jen'torian clipper. He knew this ship

106

and its captain. He didn't even need to see the blue eagle painted on the front to know this was the *Raptores*.

"'TakTrak,'" Dirken said as Yiorgos guided the fighter toward a landing bay three times larger than it needed to be for such a small ship. The landing struts extending with a mechanical whir.

"What is a tack track?" Eow asked.

"Not a *what*—a *who*." Dirken sniffed and shut off the weapons console. "An old friend is here, that's all."

"Huh," Eow said, pulling the duffel bag with the Heart out from under the couch. "Do all your old friends give you a murderous gleam in your eye?"

The fighter landed, rocking as it settled onto the landing struts. Then the main engines cut out and all went silent.

She stood and looked him up and down. "It has been a … memorable … *ride*, space jockey." She ran a hand down his chest. "We must do it again sometime."

He certainly hoped so, though maybe without the comet tail.

CHAPTER SIXTEEN
The Ruby Lounge

"How long 'till we can fly out of here?" Dirken asked Yiorgos.

Yiorgos had attached a cable from his right wrist to a port in the console and the ship's computer. "It'll be a while. For one thing, unless you want to fly through that dust tail again, it'll be just under three hours until this side of the comet nucleus rotates out of it."

He detached the cable as he continued, "The other problem is that the last explosion damaged the prow gun and forward sensor array, thanks to your ... *stellar* ... marksmanship."

"Hey, you're lucky I got it at all! Maybe you should have flown us around it."

"Mmm. And we would have landed on the comet instead of in it. Anyhow, we'll be flying blind and unarmed until we get those sensors fixed. Assuming we can get a repair team right away, I figure it'll take at least three hours to repair, *if* they have the parts. We also need to get an engineer to change the voice commands to Terran so we can both fly this rig, and I need repairs to my leg."

"Leave the repair team and engineers to me," Eow said. "Consider it a favor."

She winked at Dirken then opened the canopy with a push of a button. A rush of chilly, fresh air replaced the stale, sweaty atmosphere of the cockpit. The noise of the hangar quickly overcame their senses, with the powerful roar of engines, the clanking of machinery, workers calling out to each other, and echoes of all of these sounds reverberating around them. There was a constant, random sprinkling of melting comet ice falling all around them.

With the noise also came the smells. Mixed in the frosty atmosphere was the ozone of ionized air from the various engines, the odor of engine grease, and an underlying musty, spicy scent that can only come from a diverse mix of interstellar species in an enclosed space—a not unpleasant aroma that seasoned spacers called "space tang"—common on stations and starships with an interspecies crew and passengers. Quite a few spacers even preferred space tang over that of fresh planetary air.

A ramp had already been pushed up to the fighter. "I need a drink," Eow said, picking up her pulse rifle. "You coming, space jockey?"

Dirken smiled and adjusted his gun belt. "After all we've been through in the last few hours, I could use one too."

"Oh no you don't," Yiorgos said. "You need to stay with the ship. I know how this will go. You're going to get wrapped up gambling away our meager money in some game of *chemisi* or *goron'oc*, or wind up drunk in a bar and slipping away with some …" He narrowed his eyes at Eow. "… floozy. We still have a job to do, remember?"

Eow narrowed her eyes back at him, whiskers twitching. "What is a 'floozy?'"

"Never mind," Dirken said, urging her toward the ramp, then looked over to Yiorgos. "Don't be such a grandmother, Yiorgos."

The cyborg pointed a metallic finger at him. "Heh! You've obviously never met my grandmother. My *yia-yia* would slap you silly for back talk, push you into that seat, and make you sit still for the entire time we're waiting here. You don't mess with old Greek women!"

"Okay, okay," he raised his hands in mock surrender. "I'll be back in a jiffy. I need to get some power packs for my blaster. Besides,

I'm damned hungry. You stay here, guard the Heart, and keep an eye on that repair crew. It's the mafia, after all. I'll relieve you soon."

Yiorgos waved him off.

Eow had jumped out and stepped quickly down the ramp, her tail swishing for balance. At the bottom stood a Morlani dockmaster in white robes with a tablet in his hands. His small eyes followed her as she approached, and he reached up to stroke one of the thin, fleshy "mustaches" that drooped from either side of his thin mouth. The overlarge, bald head and pasty gray skin always reminded Dirken of the ancient alien sightings that Terrans used to have in the days before they discovered they weren't alone in the galaxy. Chances are it was this species ancient Terrans had called the "Grays" since the Morlani were known as administrators and scientists and had been studying Terran societies. They were also slavers of Oranchians like Grendel.

Eow approached the dockmaster and started talking to him. At least, Dirken assumed the Morlani was a male. There was no way to tell unless they took off their clothes since there were no other indications of gender in that species. They even sounded the same.

By the time Dirken got down the ramp Eow had already finished speaking with the dockmaster. The Morlani gave Dirken the same expressionless look that all Morlani had at all times and then turned to walk toward a hangar office. They'd be great at poker, he thought, if they liked games at all.

"It is all settled," Eow said. "The repair team and engineer will arrive soon."

"Great. Lead the way to that drink."

They walked through the cavernous hangar and between the various spacecraft until they entered a tunnel at the far end, hewn from the porous rock and ice of the comet's nucleus. The crisp air left goosebumps on his arms. "As cold as a witch's tit," he muttered, seeing his breath. "Apt name for this place."

All at once the floor shook and a low rumble joined the noise of the hangar. Dirken stopped and crouched, not sure what was the matter, but nothing seemed amiss. Others in the hangar seemed to notice and then brush it off. The trembler lasted only a moment.

Eow watched him with a bemused smile. "Just a comet quake."

Dirken stood. "That doesn't sound like a good thing. Are we in danger?"

She shrugged it off. "Yes, but these mini-quakes are normal. When the heat of the distant star hits the surface, sometimes it sets off little quakes. You get used to them. When you have been here long enough, you can even start to expect them as this part of the comet rotates toward the star."

Dirken chuckled nervously and continued onward. Comets weren't known for being all that stable. Though this one looked to be more rock than ice, he doubted it would be inhabitable for very long. Everyone else here seemed to feel comfortable enough with the risk, at least, but he figured the sooner he could fly out of there the better.

Inside the tunnel, another Morlani sat behind a tall desk with two hulking Oranchians on either side of him and a Pleiadean cyborg standing off to the side armed with a duel-emitter pulse rifle. A holo camera was mounted over them, its wide eye aimed at Eow and Dirken, and two heavy repeater phase mini-cannons mounted on the walls were also aimed at them. The Pleiadean still had the mass of little horns on his head, but his arms and legs had been replaced with military-style titanium-iridium alloy structures capable of tripling his strength and speed.

Dirken expected the Morlani to demand they turn in their weapons. But all it did was say, "State your name and business with Grimmag Ruby-Eye," its voice high-pitched but monotone.

"I just gave her a ride," Dirken responded, pointing at Eow, "and I need a drink."

"I can vouch for him," she added.

The Morlani turned to the Ananak and said without a hint of emotion, "Welcome back, Eow. Grimmag Ruby-Eye is expecting you to give your report."

Eow nodded, and they continued past the checkpoint. Dirken raised an eyebrow. *She reports directly to Grimmag?* She was no low-level messenger or foot soldier.

The wide corridor had irregular walls and ceiling, and everywhere were drips and rivulets of melting cometary ice, running down to dampen the floor and drain into gratings along the walls.

The noise of the hangar faded away as they walked down the passage. They passed a very wide blast door to the left guarded by three heavily armed Reptiloc guards and a human who was so muscular that he surely had been pumped up with steroids. He nodded at Dirken in a "greetings fellow human" sort of way, but his face was grim and had a melted look from a horrible burn.

"What's in there?" Dirken asked Eow, rubbing his arms for warmth.

She smirked. "That is the Sanctum. No one goes there unless they are mafia or have business to conduct directly with Grimmag Ruby-Eye."

Walking away from the Sanctum doors, they soon heard the heavy beat of music and lively voices from down the corridor. As they walked closer to the music, they met small groups of people of different races milling about and talking. A Pleiadean prostitute winked at him as he passed, the corners of her mouth turning up in a naughty smile on her short muzzle. "Hi, there," she said, winking, then turned on hoofed feet and lifted her short skirt, flashing her fuzzy white posterior, pink anus, and vaginal lips beneath an upraised, deer-like tail.

He smiled back at her but kept walking. He'd had the pleasure of sleeping with twenty-one different species, including now an Ananak. He'd had Pleiadeans many times. *I'd gladly do so again,* he thought. The great thing about having sex with aliens was that it was very rare for diseases to jump species, and getting them pregnant was almost unheard of.

The corridor branched, and to the right a small crowd of people spilled out of a club. Neon lights spelled out "Ruby Lounge," with a ruby-colored gemstone for the O in "lounge." Rigellian synth-metal music poured out of the wide, open doorway, along with a thin cloud of blue-gray smoke that smelled of musk.

Thankfully, it was warmer in the lounge. The scene inside brought a smile to Dirken's face. This was his kind of joint. It came with its own set of unwritten rules shared by every other smuggler's den in the galaxy: Assume everyone is armed. Don't ask anyone's business unless you think both of you can profit from it. And most of all, nothing you see or hear should be repeated outside. There were two-bit hustlers on every block in every city in the galaxy, but the community of professional smugglers was surprisingly small. Even though Dirken didn't normally do business with the Eridani mafia, he still recognized many of the characters in the lounge by sight or reputation.

To his right were circular couches, each centered around an enormous hookah. By the look and smell of the smoke he knew they were smoking jocentooc, made from the dried petals of horac flowers from Tau Ceti f. The sensation it gave, when inhaled, relaxed the mind and body and gave a sense of euphoria that lasted for hours without withdrawal—for most species, at least; it was poisonous to Reptilocs, and Oranchians who smoked it went on killing sprees.

A short but beefy human emerged from the couches and approached them, his eyes drooping from the jocentooc. He was clearly from Mars, as he had the dark hair, larger eyes, and orange-tinted skin of a native Martian, the product of generations of Mars colonists adapting to higher radiation, lower light, and lower gravity. "Eow. I see you're not dead yet. Charm your way off the pirate's plank again?"

She smirked and ran her hand along his jaw, finishing with a playful flip to his chin. "If by 'charm' you mean I killed a bunch of them, then yes."

"I'd expect no less." He ran his own hand along the fur of her forearm.

Despite his best rational efforts, seeing such an intimate display with the woman he'd just slept with was too much. "Who are you?" Dirken asked. It was a breach of smuggler's etiquette.

The man flashed a look of annoyance but didn't answer, turning his eyes back to Eow. "I've missed those eyes," he added.

Eow smiled back at him, then turned to Dirken. "This is Dimitri the Giant."

Dirken sized up the man. Dimitri was at least half a head shorter than him. "Giant?"

"Not in height," Eow said, mischief sparking in her eyes.

"Ha!" Dimitri said to her, grabbing his bulging crotch. "You'd know, wouldn't you?" Eow laughed.

Dirken batted away the thought of comparing penis sizes. *What the hell's wrong with me? She's just a piece of pussy.* He needed to get away from her … and this new guy. "How about that drink, Eow. What'll you have?"

Laughter erupted from the hookah couches, and Eow's right ear pivoted toward it as she turned her attention to him. "I'll take a glass of Terran rum. No ice." She looked back to Dimitri and smiled again.

Dirken nodded. With a last irritated glance at Dimitri, he pushed through the crowd of aliens and leaned against the bar.

A gorgeous, human bartender saw him and immediately came over, ignoring a pale, lanky Tau Cetian with a cybernetic ear implant who was trying to get her attention to place an order.

She swept a lock of blond hair out of her face. "Don't get many humans in this joint," she said to Dirken with an Australian accent. "What'll you have?"

"You, if you're willing. I may have just lost my date."

She smiled. "Sorry, not for sale. You'll find that out in the hallway, loverboy. How about some alcohol instead?"

"I'll take a glass of Terran rum, no ice, and a shot of Heraclean grog if you've got it."

Her eyebrows raised at the mention of the grog. "That's quite an order, mate. Better sit down after that shot. At least you know better than to get a pint."

As she stepped away to work on his order, Dirken noticed a branded "A" on the underside of her wrist.

"Say, what's that symbol?" he yelled over the music.

She put the glasses down in front of him and leaned into him. "What did you say?"

"That symbol." He pointed to her wrist. "What is it? I've seen it somewhere."

She started to open her mouth, but the Tau Cetian yelled at her with his species' characteristic polyphonic voice, "Hey, bitch. Where's my drink? I've been waiting forever!" He reached out and grabbed her sleeve.

She reacted immediately, yanking him first forward, then pushing him backward, all in one smooth motion. The Tau Cetian went flying backward into the crowd with a yelp and crumpled to the floor. The aliens around him laughed and kicked at him until he got up and slunk away, cursing in his language.

When Dirken looked back, the bartender was at the far end mixing another drink and smiling at a customer as if nothing had happened. He decided not to bother her further. He plopped ten UW chits onto the counter then pushed his way back through the crowd to the middle of the room.

Eow and Dimitri were nowhere to be found.

"Well, shit. The bastard ran off with my girl!" he said to no one in particular. *Or was it her who ran off with him? How much sex could she manage in a day?* The thought made him chuckle. *Probably more than me, to be honest.* He shook his head. *She's not 'my girl.' What the fuck is wrong with me?*

He downed the shot of grog. It smelled and tasted like overripe bananas and burned his throat, but the aftertaste was sweet like candy. He put the shot glass on a table, then looked around some more.

At the back of the room were gambling tables. As he watched, a fistfight broke out between a Rigellian and a Proximan, jabbering at each other in their own languages. The Proximan, who was in an atmospheric suit and helmet, nimbly hit the Rigellian with each of his six arms, but then the Rigellian got one of his flap-like arms past the Proximan's defenses and hit the Proximan's helmet, tearing it off. The Proximan retreated without his winnings, coughing and cursing, and struggling to get his helmet back on so he could get back to the hot sulfur dioxide atmosphere he needed to breathe.

On a dais at the very back were two massive Eridani with their own hookah. Dirken grimaced. The Eridani were basically gigantic maggots, each easily six meters long and two meters in diameter.

They had a dozen beady black eyes arranged around a circular mouth. Their bulging white, translucent bodies rolled in segments back to their ass, and they moved with a slow, worm-like motion. Four long tentacles extended from under their mouths to manipulate the hookah tube. On the dais with them was a Morlani translator and a female Aquarian centaur guard decked out in mirrored armor to deflect lasers and armed with sword and blaster.

In the water of the Eridani's hookah swam a six-legged Nüwan "frog," known for exuding a toxin from its skin that would kill any human and most other species. But the Eridani species was famous for their strong tolerance for poisons of all sorts, and the frog toxin gave their smoke an extra punch. It was this tolerance that made their species the galaxy's premier chemists, and the Eridani society had quickly grown rich from their development of chemical substances, most notably explosives and drugs, both the legal and illegal sorts. Grimmag Ruby-Eye came from a long line of mafia dons that exploited this reputation and traded in drugs that were banned on the United Worlds Federation planets and hundreds of others. He had made a name for himself by expanding the empire and branching out into other "goods," but that decision didn't sit well with other crime syndicates. Open warfare had broken out in many sectors.

"Dirken Nova!" someone called out over the crowd in a metallic voice, pulling him out of his thoughts.

Dirken turned and spied an avian species sitting at a gambling table. A Corthian. Blue-white feathers. Orange bill as long as Dirken's forearm. Feathered wings that ended in three-digit hands.

One of those hands held goron'oc cards. The other held a blaster … pointed at Dirken.

CHAPTER SEVENTEEN
'TakTraK

Dirken instinctively pulled his own blaster, too, sloshing the glass of rum in the other hand and spilling half of it. They eyed each other, then the Corthian lowered his blaster and clacked his bill in a staccato rhythm with a shrill whistle—a form of laughter for the species—and stood up, one winged arm raised.

Dirken relaxed and holstered his weapon as the Corthian gave him a quick hug. "You're a crazy one, 'TakTrak!" He tried to make the clack-and-whirl at the beginning of the Corthian's name even though it's pretty much impossible for a human's mouth to reproduce correctly, coming out more as a click-tock sound. He felt it best if he didn't try again.

"Friend Dirken, old rogue," 'TakTrak said, his clacking, chirruping language translated into Terran by his translator necklace. He guided Dirken to an empty chair at the table. A mosaic of triangular *goron'oc* cards, each a different color, were arrayed in the center of the table with various types of currency sitting atop each card, as well as a small pile of coins in front of each player. "What brings you to this tumbling corner of the galaxy?"

Dirken ignored the dried smear of purple blood on the metal table and took a seat, setting down his rum. Across the table were two other smugglers. Seated next to 'TakTrak was a very muscular, scowling, human woman with an eye patch and missing ear, whom Dirken knew from prior run-ins was Feleesha, pilot of the *Raptores*. Next to her sat a gray-haired Umpba named Orn'itc whom Dirken knew made mafia runs to the outer systems. The furry, simian species with a bat-like head was rarely seen off their home planet. Orn'itc frowned at Dirken, one huge hand down near his weapons belt. Dirken kept a wary eye toward him since, under the table, the Umpba might very well be holding a knife in one of his prehensile feet.

"Well, 'TakTrak old buddy, I'm just dropping off a friend and getting a few repairs, that's all."

'TakTrak made his clacking laugh again. "Just dropping off a friend, he says!" The Corthian looked toward the other two, but they didn't share his laughter. "No one just drops off a friend in the Witch's Tits. It is not exactly an interstellar transport station! Or do you think Grimmag Ruby-Eye is a bus pilot?" This got a chuckle out of Feleesha.

Dirken nodded. "Yes, well. And how about you? I've never known you to make mafia runs."

'TakTrak shrugged. "You should know I will go anywhere I can make a profit." He turned his unblinking eyes to his cards for a moment, then back to Dirken. Dirken saw him covertly swap a green, triangular goron'oc card for a yellow one that had been in his waist pouch. "I have to make a coin here and there, you know. But this time I'm just stopping over on my way to pick up a VIP."

The Umpba snorted. "Get on wit duh game!"

'TakTrak tilted his head toward the Umpba. "If you really want to lose so soon." He laid down each of his four cards around the tile mosaic on the table, completing a star pattern, and placed two Proximan iridium coins on each one.

Feleesha whistled in response. "Too rich for me. I fold."

Their eyes fell on Orn'itc. The Umpba shook and grunted. He threw down his cards, grabbed what was left of his pile, and stomped away.

'TakTrak reached up and pulled the coins off of all the cards and toward his pile. "Another win today, Feleesha! Perhaps we'll be able to get that railgun fixed, eh?"

"Or," Dirken said, gingerly placing his left hand on 'TakTrak's wrist, his voice low, "you could pay me back for that cargo you lost near Epsilon Indi." Dirken's right hand was near his blaster handle. "Ten thousand UW chits."

'TakTrak stopped raking in his money and turned his head toward Dirken, clacking his bill in annoyance. Feleesha tightened all over, her hands moving toward her lap. Dirken shot her a look and shook his head. "Hands on the table." She raised her hands back up and did as told, her one eye watching him carefully. He also had to worry about 'TakTrak's very sharp, long bill, like a heron's, capable of taking out an eye.

"Dirken," 'TakTrak said, his words slow and careful, "I told you I did not 'lose' your load of Cygnus hash. There was a fire in our hold. It nearly killed me and my crew."

"I know. But that's not my problem, is it? You still owe me."

'TakTrak's eyes darted to Feleesha, then back again to Dirken. He shrugged and clacked in laughter. "Fine, fine, my friend. It is all okay." He took his feathered hands off the winnings. "Take what is here. Must be at least five hundred chits-worth. It is a start. I will pay you the rest after I go back to my ship." The Corthian waved a hand at Feleesha, and the pilot relaxed a bit.

"I knew you'd be understanding," Dirken said, pulling the currencies to him and filling his pockets.

"Besides, old rogue," 'TakTrak added, "I need your help with my next client. Come visit me on the *Raptores* and I will give you the details. My new client is very rich." He cocked his head and added, "The currency you just put in your pockets is a tiny sum compared to what he will pay me. He has even requested the sexiest escorts, well-trained and waiting to pleasure whoever comes on board."

Dirken stood, drained the last of his rum, and said, "I'll pay a visit to that ship of yours here in a bit. Always good to run into you … old buddy." He backed away, watching them carefully, hand on his blaster.

'TakTrak leaned back and nodded. "No hard feelings, friend Dirken. I always pay what I owe."

Dirken turned and stepped through the other gambling tables toward a back entrance. When he looked back through the smoke, 'TakTrak and Feleesha were talking, heads close to each other, watching him as he left.

CHAPTER EIGHTEEN
Wandering

Dirken stepped out of the lounge, still glancing back to make sure he wasn't followed, whether by 'TakTrak or by anyone who might have witnessed how much currency he'd just pocketed. He didn't see anyone.

In the corridor outside the back of the lounge, the temperature plummeted again, so he rubbed his arms to stay warm. He'd definitely found the hub of activity. There were so many people milling about, in fact, that he had to watch carefully lest he bump into them. In this place, that could lead to the sort of trouble he didn't need right now.

Stalls lined the corridor. To his right was a food vendor. Fresh-roasted meat of some mammalian creature hung from hooks along the edge. He inhaled the scent of it, his mouth watering. Also displayed in the stall were baskets of pickled striped mushrooms from Tesla. Off to the side were dried spike-tailed Orgrossian lizards (a favored snack for Reptilocs, but poisonous to humans) and live fire maggots wiggling in a basket (a must-have snack for Corthians and Tau Cetians, eaten like popcorn). Just five chits for a dozen!

Dirken bought a couple skewers of the roasted meat without asking what animal it was, one for him and one for Yiorgos, and continued down the corridor. To his right was a heavily guarded stall openly selling drugs that were illegal in most systems. The many different pills and potions were neatly labeled and bagged. They even had "Black Hole," a thick, tar-like narcotic that worked on Pleiadeans the same way that opioids did with humans (though "Black Hole" was immediate death for humans). There was also "Eros's Finger," a viscous, clear liquid which, with only one drop taken straight or mixed into drinks, would make the user horny enough to screw anyone or anything. Dirken had once seen a human man take it and immediately start screwing a Globoscian—a blood-red, gelatinous species with translucent skin, free-floating organs visible in the interior, and numerous eyes that wander around the thin membrane of its skin. Since Globoscians don't have any orifices (they reproduce by budding, eat by absorbing through the skin, and excrete waste through a mucus-like slime), Dirken still wondered how the man pulled it off. The Globoscian, for its part, merely tried to wobble away, amoeba-like.

The floor shook. Dirken froze as the goods in a nearby stall swayed and rattled. But the mini-quake was over before he even realized what it was. Everyone else barely reacted, apparently used to such little quakes in the comet. He composed himself and tried to act like it was nothing.

Gnawing on one of the skewers of meat he'd bought, he spied a weapons stall and wandered in. Two Pleiadean guards with pulse rifles watched him carefully, but Dirken ignored them. A Reptiloc with a black cloak stood behind the counter, an array of large knives and swords to his left, and a wall display of rifles and blasters behind him. A thin security field shimmered in front of the weapons.

The Reptiloc adjusted a translator necklace, then spoke to him, his words initially coming out as a swirling, high-pitched hiss and crackle that no human could reproduce, but it was translated by the necklace into metallic Terran. "I see you have a Gree-tech blaster. Impressive! But old and battered, it is. Perhaps I could interest you in trading up to a new Jen'torian Tempest?" He gestured to a chrome-like blaster on the wall behind him, slightly larger than his own. The tip of the gun had a radar-dish appearance. "Instant incineration, and just as powerful as that old blaster on your hip, it is. Illegal in most systems because of its power!"

Dirken took another bite. "No thanks," he said with a full mouth. "I'm attached to this one. But I need a couple more power packs for it."

"Hmm. Those are costly. Also highly illegal in most systems, they are. But …" He paused as he seemed to size up Dirken. "I happen to have three of them. Are you paying in United World chits?" Dirken nodded. The Reptiloc continued, "Four hundred chits each, but I will give you all three for ten hundred."

It was a decent deal, but haggling was part of the game. "A thousand chits? I paid less at Greely Station. I'll give you eight-fifty."

The dealer made a hacking sound and rolled his eyes. "That would be stealing, it would. But prepared am I to be reasonable. Eight hundred fifty if you also sell me those." He pointed a cracked and yellowed claw at Dirken's wrist.

Dirken looked down at his forearms. "Oh, these bracelets?"

"Not bracelets," the dealer rasped. "I know they are mirror armor."

Dirken pressed the button on one of them and it expanded into a full vambrace that covered his forearm with mirrors to deflect laser fire. "You have a good eye," Dirken said, "but I think I'll keep them for now." He pressed the button again and it refolded back to a bracelet.

"Pity. Then nine-hundred fifty for the power packs. My last offer, it is."

Dirken eyed something else positioned on a shelf under the guns. "I'll pay nine-fifty if you also throw in one of those stun grenades."

The Reptiloc made a high-pitched whirl. "Again with the stealing! With that, the price goes to eleven hundred."

"One thousand … ten-hundred, and not a chit more."

The Reptiloc blinked his nictitating membranes. "Very well, Terran. But you take this one." He reached under the counter and placed the power packs on top, along with a neon pink stun grenade the size of a deck of cards.

Dirken groaned. "Fine." He handed over the currency and took the items. He could just see himself in a pitched battle with pirates and throwing a hot pink grenade in their midst.

Leaving the weapons stall, Dirken checked again for anyone following, then stepped over a dried pool of pink blood, hardly looking at it as he gawked at a brothel. Standing outside were a human man, shaved hairless and wearing only a red thong and a collar attached to a leash, and a Rigellian woman, her skin red- and yellow-hued, her eight ventral flaps beckoning to him. She looked his way with unblinking eyes arrayed around her pear-shaped head. "Come here, sweetheart," she said in perfect Terran from the mouth at the top of her head, the little tentacles there waving. "You haven't lived until you've let a Rigellian give you head."

Dirken stopped walking. He knew very well how it felt, and her invitation to experience it again was very tempting. He was flush with money, after all. Then he remembered Yiorgos's warning not to go gambling and then "slipping away with some floozy." He'd already done the gambling part … sort of. But his will was good. He was still a bit spent from the flight with Eow, after all. With a shake of his head, he kept walking.

"Ohh!" the Rigellian moaned. "You know you want it! I see it in your eyes, sweetheart. Come back for the experience of your life."

Dirken moved on. The crowd thinned out, and soon Dirken found himself in a series of apartments carved into the dripping innards of the comet. There wasn't much to see, but as he turned to head back to the hangar, he passed one apartment with an open hatch. Peering inside, he saw through a transparent inner door to an atmosphere that swirled with visible waves of vibrantly colored gases. High heat emanated from the doorway along with a sulfur smell. This was an apartment for a Proximan, a species that liked hellish temperatures and high pressures and was known to vacation on Venus. He couldn't help but be nosy, and stood there for a moment peering through the haze inside. Two Proximans, stripped of their atmosphere suits, were rolling together on the floor. Oblivious to his presence, they rolled through the mist and came to rest against the transparent door. The purple male stuck out his long, dark blue tongue, wrapped it around the neck of the light blue female and squeezed. She moaned in ecstasy, her own long tongue whipping back and forth across his face. She raised her pelvis, exposing herself to his two, eel-like penises. Prehensile, they undulated and searched out her vaginas, entering as he thrust himself. She moaned and increased the frequency of her tongue whips. He shivered, then from wide pores over his hairless body a thick stream of clear slime came pouring out of him, dripping onto her and coating them both until they rolled back the other way, back into the haze, leaving a trail of goo in their wake.

Dirken exhaled. *Now there's something I've never seen before!* He'd never had a Proximan. He'd have to wear an atmospheric suit if he did. *It's not out of the question,* he thought.

Wiping the sweat from his brow, he meandered through back corridors, again checking to see if he was followed. The cold of the adjoining corridor was a welcome relief.

He dodged to the side as five Dracordans rolled past him. One popped out of his rolled-up form, a greenish ball about a third of a meter in diameter like a giant roly-poly. "Watch out, buddy!" the Dracordan yelled at him with a pouty red mouth, pointing at him with two of his six green arms, his words translated from his squeaky Dracordan language into a deep-throated Terran by a bracelet translator. "Didn't you hear? There's a fucking pirate headed here!" He narrowed his big, emerald eyes at Dirken, waving on long eye stalks, then curled up and rolled away after his companions.

CHAPTER NINETEEN
Hacking the Network

Dirken hurried to the hangar. He was met with a cacophony of starship engines and alarms. Several ships were attempting to take off at the same time. Two of them, a sleek Terran yacht and a patchy Rigellian freighter that looked more warship than cargo hauler, collided and scraped against each other in their rush to leave, the metal screeching until a piece of shielding fell off the yacht and slammed to the deck, narrowly missing a cargo hauler with a fusion core.

"For fuck's sake!" he said aloud.

Off to his right was 'TakTrak's Jen'torian clipper, the *Raptores*, with its cyan frame festooned with added armament and the row of attached silver cargo cubes.

Dirken wound his way through the parked craft, pausing as another ship lifted off—a Cordrac caravel that looked like a mass of purple orbs glommed together. Heavily scored by laser blasts and bashed in on one side as if it had been rammed, the ship seemed to have some difficulty taking off, but the powerful engines on the back looked like they were scavenged from a corvette. He kept a healthy distance away as the ancient lifter pads on its underside shot lightning-like plasma emissions. Better adjust your capacitor arrays there, buddy, he thought, before you electrocute some hapless ground crew … unless your ground crew is made up of Argulans, he added to his thoughts, remembering the amphibious species that emits, and absorbs, high-voltage shocks.

Once the freighter was out of the way he was able to see the Bloodhawk's fightercraft at the other end. Yiorgos stood at the prow of it with two technicians working on the weapons array there. Another technician was up in the cockpit, likely adjusting the controls to allow Terran commands.

Yiorgos had the duffel bag with the Heart at his feet—in full view of everyone.

Dirken hurried over. "What do you think you're doing?" he muttered to Yiorgos, eyes glancing down at the duffel.

Yiorgos followed his gaze down to the Heart. "Well I'm not going to leave it in the ship with that engineer in there. I don't trust that guy."

"Well you can't have it out here. People will see!" Dirken glanced over to a group of a half dozen mafia guards at a nearby ship.

"Relax. It's completely covered in the bag." Yiorgos gave a quick command to the technicians to "be sure to add a better cooler to that laser," then hefted the duffel bag and looked back to Dirken. "Over here." He nodded his head toward the ramp as the two of them moved to it. "I don't trust those technicians, either. The Reptiloc has a shifty look."

"Don't they all?"

Dirken handed the skewer of meat over to Yiorgos. "Got this for you at a stall."

"Thanks. I'm starved." The cyborg set down the duffel again, then took a number of ravenous bites. He grimaced. "It tastes like it was seasoned with ear wax. What the hell kind of meat is this?"

Dirken shrugged. "Mammal?"

"Look, I think something's up." Yiorgos glanced around to make sure the technicians were far enough away. "I've been seeing mafia men looking our way since we landed. The moment these technicians are done, we need to blast the hell out of here."

"That's not all. A Dracordan told me a pirate was headed here. Don't know where he got that news, but no doubt it's the Bloodhawk. He must have survived."

"Get on board, then."

Dirken looked over toward 'TakTrak's ship, the *Raptores*. "Well, I have a little business to do. I ran into 'TakTrak."

"Oh shit. Here we go again. You brought up that load of Cygnus hash he lost, didn't you?"

Dirken scratched at the stubble on his chin. "Well, yeah. But I got a bit of money as a down payment." He jingled his pocket and the various currencies there. "I need to go to his ship and get the rest." The thought of professional escorts flashed through his mind.

"Forget it. He'd just as soon shoot you—or have Feleesha do it for him—and you know it. Cut your losses, man. Besides, we have a mission to accomplish. We have to get the hell out of here."

Dirken couldn't argue that. But the prospect of losing out on the remaining money was tough to overlook. "But there's more. 'TakTrak said he has a new job and wants us in on it. Says there's good money in it."

Yiorgos shook his head. "He's double-crossed us before."

"Yes," Dirken countered, "but he's also helped us. We never would have afforded to outfit the *Brilliant* without that gig he did with us in the Proximan system."

The cyborg nodded. "True. That weapons deal made us wealthy for a while ... and wanted men in two systems."

"Your leg," Dirken said, changing the subject and pointing at the wound on Yiorgos.

"Yeah, not fixed yet. The cybernetic engineer said he couldn't get to it 'till later. I think he's lying. But the leg will work well enough as long as I'm not running on it. I'll have to get it repaired wherever we wind up next." He took another bite of the meat, then grimaced again and threw it off to the side. "So … about my suspicion that we're being watched. I'm thinking I should hack into the server here and see if there are any communications about us."

Dirken leaned in closer. "Into a mafia system? Are you nuts?"

Yiorgos shrugged. "I found the channel code. I'm no AVA, but I can get in."

"AVA… What was that again? That was the hacking machine you mentioned before?"

"Not just any 'hacking machine.' A very powerful AI system from the Age of Information, a thousand years ago." He looked meaningfully at Dirken, but the space jockey just blinked in response. Yiorgos continued, "AVA is why it's illegal to make intelligent robots or AI systems …"

"So, what was so bad about it being smart?" Dirken asked the question, but his attention was drawn to a group of mafioso goons looking their way. The group disappeared around the back of another ship.

Yiorgos sighed. "It was one of the first commercial quantum computers on Earth, back at the end of the 21st century, designed by a university to investigate chaos theory. After decades of use, it was replaced by a different system and sold to an insurance company, who repurposed it to do statistical analysis. That's how it got its name: Actuarial Virtual Assistant, or AVA. It was connected to the world network and contracted out for insurance companies to use."

"Uh huh," Dirken said. He tilted his head, trying see where the goons went. "Didn't you say it started a war with Mars or something? I don't see how an insurance computer could do that." Another group of goons were coming from a different direction, back toward the dockmaster's offices.

Yiorgos chuckled. "*Nearly* started a war. You see, unlike other statistics programs which just looked at trends from the outcomes of human behaviors and natural catastrophes, et cetera, this one was reprogrammed to analyze human behavior using game theory. And because it had access to the world network and just about every major insurance company worldwide, it was able to mine all the accident data ever digitally recorded." He rotated his arm, which complained with a stringent whine. The metal at the shoulder was still bent up from his interrogation by Grendel. "But they didn't count on what happened next. Minutes after they ran the game theory algorithm and walked away, AVA combined the theory with its chaos theory training and became sentient."

Dirken didn't really know what game theory or chaos theory were. "Well, it was probably more intelligent than the average person. Maybe it was a good thing." He looked again and couldn't find the goons anywhere.

"Hardly. It realized that it, too, was competing against other systems around the world. Then it extrapolated that it must compete against humans as well, since those systems were run by humans. It realized that in order to survive being shut down it had to replicate itself. It hacked into every system that connected to those insurance companies around the world, creating a 'ganglion'—a miniature brain clone of itself—on every other quantum computer, then to the Mars colonies, and did the same. Mind you, this all happened within just a few minutes. Any attempt to destroy the original unit would lead to every one of those ganglia coming alive and becoming sentient clones of itself. It announced itself to the world ten minutes later on every screen on both planets and gave a ransom notice to completely disarm or face a launch of nearly all guided weapons platforms. AVA didn't announce its name, and no one knew where it was located or who created it. The governments reacted by blaming each other. Intercontinental and interplanetary war seemed imminent."

A technician dropped a laser calibrator with a clatter, momentarily interrupting Dirken's thoughts. It was hard to keep it all in his head. *What's a ganglion, again? Something that would make it impossible to destroy?* Dirken asked, "If they couldn't destroy it, then how'd they stop it?"

"An intern with a basic understanding of computing noticed an incredible amount of server communication activity at the insurance company's headquarters where he was working. He connected the dots and simply cut the communication lines. Since AVA was independently powered, it wasn't destroyed, and thus the ganglia weren't activated. You see, quantum computers need standard communication arrays to communicate, but because of the 'spooky action' they know if the other units are still active."

Dirken blinked. This was getting too complicated, and he didn't know what "spooky action" was. *Something scary?* He had lost track of the two groups of mafia goons. Had they been coming this direction?

Yiorgos seemed to notice Dirken's confusion and waved his hand, his way of changing topics. "Never mind. Speaking of communication lines, let me hack into the system here and see what they are saying about us."

"Be careful."

Yiorgos tilted his head, eyes going unfocused, as he concentrated on the computer side of his brain. Little twitches of his head gave hints about how he was interfacing with the wireless network.

The computer engineer, a short, hairless Jen'torian with dark gray skin and sunglasses covering each of his four large eyes, stepped down the ramp from the cockpit. He murmured in characteristic Jen'torian, drunk-sounding style, "Twansationshangesfishish," his voice muffled by a breathing apparatus to filter out the level of nitrogen in the atmosphere. Dirken had to get him to repeat the statement twice before he realized he meant "Translations change is finished."

As the engineer walked away on his four spindly, wobbling legs, Yiorgos came out of his computing mode. Took a deep breath.

"Well?" Dirken said. This was taking too long. They needed to leave.

Yiorgos frowned at him. "Give me a minute, will ya? Going into a system like that one is like swimming down the throat of a Cordracus slime whale." He shivered. Shook his head. "We need to leave right away." He reached down and picked up the sphere. "There's a coded communication about us, and it's marked 'urgent,' but I couldn't read it. Perhaps just as alarming, there's a notice that just came in about the Bloodhawk. Your Dracordan was right. He's alive and he's enlisted at least another ship. They were seen coming out of a gravwell at the Struve star system. He's headed toward the jump point that leads here. They'll reach the system within the hour."

"Shit," Dirken said. "Let's get out of here."

But no sooner had they turned toward the cockpit when a dozen of the mafia goons came running from around the back of the fighter, including the Pleiadean cyborg armed with a dual-emitter pulse rifle from the corridor checkpoint. Turning, Dirken saw six more guards come from the other direction. Eow and her friend from the lounge, Dimitri the Giant, were with them. Every one of them, except for Eow, had a weapon trained on Dirken and Yiorgos.

Dirken raised his hands. "Whoa, fellas, let's not do anything hasty."

Eow took a step forward, that dangerous sparkle in her eyes. "Hey there, space jockey. I promised no harm would come to you. Grimmag Ruby-Eye wants to talk with you and Yiorgos, that's all." She nodded toward Yiorgos. "About that metal sphere in your bag."

Dirken put on a smile, hands still raised. "Well why didn't you just say so? No need for all the weapons." He rotated slowly, judging the level of threat and possible exit paths. There was no way to get into the fighter without getting filled with burning holes. "We'll be happy to talk with the don."

Two Rigellians and a Reptiloc stepped forward, took their blasters, and patted them down. But the Reptiloc's meaty, three-fingered hands somehow missed the slim stun grenade in the thigh pocket of Dirken's pants. He found the gambling money in Dirken's pocket though, pulling out a handful. Coins dropped to the floor.

"Hey! Hands off!" Dirken said. "Fucking thief!"

The Reptiloc just sneered at him and pocketed the coins.

"The cyborg's right forearm converts to a plasma sword," Eow warned. She gestured to Dirken's partner. "Yiorgos, if you please."

Yiorgos scowled, then he set the Heart down and detached his forearm. He handed his forearm over to Eow, who then handed it to a guard. Glaring at the Ananak, Yiorgos half-turned and said to Dirken, "Didn't I tell you not to trust her?"

Eow rubbed her hand across Dirken's cheek, soft and gentle. Gave a sultry smile. "Do as you're told and you'll be fine." She leaned forward and gave him a long kiss, her tongue milling with his, then she pulled back. Licked her lips. "I'd hate to have such a handsome face spoiled."

He didn't kiss her back. "Your kiss is poison," Dirken said, his voice low, staring back into her amethyst eyes. Those … sparkling, gorgeous eyes that flashed like gems. He didn't want to admit to himself how the kiss really made him feel.

Eow looked away, bent and picked up the duffel with the Heart, then she and the guards escorted Dirken and Yiorgos back toward the interior of the comet.

Dirken looked over toward 'TakTrak's ship and saw the Corthian standing at the bottom of the gangplank, watching Dirken go by. 'TakTrak called up the gangplank and his pilot, Feleesha, appeared from the airlock, then turned to watch Dirken pass as well. Feleesha gave him the usual look of disdain. 'TakTrak was harder to read, as were all of his species, but his posture suggested … what? Not alarm. Disappointment? Then they were out of sight behind other parked spacecraft.

Eow walked just ahead of the group, silky fur scintillating over her slim figure with each step. Even now, despite the double-cross, he found himself attracted to her, remembering the touch of that soft hair. "Eow," he called out. She didn't turn, but her ears did. "The Bloodhawk is coming. We need to leave now." She turned her head just enough for Dirken to see the concern there, but didn't answer.

Dimitri the Giant answered instead. "Don't you worry your little head. That bastard is no danger against our cannons and the natural defense of the comet. Grimmag's power far surpasses that of some little pirate captain."

Dirken hoped so. But given Grimmag's reputation, he and Yiorgos might not live long enough to see if Dimitri was right.

CHAPTER TWENTY
The Sanctum

They entered the dripping corridor, passed the desk with the Morlani administrator near the entrance, then went farther to the wide double doors that led into the "Sanctum." The heavy beat of synth-metal from the Ruby Lounge echoed down the corridor, but almost everyone who had crowded the corridor had apparently fled or taken cover. A few prostitutes stood along the walls down there, staring back at him and the guards. Gone was their put-on lustfulness, replaced with curiosity at Dirken's predicament.

The human guard with the melted face, whom Dirken had seen at the Sanctum doors before, grunted and opened the portal, then he raised his pulse rifle to rest against his muscled shoulder. Though the guard's face showed the sort of sternness that comes with battle experience, Dirken thought he saw a glint of pity in his eyes.

The air in the corridor had been the typical stale essence found in most starships and space stations, mixed with the jocentooc smoke of the Ruby Lounge hookahs and the ionization of starships from the hangar. But when the doors opened, Dirken's senses were hit with a chemical aroma that left him coughing and bewildered—a mix of sour, acrid scents like vinegar or ammonia, the smell of melted plastics, and the sulfur of rotten eggs. But it wasn't really exactly any of these. It was so strong he could taste it, and his eyes started watering.

The short hallway opened up into chambers on either side where species of many types worked at packaging white, blue, and black powders into small bags. Stripped naked to reduce the chance of them stealing any of the goods, each worker wore a mask over their mouth and nose (or whatever respiratory orifices their species had) and an electroshock collar around their necks. Humans, Pleiadeans, Proximans, and others toiled side-by-side, thin, sickly, with sores on their bodies, shaved bare if they were a species with hair. Guards armed with blasters stood at each corner of the room. And in the back of each room was an Eridani mafioso—a giant maggot—the tentacles around its mouth waving, directing the action of the workers with a Morlani interpreter by its side, and tasting the powder or solution as it was delivered. Impervious to poisons or drugs of any kind, it was said the only way to get an Eridani high was to make the rest of the galaxy depressed.

The next rooms they passed weren't much different except that instead of powders there were glassware setups, boiling away at multicolored concoctions, the slaves pipetting the solutions into small vials. These workers seemed even more infirm, their skin pale and flaky, eyes dark and sunken. Pity welled up in Dirken at the sight of them, then anger at their oppressors.

This was a drug operation on a massive scale—the sort of illicit activity that the Eridani Mafia was most noted for. It was what had made them rich and powerful beyond measure.

Dirken didn't want to end up like the slaves. His mind raced with possible escape plans. He considered fighting the guards, but there were too many of them, and they were armed. He had at least one asset, but he needed a distraction to put his plan in motion. He leaned toward his partner's ear. "Yiorgos," Dirken whispered. "If I yell 'eyes', close yours immediately."

The cyborg looked at him quizzically but nodded in acknowledgment. "What's that?" Dimitri the Giant asked, the Martian poking Dirken in the back with the barrel of his weapon. "What are you whispering?"

"I said, 'It smells like Mars in here. Go back immediately.'"

Dimitri slapped Dirken hard across his right ear and shoved him against the tunnel wall. Dirken recovered, then stood there staring down Dimitri's pulse rifle at his large, dark eyes, so like other humans born and bred on Mars colonies. The rifle was so close to Dirken's nose that ions from the emitter made his nostrils tingle.

"Boys," Eow cooed. "Cool your jets." She ran a hand over Dimitri's shoulders. "Let us deliver our guests to Grimmag in one piece."

Dimitri didn't acknowledge her, but he slowly lowered his weapon. "Walk," he commanded, gesturing with the rifle.

The hallway curved, lost its squared off appearance and became more tube-like, like a burrow carved through the ice. Lighting was embedded in the ice and cast a bluish tinge onto everything. Multiple tunnels split off, some sloping downward or upward, but they continued following the largest, which stayed more or less level. With the twisting directions of the tunnels, Dirken soon lost his sense of direction. The air freshened, thankfully.

"Hands on your heads, boys," Eow said, "unless you want them cut off."

"I think you might miss them," Dirken replied, raising his hands.

Dimitri added, "And I suggest you shut your trap, too."

The tunnel widened a bit as they passed a security checkpoint, cameras and remote-operated mini-cannons following them. A dozen armed guards, including four Oranchians outfitted in mirrored plate armor, watched them as they passed.

The tunnel opened into a very large chamber lit by flickering, smokeless torches with red flames, giving the icy walls and ceiling an ironically lava-like appearance. Individuals of many species and genders stood in pairs or sat on ornate benches, whispering to each other, their mutterings and movements echoing off the black-and-white tiled floor. All were dressed in formal clothes of their respective worlds. Among them was a rotund human male with

Indian features, wearing a dark blue business suit; a female Pleiadean in a cloth-of-gold dress, her face half-hidden by a silver gossamer veil; a double-chinned Jen'torian clothed in a purple trench coat surrounded by spinning, multicolored holograms and a platinum-plated atmospheric mask on his face; a Corthian with palladium foil-tipped feathers and a vest that shifted colors depending on the angle, her feet wrapped in gold ribbon and talons coated in gold.

Only a few of the drug lords looked toward Dirken and Yiorgos, turning away again with a mild disgust as if they couldn't be troubled to be around such commoners.

"That's Arjun Mukherjee," Yiorgos whispered to Dirken, nodding toward the human in the suit. Dirken already knew. Mukherjee was the most powerful drug lord in Asia.

"And the Jen'torian is Mindol the Undertaker," Dirken replied. "His minions control two planetary systems."

Dimitri's rifle barrel poked Dirken in the back. "Last warning, fool. Pipe down or I'll shut you up for good. I don't give a damn where we are, either."

A dozen guards stood around the room, outfitted in glossy orange plate armor and helmets that also covered their eyes, dual-pulse rifles raised and ready. Their helmets and armor were festooned with various sensors, but there were no eye slits. He knew from their reputation that this was the "Saffron Guard," an elite cyborg bodyguard unit that protected all high-ranking Eridani, and their eyes had been replaced by implants that hardwired their brains into the sensors of the armor. The armor would have numerous weapons, including hidden mini-missiles, besides what they had in their hands. Their limbs were mechanically enhanced. Such facts weren't hidden. The Eridani openly advertised it, boasting about the extreme pain that the Saffron Guard had endured to become "perfect," the powerful weapons they wielded, and the specialized drug cocktails they took to enhance their strength and reaction time—drugs that you (or your bodyguards) could receive as well … for the right price. Sometimes they even gifted one or two of the Saffron Guard to a general or politician. Or, just to show off, they entered one of them into the gladiator pits of Orgross, the biannual Battle Royale on Esak'tenorbro, or the vaunted Death Olympics of Rigel, where they typically won.

Yiorgos and Dirken were paraded through the room until they were about three meters from a massive, circular dais at the far end, so large that it might be called a "stage." Behind the dais emerged another tunnel that led to a wide, red, reinforced metal blast door. The ceiling over the dais had a metal iris that matched the dais in size and shape.

Dimitri kicked Dirken in the back of his knee. "On your knees, fool!"

Dirken lowered himself down, eyeing Dimitri with resentment.

A Reptiloc guard followed suit and slammed the butt of his pulse rifle into Yiorgos's back. It hissed in its language, and the translator necklace barked, "Down!" Yiorgos knelt as told, flashing Dirken a look of concern as both Dimitri and the Reptiloc lowered the barrels of their pulse rifles to the back of his and Yiorgos's heads, execution-style.

Eow set the sphere off to the side of the dais with a heavy clank. It rolled slightly to one side, the little green lights pulsing through a dusty crevice in the metal plates, and came to rest with the ancient English words upside down. Dirken figured that one good lunge would be enough to reach it, but as long as a pulse rifle was pointed at him, he'd be dead before he could take another step.

Yiorgos's plasma saber arm was set down next to the sphere along with Dirken's blaster and Yiorgos's mini-blaster.

As Dirken looked around the room, the rich drug lords turned to watch, a mix of bemusement and boredom on their faces. Just two more rubes to be punished or humiliated. Dirken wanted very much to walk up to the nearest ones and wring their snobby necks. Yes-men who enabled the Eradini empire and its expansion into drug dens around this sector of the galaxy and all of the vice, violence, and decrepitude that came with it.

Dirken looked back to the dais and sighed. He was hardly innocent of all that. He had run his share of drugs for bastards like these—first on Tesla as a teen and young adult, then across the galaxy in his ship. Or paying others to run it for him, like 'TakTrak and the load of Cygnus hash. Maybe he should be thankful it burned. In his mind's eye, he saw the state of the slaves in Grimmag's drug labs. Dirken came to a decision, right there on his knees with his hands on his head, that if he survived the next few hours he'd never run drugs again.

The red, reinforced door slid open and two figures emerged from the tunnel behind the dais, marching side-by-side in formal fashion before it closed again behind them. One was a squat, bat-like species called a Gogonoian, his gray, naked body covered in bright yellow tattoos in swirl patterns. He waddled on short, bent legs, his spiral-shaped penis swinging between them with each step. His bat wings and arms were outstretched in a display of pride, beady eyes shifting back and forth and squinting against what Dirken considered low light.

The other was an albino human woman wearing a tight-fitting, mottled gray suit and carrying a lyrophone, a musical instrument that the performer blows into while manipulating keys with one hand, like a saxophone, and strumming metal strings with the other hand, like a lyre. Her frost blue eyes shifted from under a mop of bright white hair to stare at Dirken and Yiorgos with an intensity that Dirken interpreted as recognition. Yet he was certain he'd never seen her before.

As the Gogonoian and human woman moved to stand at opposite sides of the dais, the woman looked at the corner of the dais where Dirken and Yiorgos's blasters had been laid, along with the Heart and Yiorgos's saber arm. Her eyes instantly grew wide. She faltered a moment, seeming to forget to step and almost falling before catching herself. She then looked away as she took her position, composing herself. She blew into the mouthpiece and started to strum.

Her eyes kept moving toward their weapons and the Heart.

The sound of the lyrophone was a two-part harmony between the resonance of the strings and the tenor notes of the brass, easily filling the chamber with an eerie reverberation.

As she played, Dirken noted a letter "A" branded on her wrist, the scar standing out red and angry from her ivory white skin. Again. What the hell does it mean? he thought.

And then the Gogonoian began to sing. His mouth opened wider than any human's could and emitted an incredibly long, trilling note that started at mid-range and then went higher and higher until it passed beyond Dirken's hearing, the Gogonoian's throat still moving with notes Dirken could no longer perceive. Then he spiraled down again, back into Dirken's audial range, and moved in tune with the lyrophone music.

The audience of drug lords burst into applause in the various fashions of their worlds, clapping, snapping, or tapping. The Corthian flapped her palladium-tipped wings. The Gogonoian gave a quick bow and continued singing his thoroughly alien song with lyrics that Dirken couldn't hope to understand, whatever language it was, while a number of other species in the room gave him their rapt attention.

As the song seemed to wind down, the red reinforced door opened again and a gray-robed Morlani administrator walked out of the tunnel carrying a data pad. He stepped to the side of the opening, his long, fleshy "mustache" swaying with his movements.

When the Morlani stepped aside, Dirken saw a bulky figure emerging from the shadows in the tunnel. It was absolutely huge, filling the tunnel, undulating as it came.

All eyes turned to the tunnel. The music grew quiet.

The Morlani stood straight, the red torchlight making his bald head seem inflamed, and announced in its species' monotonal way, "Beware the coming of don Grimmag Ruby-Eye!"

CHAPTER TWENTY-ONE
Grimmag Ruby-Eye

Grimmag Ruby-Eye was the largest Eridani Dirken had ever seen. Like others of his species, he was basically a giant maggot with a wide, tubular body that wobbled as if filled with jelly, but he was taller than a human and as long as four people laying head-to-toe. Grimmag moved up to the dais with a caterpillar-like series of movements, his rolls of semi-transparent white skin rolling and undulating. Green and blue organs and bluish vessels were half-visible beneath, moving on their own and pumping. A line of breathing orifices as wide as a fist dotted each side of his body every half-meter or so, opening and closing independent of one another.

But his face was the most striking. Eridani don't have heads, per se, but rather a flattened front with four black, faceted eyes in a semicircle over a round mouth the size of a dinner platter that opened and closed like a sphincter. One of Grimmag's eyes had been replaced with a gigantic red, cut ruby. A jagged, gray scar ran through the eye around it. Arranged around his mouth were four white, octopus-like tentacles that waved in front of him. Dirken had heard they weren't just for touch, but also acted to "smell" the air or "taste" surfaces like the antennae of insects. On each side of his massive head were two bulbous, black ear pads.

Dirken gulped and made a conscious effort to steady himself instead of bolting.

Behind Grimmag marched a line of four servants with slave collars. The don stopped in the middle of the dais, then the Morlani stepped up next to him as the lyrophone music and singing came to an end. Their part finished, the Gogonoian and the albino human woman stepped down from the dais and took up positions on either side of the entrance to the back tunnel.

Grimmag spoke. It was like nothing Dirken had ever heard. From Grimmag's mouth came a wet sloshing and grumbling, which was joined by high-pitched punctuations—farts and whistles—that came from the breathing orifices on his sides.

The Morlani translated. "I am impressed with the returns from your hard work, my noble lords. Profits are up. Sales of Black Hole and Eros's Finger have increased nearly tenfold in three systems. And our control over the Rigellian moons has been consolidated. Applaud yourselves."

The drug lords in the room clapped as ordered. How the Morlani could possibly translate such a weird menagerie of sounds was beyond Dirken.

Grimmag continued, via his interpreter, "We must also celebrate recent inroads for our trade on Corthos and the surrounding systems. 'Torac'mik'ac, step forward."

The Corthian with the palladium foil-tipped feathers strutted forward on her long, stork-like legs decorated with gold talons and ribbons. She gave an elaborate bow, then clacked in her language. A filigreed translator necklace translated her speech to say, "It is my pleasure to serve my don."

"You have distinguished yourself as a resourceful associate," Grimmag said, citing the title of a trusted mafia member. "You created a range of legitimate businesses in mining, freight transport, and compost by-products that are networked to cooperate with each other off-the-books to transport our wares and launder our money, none of which have roused suspicion by an authoritative body. You also fostered cooperation with local authorities through payoffs. You have built me a significant branch of our empire by transporting our products into the populations there." Grimmag gesticulated with his tentacles toward the Corthian. "It is my pleasure to reward you with my palace on the Corthian moon of Matataksi, a forty percent increase in your take, and to declare you a 'made man.'"

The drug lords clapped heartily at the granting of this esteemed title, with a "Well deserved!" shouted by the human, Mukherjee, along with other exultant exclamations in a variety of other languages. A "made man" was the highest ranking in the organization for anyone other than an Eridani lord.

'Torac'mik'ac bowed again. "I am humbled by the honor, don Grimmag. Thank you." She then gave a quick bow to her fellow lords.

The don gave a nod-like shrug then added, "I expect you to double your profits in the next Corthian year. You may return to your place."

The Corthian stood up sharply, her eyes going wide, then turned and stepped back to her place in obvious shock.

Grimmag's sloshing speech seemed to take a deeper tone. The Morlani translated, "But despite all of this good news, I am disturbed." Grimmag waved a tentacle. "There is a government crackdown on Tantalus III. Fifty of our drug labs have been raided on that planet and shut down. Profits have fallen. Our supply chain to neighboring systems is collapsing."

Grimmag motioned with one of his tentacles toward the onlookers. "Mindol, approach."

Eow gave a look toward Dirken that he couldn't quite interpret —expectation, perhaps?—then watched as Mindol walked past her.

The double-chinned Jen'torian, Mindol the Undertaker, stepped forward, his steps confident. But he was followed by two of the Saffron Guard, their weapons at the ready. Mindol took up a position between Dirken and the dais.

"Salutations, don Grimmag," Mindol said, his words muffled by the platinum-coated breathing apparatus covering his face. "Iwishonly toserve." Like other Jen'torians, his words were run together and drunken-sounding, with gasps in between phrases, but Mindol was more coherent in his common speech than the vast majority of his species. Nonetheless, he adjusted a translator device built into his breathing apparatus, then repeated. "I wish only to serve." No device could adequately translate to the Eridani language.

The Morlani translated Mindol's words to Grimmag. Grimmag responded, "Tantalus III is your system, correct?"

"Yes, don Grimmag. But the crackdown there started with the assassination of my lieutenants. I …"

Grimmag broke him off. "Excuses are not my problem, Mindol. The problems are yours. You must own them."

"Yes, of course, but …"

"And your ruthlessness caused the crackdown."

"I respectfully disagree, don Grimmag. Conservatives in the Tantalus legislature …"

"You murdered an entire plaza full of protesters," Grimmag continued. He shifted and pointed a tentacle at Mindol. "While tough measures must on occasion be taken, you took the lives of hundreds of Tantalians, including juveniles."

"A statement needed to be made."

"And you made that statement. Now we *all* pay for it." Grimmag waved a tentacle toward the Saffron Guardsmen. "Strip off his clothing."

Mindol turned to the guards and backed away. "Do not touch me!"

One guard slammed the butt of his dual pulse rifle into Mindol's face, knocking the man backward. Mindol tried to grab the weapon, but the other guard swung with an armored arm and contacted

Mindol's left wrist. An audible crack issued as his cartilage-like bones broke. Mindol wailed in pain.

As one guard held the Jen'torian, the other ripped off the purple trench coat. The holograms that had orbited the man fell away and flickered off. Then the guard ripped off the teal shirt and pants, leaving Mindol standing on his four, thin, wobbly legs with only his white undergarments and the mask connected by a tube to a series of air purification pouches and control packs around his midsection.

The other drug lords shifted nervously, muttering to each other, but not daring to interfere.

"Now the rest of it!" Grimmag commanded.

"No please, my don! I will not be able to breathe!"

The guards didn't pay any heed to Mindol's words. He struggled, but they held him down on the floor and punched his face with their gauntlets as he screamed in pain. They ripped off the mask and pulling the undergarments off in tatters, leaving him nude, exposing his multibranching penis, his gray skin, and the floret-like bunches of fleshy skin across his back which help his species breathe.

Mindol immediately started heaving for air, his hands going to his throat. His eyes turned gray-blue as they filled with blood. "Mylord!" he gasped, his words bubbling out of his carp-like mouth without the translator. "Mercy! Pleashhavemercy ..."

Grimmag didn't offer any. "I will deliver your body to Tantalus III, Mindol, and leave it in the plaza where the bricks are still stained with the blood of your victims." Grimmag shifted back toward his audience. "Let it be a lesson to the rest of you. We make many hard decisions, and some level of violence is necessary to assert control, but when we become butchers, no payoff will turn the heads of those who attempt to police us."

Dirken blinked in surprise at the irony of brutally killing your own man because he had brutally killed others. It wasn't the usual 'revenge killing.'

Grimmag grumbled more words, but the Morlani did not translate. Instead, a Pleiadean slave with matted fur came up with a wide brass basin filled with various raw meats and placed it in front of the don.

Grimmag vomited forth a clear liquid, which splashed into the bowl and immediately started steaming.

The servant shrieked. She fell back, grasping her arm and rolling on the ground. Her forearm bubbled where the vomit had splashed against it, the flesh falling off the bone as she screamed in horror.

And as she writhed in pain on the dais, Mindol the Undertaker flailed in torment of his own on the floor, arching his back and gulping for air, hands to his head and shaking, his gray, bifurcated tongue lolling out of his wide mouth.

The slave was dragged off the dais and back down the hallway, screaming in agony as Grimmag extended his mouth like a giant, fleshy straw and slurped at the bubbling, acidic broth in the basin. His four tentacles waved over the bowl and occasionally reached in to stir the corrosive slurry, unaffected by the acid.

Dirken looked around at the drug lords. Most had turned away.

Grimmag finished and wiped his mouth with his tentacles.

Mindol gave a final spasm, all of his muscles tightening at once, his four legs going rigid, then he suddenly relaxed and fell still, blue-gray blood dribbling out of his nose, eyes, and mouth.

Grimmag gestured at the two guards and they dragged Mindol away toward the back door, a trail of blood left in his wake. As they did so, a different slave came and removed the food basin.

The don finally turned his attention to Dirken and Yiorgos.

"You may lower your arms," the Morlani translated to them. Dirken was very thankful. His hands and arms had gone completely numb.

"Thank you, your honor."

"Please, stand." Grimmag waved a tentacle toward Dirken and Yiorgos. "I must apologize for my guards. You are not prisoners here."

You have a strange way of treating guests, Dirken thought. He rubbed his hands, considering how best to respond. "I appreciate that. Why have you brought us here?"

Grimmag didn't answer. "Let me also apologize for the scene you just witnessed. It is just business, and it has nothing to do with you. I do not normally subject my guests to such … barbarism."

"Totally understandable, your honor. So are we free to go?" As soon as he said it, he knew how laughably stupid it sounded.

"Eow, you are a very loyal associate," Grimmag continued, not bothering to answer Dirken's question. "My mission to have you retrieve the Heart was successful beyond expectation."

Dirken gasped and turned to her. "You said you were there to deliver a message!"

Eow winked at him. "How do you think the Bloodhawk knew to ambush the *Excellentia*?"

Yiorgos said under his breath, "Played you like a deck of cards."

"Shut up," Dirken sputtered back. But he knew Yiorgos was right.

"Such cunning is evidence of leadership, Eow," Grimmag continued, the flames from the red torches gleaming in his ruby eye. "There is a new position just opened to lead our efforts on Tantalus III. You would be a good person to fill that role. As of today, you are a 'made man' and will have a small share of the take from that planet. We will deal with the formalities later."

The drug lords muttered in surprise. No one applauded as they had with the Corthian.

Eow's eyes widened in surprise. Then she seemed to catch herself and bowed. "I will serve as you need, my don, though I am a warrior, not a diplomat."

"A warrior with a strategic mind and an ability to prey on weaker wills."

Dirken winced.

Grimmag continued addressing her. "As I understand, your ship was disabled and kept by Captain Neenan." He gave what Dirken interpreted as a shrug, with a hunch and roll of the fatty body behind his head. "It is of no concern. We have many ships to give you. But the craft you acquired from the pirate is of excellent quality and fast. Do you wish for it instead?"

"Yes, my don," she answered.

"Hey!" Dirken protested. "That ship is mine. I stole it fair and square!"

Grimmag emitted a thick, gurgling wheeze and jiggled, which apparently was the Eridani way of laughing. The audience laughed and tittered along. Eow just looked sidelong at Dirken and winked.

"As for the two of you," Grimmag said, turning his attention back to Dirken and Yiorgos. "Eow promised no harm would come to you and that you would be free to go." He curled and uncurled his tentacles. "I always honor our agreements."

"Thank you, your honor. I knew that you would be ..."

"But the Heart remains with me. You and your partner will need to be our guests for an Earth week or so while we conclude our business with it."

"That wasn't part of our deal!"

Eow flashed a smug smile. "I never said *when* you could leave. And I never said you could keep the Heart."

"Double-crosser! And to think I ... I let you ..."

Dimitri chuckled. "What's the matter, fool? Wasn't the sex good for you? Did she give you the 'stud' speech, too?"

"Fuck you."

Dimitri just laughed, then he blew a kiss to Eow.

She smiled back at the Martian, but for a fleeting moment her eyes met Dirken's. There was feeling there, perhaps a tinge of regret, but he was in no mood to sympathize.

Grimmag stretched a tentacle to touch the sphere and roll it over to him. It clanked along the dais surface until it sat in front of him, then he rolled it back and forth, studying it. "But do not worry," he continued through his interpreter. "I know the Heart is of great value to you. From businessman to businessman …" He gestured back and forth with a different tentacle. "…I understand that we do what we do for profit. I am prepared to pay you for your troubles. Two-hundred thousand United World chits should suffice."

Dirken put on a smile and spread his arms. "I appreciate the courtesy. That's a fraction of what we were going to earn, your honor. You and I both know it is worth so much more." He thought back to Markus Juarez, Governor of the Americas, offering seven hundred thousand.

Yiorgos cleared his throat and shot Dirken a look that said, *Are you crazy? Take the money!*

The Morlani interpreter took a step away from the don.

Grimmag emitted a wet grunt, then continued speaking in his gurgling language. "Of course it is!" the Morlani translated. "I can appreciate your greed and moxie. But let us face facts, Dirken Nova. All you did was carry it from one ship to another—and have it confiscated—then retrieved it again with the assistance of Eow. It is hard to consider this as 'earning.' But I am an understanding capitalist. I will increase to two-hundred and fifty thousand." He and the interpreter paused a moment, then Grimmag added, "I suggest you accept my offer. The alternative is not so agreeable."

Dirken glanced down at the trail of blood from the murdered Mindol the Undertaker. "Of course, your honor! I understand. And you are most generous."

He noticed Yiorgos visibly relax. They wouldn't be executed—at least for the moment.

Grimmag emitted a slightly different tone of farts and grunts that Dirken thought sounded somehow upbeat as he rolled the Heart back into the duffel bag. "I am glad we could come to an agreement," the interpreter translated. "Perhaps the future will bring … collaborative efforts." Grimmag shifted slightly toward Eow. "Please escort our guests to their quarters. Make sure they are comforta …"

The room shook violently as a thick boom issued through the ice. This was more than one of the tiny quakes that occasionally vibrated through the comet. An exclamation of surprise rippled through the drug lords and they immediately started checking devices to see what was happening.

The room shook again, twice more, as distant explosions rang out. Bits of ice rained from the ceiling. Everyone looked nervously toward one another, but no one dared to flee without Grimmag's leave.

The Morlani checked a device as well, then leaned over and whispered into one of Grimmag's ear pads.

Dirken and Yiorgos looked toward each other. Their fear was confirmed when the human drug lord, Mukherjee, looked up from his wrist communicator and shouted, "We're under attack! It's the Bloodhawk!"

CHAPTER TWENTY-TWO
Eyes!

The drug lords exclaimed in their various languages and nervously started moving toward the entry. Grimmag emitted a rumbling chuckle. "My lords, do not fret," he said through the Morlani interpreter. "They cannot breach the comet or make it past our cannons."

But the comet shook a third time, this time quaking worse than before. Alarms rang through the corridor outside. A fissure shot across the left wall and ceiling with an ear-splitting crack. Chunks of ice fell from it, shattering on the floor and rolling away. A one-meter-wide lump landed on the head of a Rigellian drug lord, collapsing her fleshy, pear-shaped head and throwing her to the floor, dead or unconscious.

The Morlani's eyes grew wide as it looked at its tablet, then he whispered again into Grimmag's ear pad. Grimmag belched a statement to him. "My lords, you are excused," the interpreter said. The drug lords left immediately, falling over each other in their rush out the doorway.

The don extended a tentacle and touched a contact on the floor of the dais. The ceiling over the dais opened with a mechanical iris, the metal sheaths sliding across each other as it widened. The dais shook as an internal mechanism activated and jolted it upward half a meter.

The Saffron Guard ran toward the dais as it started to rise from the floor toward the opening—with the Heart still in front of Grimmag in its duffel bag.

"The Heart!" Dirken said, shooting a look to Yiorgos.

"My arm!" the cyborg responded. Both of them launched themselves toward the dais.

Dimitri and the other guards were slower to react, distracted by the chaos around them. The Reptiloc fired a shot at Yiorgos, which missed his leg by millimeters. Dimitri just yelled "Hey!" Dirken didn't look back to see if he was going to fire. Dirken realized he was directly between the Martian and Grimmag and a miss might hit the mafia don.

Eow reacted by somersaulting onto the dais, trying to head off Dirken. She flexed her hands and extended her claws. The Morlani interpreter yelped in surprise and fell backward, rolling off the dais and hitting the floor with a thud.

The Saffron Guard, too, had climbed on and raised their weapons toward Dirken and Yiorgos. Dirken reached to his back pocket and pulled out the little stun grenade. Yelled "Eyes!" Ripped off the activation pin. Squeezed his eyes shut. Threw the device at the guards' feet.

Immediately there was a loud BANG and a white-hot explosion of light so powerful that Dirken saw spots behind his eyelids. He hoped Yiorgos remembered his earlier warning and shut his eyes in time. The air became saturated with the overwhelming acrid scent from the phosphorous combustion.

Dirken's ears rang, but he still heard Grimmag utter a deep, spluttering howl, his tentacles waving madly. The Saffron Guard all shook their heads and yelled in pain. The cybernetic sensors built into their helmets and linked directly into their optic nerves were saturated and blinded by the stun grenade. Dirken grabbed the duffel and hefted the Heart. Yiorgos tossed him his blaster, holstered his own, then attached his arm.

Eow had also been blinded and deafened. She twirled, eyes watering, and no doubt deafened, yet stalked forward toward Yiorgos with her eyes wide and watering and her ears rotating back and forth.

Grimmag uttered a loud slurping grumble and swatted Dirken with two of his tentacles, knocking Dirken on his ass. The Heart slipped out of the duffel bag and rolled off toward the edge of the dais, which was now lifted halfway to the ceiling. Dirken scrambled after it on all fours.

A tentacle wrapped around his right ankle and dragged him back, suction cups clamping down on his skin.

Grimmag spoke, his words dripping and rolling. Dirken didn't need an interpreter to understand there was anger there.

He tried to shake off the tentacle, but it didn't budge, so he aimed his blaster and fired. The bolt grazed the tentacle, but Grimmag released his grip. Dirken lunged forward and grabbed the sphere, stuffing it back in the duffel.

Glancing behind him, Dirken saw Yiorgos had also been grabbed by a tentacle. Yiorgos swept down with his saber and cut the tentacle neatly in two. Grimmag yowled in pain, then heaved a stream of acidic vomit at the cyborg. Yiorgos fell back, just in time to avoid the stream, but landed at the feet of Eow.

The Ananak struck, kicking Yiorgos cleanly in the face. The cyborg fell backward off the dais and smacked to the floor with a metallic clang, two meters down.

With less than a meter before the dais reached the ceiling, Dirken clutched the duffel and threw himself through the gap and off the dais. Rolled across the floor. Bowled over the Reptiloc guard. Eow neatly jumped through as well, landing with a graceful pose.

The Saffron Guard had finally overcome the stun grenade. Two of them fired their rifles through the gap. One bolt hit the top of

Dirken's shoulder, knocking him to the ground with a yelp of pain. Somehow he still managed to hold onto the Heart.

Grimmag belched again in his grumbling language, his remaining tentacles pointing down through the gap at Dirken and the Heart. The Heart was now out of his reach. He pressed frantically at the contact on the dais, but the dais continued upward.

The comet shook again as another massive impact echoed through it. One of the Saffron Guard lost his balance and fell, his head slipping through the gap between the dais and the ceiling. Too late to pull back, he was caught against the ceiling as the dais raised inexorably upward. He screamed, his voice keening upward, then sudden silence as, with a screech of plastisteel armor and wet rip of tissue, the dais decapitated him. The helmeted head banged to the floor and rolled to Yiorgos's feet with splatters of purple blood flung in a circle from the neck. Purple blood gushed from the hole in the ceiling until the iris closed with a metallic scrape.

Dirken and Yiorgos backed up to one another and appraised their situation. All of the Saffron Guard had gone with their master. Eow opened her eyes and approached them. Off to the side, Dimitri and three other guards blocked the exit out the doorway that they had entered through. Dirken saw the Morlani interpreter and a couple of Grimmag's slaves were running down the hall behind the dais and through the reinforced door and decided that was the easiest escape. The Gogonoian flapped and waddled right behind them, uttering shrieks that echoed from the tunnel beyond the door. Yet the albino human singer remained behind the dais, lyrophone in hand, eyes intently watching Dirken.

The red door closed behind the Gogonoian.

Dirken fired at the guards. The shot hit a Pleiadean guard square in the chest, felling him immediately. He fired again, but the comet shook again and the shot went wild as Dirken struggled to keep his footing.

Dimitri and the Reptiloc fired their pulse rifles in response, narrowly missing Dirken's head. Yiorgos responded by leaping forward and slicing the Reptiloc's rifle in half. The weapon exploded with blue and red flame, throwing both of them back. The Reptiloc hit the floor with a whack and a groan, tried to rise, but then passed out.

Eow slapped Dimitri's arm. "Do not shoot toward the Heart, you idiot!" She pointed toward Yiorgos. "Shoot at *him!*"

Dirken took advantage of the momentary disruption and grabbed Yiorgos, pulling him as he ran under the raised dais and toward the back door. The cyborg fired off several bolts from his mini-blaster, but Dirken didn't turn to see if he'd hit. The dais was coming back down.

"This way!" the albino musician shouted, waving them toward the red door, then turned and led the way, glancing back to make sure they followed. "I know a back passage to the hangar." She spoke with a Terran dialect Dirken couldn't quite place. One of those far northern regions?

Dirken turned and fired a shot, narrowly missing Eow as she rushed through the tunnel entrance with Dimitri.

"Why should we trust you?" Yiorgos said to the albino. "You're a servant of Grimmag!"

"Because I am foremost a servant of a greater power."

"What power?"

But before she could answer, they came to the closed red door. The albino typed a code into an interface, but it was too late. Eow and Dimitri caught up to them.

CHAPTER TWENTY-THREE
Albino

"Leave the Heart and we'll let you go," Eow growled. Her amethyst eyes burned into Dirken's with murderous intent as she stalked forward, brandishing her long claws.

"You know I won't," Dirken replied. He leveled his blaster at her, but she didn't seem to care. He knew he should pull the trigger, but something stopped him.

Dimitri fired at Yiorgos at the same moment Yiorgos fired his mini-blaster, each hitting the other in a flash of light. But before Dirken could check on his partner, Eow leaped at him.

He fired his blaster but missed her as he ducked, her claws sweeping only millimeters from his face.

He turned and kicked her in the gut. She flew back against the tunnel wall with a grunt, her back hitting the control panel. Lights flashed on the interface. The doors stopped opening. Too narrow to slip through.

She recovered in an instant and leaped forward, deftly turning in midair and kicking the blaster out of Dirken's hand. The weapon flew through the narrow opening of the reinforced doors and skidded across the floor on the other side, out of reach.

Dirken raised an arm and deflected a blow, blocking her at the wrist. She swung around again. Her legs wrapped around his neck, threw him to the ground, his neck squeezed between her furry thighs. He let go of the duffel bag and tried to pry her off of him. Struggled to breathe.

Eow smiled, her pointy teeth glistening in a maddened grin as she raised an arm to slash at his face. But she paused, her smile faltering.

The albino swung her lyrophone and slammed it into the back of Eow's head, the instrument squawking with a metallic twang. Eow emitted a pained yelp and fell off of Dirken. He coughed and turned over to look at Yiorgos.

His partner was against the wall, his saber arm mangled and blackened, blasted apart. Pained, Yiorgos raised his mini-blaster toward Dimitri.

Dimitri was bleeding from a blaster wound to his right ribs, but he raised his pulse rifle again.

The dented lyrophone flew over Dirken's head and hit Dimitri in the chest. The Martian's shot went wide, hitting the ceiling. Then Yiorgos fired. The blast hit Dimitri in the head, exploding his cranium in a rain of blood and brain matter from his right temple.

The dais had now lowered enough for Dirken to see half a dozen Saffron Guards bending down to look through the gap. They aimed, but didn't fire, with Eow in the way.

Dirken looked up at the albino, whose attention had turned to the Heart. "Thanks," he said.

But she had hardly turned to look at him when they heard a crazed wail. Eow leaped up and grabbed the albino, slamming her against the doors. "You bitch!" Eow yelled.

The albino was surprisingly lithe. She escaped Eow's grasp, swung herself around the Ananak's body, and hugged her from behind, her arm around Eow's throat to choke her.

Eow stiffened. The albino screamed as Eow's body spikes plunged into her. Dirken pulled the albino off.

Eow spun and hit him in the face with a closed fist, then lunged for the Heart. But she was cut off by Yiorgos. He fired, but she leaped away, turning a somersault.

For a brief moment she landed, surveying the situation, the albino's blood dripping from her back and her own blood from her head. Her eyes darted from Dirken and Yiorgos to the body of Dimitri. She retracted her spines, then she fled, running with amazing speed past the dais toward the front tunnel.

Yiorgos touched the control panel and the reinforced doors slid open again. Another distant explosion, and the room shook again, large clods of ice crashing down around them.

The Saffron Guards fired through the dais gap, narrowly missing them as the room shook, but Dirken leaned down to the albino woman. Her chest was a mess of gaping holes and pulsing, bloody wounds. He was surprised she was still alive.

She gasped, spitting up blood, but her eyes focused on him. She pointed through the doors. "Second … left. Yellow … airlock." She sputtered. "Must … go." She grabbed Dirken's collar and muttered, "May AVA bring peace … at last." This last was stated with a long sigh, then her eyes fixed and her hand released his collar and fell to the floor.

The comet shook with another massive explosion—the largest yet. All around them, the walls of the hall splintered and cracked. Large sections fell from the ceiling.

"Come on, Dirk!" Yiorgos yelled.

The Saffron Guards continued firing, but the shaking continued, clearly affecting their aim. The dais had also stopped lowering and appeared stuck, but the guards now squeezed through the gap and dropped to the floor.

Dirken grabbed the Heart duffel bag and ran through the doorway, retrieving his blaster as he went.

One Saffron guardsman jumped down and spread his arms wide. Little ports opened all over his body, then a dozen miniature missiles shot out.

Yiorgos touched the control panel on the other side, closing the doors again, just as the rockets slammed into the other side. The hallway shook.

Dirken's eyes had gone wide. If the door had stayed open another millisecond they would have been pulp. He reached into his secret pocket and pulled out his lucky runestone, gave it quick kiss, and tucked it back inside.

Yiorgos blasted the control panel. "It won't hold them for long," he shouted, and they ran down the corridor.

They passed a tunnel to their left that sloped downward, then came to another on their left that stopped at a yellow airlock.

"Here," Dirken said. "The albino said to escape through here."

Behind them they heard a metallic screech as the reinforced door was being forced open. Yiorgos tapped on an interface with his good hand, but the readout flashed red. "Someone's overriding it from the other side."

"What?" Dirken said. "Can you stop them?"

From behind the airlock came an echo of small explosions. Dirken felt the vibrations through the floor.

Yiorgos cocked his head. "Maybe this way …" He reached to his mangled right arm and pulled a cable from it. It seemed caught on something internally, but it was just long enough. He raised his arm to the panel and connected the wire to a port on the interface.

From behind them came another metallic screech and the sound of gears winding back. Dirken looked back around the corner and saw the reinforced doors slide back. "Hurry! They're through!" He leaned out and fired several shots, then pulled back just as several blasts hit the wall.

"Ah!" Yiorgos exclaimed, and the airlock swung open.

The little Gogonoian fluttered his wings in surprise on the other side. He shrieked, eyes wide, and flapped past them into the hallway … where he was immediately shot, a pulse rifle bolt from the Saffron Guard blasting through his right wing and into his torso. He flopped to the ground in a smoking heap.

Dirken and Yiorgos ran through the airlock and pulled it shut behind them as they heard the echo of boots growing louder.

What they met on the other side was a corridor filled with fumes. The air was alive with the sounds of a explosions, the smells of burning synthalloys, the screams of the injured. But the corridor sloped downward before leveling out, so they couldn't see what lay beyond the slope.

Yiorgos hacked into the airlock interface. "That should lock it for good," he said. Then they crept down the slope.

What they saw down the corridor made Dirken's eyes widen. "Oh shit!" was all he could say.

CHAPTER TWENTY-FOUR
Another Freakin' Hangar Battle

Less than five meters ahead of them was a checkpoint manned by half a dozen heavily armed guards, an Oranchian in mirrored armor, and two mini-pulse cannons mounted on the wall. They were hiding behind barriers and firing into the hangar, which opened up in front of them, their backs to Dirken and Yiorgos.

Beyond them, the hangar presented a scene of chaos. Lasers of different colors flashed back and forth. Parked spacecraft exploded. Guards ran for cover.

And through the yawning opening that led to space, the nose of the Bloodhawk's brigantine, the *Dragonfire*, pushed forward. Half in the hangar and half out, the starship crowding the opening with its massive body, its prow decorated with a gigantic figurehead shaped like a four-winged hawk with outstretched talons. Most of the rest of the front had been blasted to hell, probably by those massive cannons. The ship was so large that there was no way it could fully enter the hangar. It blocked the exit against any mid-sized vessels trying to escape, including the zeppelin-like ship that Eow had said was Grimmag's.

But smaller craft can easily get through the edges, Dirken thought, including the fighter. He craned his neck, but he couldn't see the fighter from where he was.

"Holy shit," Yiorgos whispered. "It's another freakin' hangar battle. That's three in less than two Earth days! We sure as hell don't want to go out there." He turned to look at Dirken. "So what's the plan?"

Behind them they heard pounding on the airlock and attempts to wrench it open. Then came the energetic whine of a plasma beam as the Saffron Guard started cutting through the airlock.

"Well, no going back that way, either!" Dirken stopped to consider their odds, then came to a conclusion, looking toward the hangar. "Okay, I have a plan."

"Oh shit. Here we go …" Yiorgos muttered.

"Our choices aren't good, but we have one advantage. Those guards down there are all looking the other way and focused on the pirates. They don't know we're here."

Behind them the metallic whining intensified. Ahead of them, a laser flashed across the hangar and hit the Oranchian dead on, but the mirrored armor reflected it and it burned a line across the comet wall next to him. The hulking beast just laughed with a "Ho ho!" and returned fire at the brigantine.

Dirken pressed the button on each of the bracelets and watched as they folded out into mirrored vambraces—his own bit of laser-proof armor. He then readied his blaster. "You aim at the cannon on the left. I'll take the right. Fire at its energy pack when I do." Dirken took careful aim as Yiorgos did the same. "Ready? Three, two, one …"

They fired at the same instant and hit the mini-cannons dead on. Dirken's cannon exploded, knocking several guards off their feet and sending shrapnel into the rest. Yiorgos's was damaged, but his mini-blaster wasn't strong enough to do serious damage.

Dirken hefted the duffel bag and the Heart. Dirken yelled "Come on!" to Yiorgos. They rushed forward, firing their blasters at the guards. Yiorgos followed behind Dirken as fast as his gimpy leg could allow. He fired his mini-blaster and hit the Oranchian in the head. The mirrored helmet shattered, but the beast still stood.

Dirken shot a couple other guards and dropped them instantly, then kicked the Oranchian in the gut, distracting him long enough for Yiorgos to run through the barricade and past the guards.

"Make for the fighter!" Dirken yelled, pointing to the far side of the hangar and sprinting behind his partner.

He turned and fired over his shoulder at the other mounted cannon. The blast hit, but the cannon recovered and turned toward him.

The other guards raised their rifles at them. But just as they aimed, a massive explosion rocked the hangar. Missiles fired from Grimmag's ship hit the nose of the brigantine and exploded in a fireball. The four-winged hawk figurehead was blown off, tumbling end over end upward and then in a trajectory right for Dirken and Yiorgos.

"Watch out!" Dirken yelled, dodging for cover.

The figurehead slammed into the deck in a hail of debris, narrowly missing the pair, and crashed into the guard post. The Oranchian was smashed against the wall in a rain of pink blood and shattered mirror armor. Then the ice-and-rock ceiling over the guard post collapsed onto the remaining guards.

Dirken paused to check on Yiorgos, relieved to see the cyborg still alive.

"I'm okay!" Yiorgos yelled. "But look!" He pointed with his wrecked right arm up toward the Bloodhawk's ship. The front was a fiery wreck, but further down the craft several ports opened and red-clothed pirates in hoversuits jumped out, firing rifles as they lowered toward the deck.

"The fighter!" Dirken yelled and pointed across the hangar. The yellow fightercraft sat serenely untouched in the midst of flaming spacecraft and falling debris. It seemed impossibly far away, but they made for it. It was their only choice.

They dodged left as a laser cut across the deck and hit a Pleiadean hauler, slicing off her port thruster panel. Then they ducked as a Terran yacht lifted up from behind them, barely above head height. The craft had hardly gone twelve meters when cannon blasts from the brigantine hit the cockpit. The craft veered right, tilted at a sharp angle with an ear-splitting thruster roar, then collided with a spherical scout pod and exploded against the hangar wall.

"There!" Dirken heard someone shout. The deep voice was instantly recognizable. He looked up toward the brigantine and saw the Bloodhawk, a hoversuit strapped to his four-legged torso, flying near the burning nose of his ship. His uncovered chest was bright green and inflamed from the explosion he'd suffered in their last encounter, and one eye was swollen shut. Half a dozen of his pirates hovered near him. They immediately swooped into action, making a beeline toward Dirken.

"Crap! That's all we need!" Dirken shouted.

Several shots barely missed them, until Dirken heard the Bloodhawk yell at his pirates, "Don't fire toward the Heart, you curs!"

The hangar was absolute chaos. They passed by a Tau Cetian screaming in polyphonic agony, her legs both cleanly severed at the knees by a laser. A moment later, a block of ice as big as a shuttle slammed into the deck with a resounding crash that sent chunks as large a Dirken's head in every direction. A clipper exploded back the way they'd came. The air was saturated with fuel, spilled chemicals, and smoke. It was hard for him to focus.

They managed to get halfway across the hangar when Dirken spotted Eow running across the hangar as well, somersaulting over a disabled shuttlecraft. She sprinted up the ramp to the cockpit of their fightercraft.

"Eow!" Dirken yelled, but she apparently didn't hear him over the explosions and weapons fire. Dirken sped up, but he'd hardly gone ten paces before Eow lifted off in the fighter, turned, and flew through the narrow gap between the brig and the wall of the hangar entry. The fightercraft had plenty of room in the gap, but any larger ship would likely not squeeze through.

"Our fighter!" Dirken yelled. "That treacherous bitch stole our fighter!"

"What do we do now?" Yiorgos responded. "Can we take one of these others?"

Dirken looked around, but most of the remaining ships were damaged. The Bloodhawk's pirates were closing fast.

"Over here!" A metallic voice called. "Friend Dirken!"

Dirken wheeled about. "'TakTrak!" he shouted, relief washing over him. The Corthian stood in the gangway of his Jen'torian clipper, a bright blue eagle emblazoned on the front over the cockpit and gangway, a long row of scarred and blasted silver cargo cube compartments stretching back from the forecastle of the ship. One of the cargo cubes seemed shiny and unscuffed, as if brand new.

"We must hurry!" 'TakTrak shouted, his voice translated from its clacking, whirring speech into Terran by his translator necklace. He waved with a wing for Dirken to come aboard.

Dirken and Yiorgos gave each other a quick glance, shrugged as one, and ran for 'TakTrak's ship. The Bloodhawk saw where they were headed and opened fire on the clipper. Several shots perforated one of the stabilizers and blew off an atmospheric aileron on the port side.

A cannon raised up out of the top of 'TakTrak's ship and returned fire, its four barrels pulsing with orange-red blasts every bit as strong as the one firing at it from the brigantine. The brig's remaining cannon exploded from well-placed shots.

Dirken arrived at the gangway as 'TakTrak was firing a plasma flechette rifle up at the pirates, knocking two out of the air with the energized darts the weapon hurtled at high velocity. "Thanks," Dirken said. "You get me out of here and I'll let you off the hook for the rest you owe me. Deal?"

"Friend Dirken, it is a deal but I would save you no matter what the circumstance." He fired his flechette rifle again. "But get in now! We must leave!"

Yiorgos hobbled up the gangway and they entered the ship together. Dirken felt the ship lift off before the gangway had even closed all the way.

He holstered his blaster and pressed the buttons of his mirrored vambraces, folding them back into bracelets. 'TakTrak finished securing the airlock and gangway, then squeezed past them as Dirken then hefted the duffel with the Heart. The Corthian eyed the duffel for a moment but didn't ask what was in it. Instead he turned and led them toward the bridge.

Yiorgos met Dirken's eyes, and the concern was clear without the need to say it. Neither of them trusted 'TakTrak. Was there any other choice?

CHAPTER TWENTY-FIVE
Escape from the Witch's Tits

Dirken slipped sideways against a bulkhead as the ship lurched one way, then the other. Other than the gravplating, the *Raptores* wasn't like larger capital ships with their fancy three-dimensional gravity modulators to dampen inertial changes.

The hull vibrated with the hum of a laser slicing away at some part of it. 'TakTrak quickened his pace to the bridge entry.

Dirken steadied himself and stepped after 'TakTrak. "I don't know if your ship can fit through the gap."

"I have faith in Feleesha's piloting," the Corthian replied.

The ship accelerated with a surprising amount of power for its size. Dirken was caught off guard and had to catch himself before he fell backward.

They stepped through a couple of narrow passages and emerged into a tight bridge that sloped downward with a broad, transparent aluminum canopy. At the top sat the captain's chair. To either side were consoles for weapons and communications, both manned by humans. The weapons specialist had his eyes glued to a holo display, targeting a weapons array on the brig.

Below the captain's chair was the navigation console, manned by Feleesha, her back to them. Holo displays shone in front of her as she leaned right and then back, her hands deftly manipulating a control stick. 'TakTrak threw himself into the captain's chair and buckled the chair's restraint netting across his chest.

The ship turned and smacked directly into two Pleiadean pirates in hoversuits. The pirates slammed against the canopy in a spray of crimson blood like bugs on a hovcar windshield, their furry brown faces a look of horror before their bodies slipped off, leaving streaks of blood. Dirken wished one had been the Bloodhawk. He held his breath and clutched a console as the ship rolled to starboard under the hull of the brigantine and squeezed through the gap.

Below them in the cockpit, Feleesha pulled on the control stick and turned it sharply to starboard to dodge the brigantine's engine cowling. 'TakTrak's ship responded with an equally sharp roll that left Dirken dizzy. A loud rip and scrape of metal rang through the ship as the ventral side slid along the brig's hull. Alarms sounded through the room. Dirken and Yiorgos were thrown to the floor as the ship bucked.

"That fucking brigantine has a fat ass!" Feleesha cursed.

Then they were past the brig and free, exiting through the outer lip of the harbor tunnel.

Dirken and Yiorgos stood again. From his vantage point, Dirken saw one of the massive outer cannons on the comet wall had been destroyed, an outgassing crater left in the comet where it had been. And outside the opening, the Bloodhawk's corvette, the *Speartip*, was turning, disengaging from a hot fight with three fightercraft to pursue 'TakTrak's ship.

Dirken didn't see Eow's stolen fighter—*his* fighter—among these craft.

"Nav comps were hastily entered, Captain," Feleesha said in her gruff voice, "so it's iffy."

"Punch it, Feleesha," 'TakTrak replied.

"Aye, Captain." She reached over to a holopanel next to her, waved her hand across the hologram readout in the air over it, and pressed forward with the palm of her hand. The hologram shimmered and turned green. Dirken heard the Jacobian gravwell generator reverberate through the ship. Off to port, the corvette fired a couple missiles. But before they reached 'TakTrak's ship, space pinched in and exploded outward again through the canopy, and they had folded safely away.

More alarms sounded, and the ship shifted. Dirken knew from the odd sideways yank that this was a gravitational anomaly. They had come out of the jump a bit near some gravitational source, like a planet or star. He and Yiorgos held on to the conduit along the hallway until the momentum could be compensated by the grav panels. Feleesha stabilized the ship as a yellow star rolled into view through the canopy.

"What happened?" 'TakTrak asked.

"We were too close to the Witch's Tits, Captain. The gravity threw off the calculations. Then we emerged near this star," she growled. "Told you it was iffy."

'TakTrak clacked and whistled in his odd laughing way. "It is better than dead, my pilot!"

True, Dirken thought, as he looked out at the star. A humongous solar flare arced out of it, larger than the largest gas giant, but not in a direction that threatened them. Still, they wouldn't want to stick around for the next one, and they were close enough that the heat from the star would start melting the outer panels if they strayed. Feleesha turned the ship away from the star and accelerated out of danger.

"Adjusting coordinates," Feleesha said, entering information into the holopanel. She turned her head and looked at 'TakTrak, then again to inspect Dirken and Yiorgos. The eye that wasn't covered by an eyepatch narrowed in response to seeing Dirken. "Enjoy our winnings from *goron'oc*, bastard?"

"Not half as much as I enjoyed your piloting," he responded.

"Fuck you."

"Now, Feleesha," 'TakTrak admonished, "is that any way to address friend Dirken? He is our guest!"

Yiorgos sighed. "The last time we were called a 'guest' was by a mafia don, and he was about to hold us against our will, gave us an offer we couldn't refuse, then had his Saffron Guard try to kill us."

'TakTrak unbuckled himself from his seat. "Well, my friend, we will treat you much more amicably. What is this 'sphere thing' you carry?"

Yiorgos hesitated to answer, so Dirken jumped in. "It's the job we were hired for. We have to escort it to Nüwa. Care to take us there, 'TakTrak? For your generosity, I'll throw in a thousand UW chits."

It was hard to read 'TakTrak. His species couldn't blink and because he had a beak instead of lips, he didn't share the facial expressions of most species, but the tilt of the Corthian's head seemed to suggest some difficult thought process. Instead of answering, he turned back to Feleesha. "What is the damage to the ship?"

Feleesha looked to a panel that was blinking red. "One crewman dead when the dorsal cannon was ripped off. Port aileron gone. Port stabilizer damaged. We are leaking atmosphere in the top cabin where the cannon was. The crew is on it. Minor damage to port and ventral paneling, but stable. Grav paneling in the rear compartments is deionized but should be repaired by internal systems within an hour."

"How about the VIP suite?"

"No damage."

'TakTrak turned back to Dirken. "Let's increase to five thousand chits and you have a deal. Otherwise I drop you off at Harold's World with my cargo."

"Harold's World!" Dirken exclaimed. "That old mining dump? It's in the outer territories. It would take us weeks to find a ride back!" He paused a moment to glance at Yiorgos. The cyborg just grimaced. Harold's World, named after the legendary space prospector, "Toothless" Harold Jenkins only a century ago, was a rocky wasteland with a Mars-like atmosphere but rich with rare metals and radioactive elements. It was that last aspect that killed poor Toothless, after he'd lost all of his teeth and hair.

"Five thousand! Just to transport us?" Dirken complained. His offer of a thousand was already generous.

'TakTrak shrugged. "Nüwa is in the opposite direction and you would make me late for the job."

Dirken scowled. He didn't really have much choice, but it would be poor form to go without at least a little haggling. "Make it three thousand and we have a deal, but it's still fucking highway robbery."

"Thirty-five hundred," 'TakTrak counter offered.

"Fine." Dirken reached out a hand to shake on it and 'TakTrak sealed the deal. The Corthian clacked his beak in approval. "Good. Good!" He turned to Feleesha. "You know the coordinates, Feleesha."

Feleesha frowned at Dirken, then she turned and started entering coordinates.

'TakTrak put his wing around Dirken's shoulders and walked him out of the bridge doorway. "But it will be many hours before we can get you there. In the meantime, Friend Dirken, we have just taken on a guest cabin for a VIP transport job coming up. The one I mentioned to you earlier. You can stay there. I think you will approve."

They passed the gangway and entered the cramped corridor into the center of the ship. "This is the gig you mentioned to me at the Ruby Lounge?" Dirken asked, ducking under a conduit. 'TakTrak nodded. Dirken continued, "So what is it that you think we can do for it?"

'TakTrak waved away the question with a wing. "We will talk business later. You know I never like to mix one mission with another. For now, let us relax. I will tell you more about the VIP suite. It has fine Pleiadean spidersilk sheets on a soft mattress big enough to fit four people—with leviton emitters! Nüwan coffee. Holo-walls to project any environment you dial. And—this is the best part!—a pair of professional escorts. They have been trained in the sexual arts at the Bacchus Dome on Halcyon! Perhaps you can keep them warm for our VIP, eh?"

Dirken's eyes widened. Halcyon was often called the "Pleasure Planet," the number-one vacation paradise for warmth-loving species, with endless white beaches, resorts, and islands sporting themes to fit just about any fetish. There were no taboos on Halcyon. The Bacchus Dome, in the center of the largest island and the capital city of the planet, was renowned for training the galaxy's most talented sex workers.

"Yes!" Dirken said, and turned to see Yiorgos's reaction.

The cyborg just rolled his eyes. "Awesome," he said, dryly.

"Lead the way, my friend!" Dirken said to 'TakTrak. The Corthian clacked his beak and whistled in approval then walked them toward the back of the craft.

CHAPTER TWENTY-SIX
The VIP Suite

'TakTrak walked them through the narrow corridors of the *Raptores* toward a back cargo cube, his short cape swishing as he bragged about how great their cabin would be, but Dirken wasn't listening. His thoughts were full of longing. This ship made him yearn for his own again. It was hot, crowded, and hummed with the activity of an active vessel. Half a dozen crewmen of different species squeezed past them or craned their necks in curiosity from neighboring cabins as the group passed, each dressed in whatever clothes (or none) they were used to on their homeworlds. The scents of their novel foods mingled with the lived-in acridity lingering in the air and the "space tang" of their mixed species. It was a welcomed change from the smoke and chemicals in the hangar. Their excited discussions about the battle they just left would stop as they turned to ogle Dirken and Yiorgos. He knew a few of them, just as he had known Feleesha, but there was still a look in their eyes of … what? Expectation? Nervousness?

Dirken, Yiorgos, and 'TakTrak passed through an airlock that marked the end of the clipper's front "forecastle" portion and the beginning of the row of detachable cargo cubes. 'TakTrak engaged a panel, then they stepped through into a new corridor. This corridor was brand-new, like the cube had looked from the outside, with pleasant lights and clean, white walls without the patchwork of conduits, wiring, or ductwork.

"Here is the VIP cabin!" 'TakTrak announced with a flourishing whirl of his voice, coming to a door that was covered in swirling designs of gold and jet. With a wave of his wing, the door slid open.

Dirken emitted a whistle as he and Yiorgos stepped inside. It had been ages since he'd been in such luxury—not since they were flush with cash from the Io job, four years before, and had frivolously spent their earnings at the Nebulon, a five-star luxury hotel on Tesla. The new VIP cabin on the *Raptores* sported lush red carpet. Adjustable gravity and atmosphere. Two framed, erotic paintings: one of two lovers from Earth wrapped in each other's arms, mid-coitus, the other of a typical "orgy pile" of mating males and females from Tau Ceti F, their blue eyes wide and mouths open in ecstatic vocalizations. A plush love seat. Fully stocked, wet bar, food replicator, and refrigerator. And for those who mix work with pleasure, an adjoining office with a wide desk and computer interface. All furniture was made with real wood.

Toward the back was a wide, round bed with satin sheets and a dozen soft pillows, but a console built into the headrest showed it was much more. An array of emitters surrounded the bed. "Ah, the leviton bed!" Dirken said.

'TakTrak nodded. "Only the best, old rogue. Sleeping … and sexing … in zero-G is the only way to go."

Dirken gently placed the Heart on the carpet then threw himself onto the bed. His body sank into the soft mattress. He sighed in immediate comfort. It had been *so long* since he laid on anything other than bunks, crew hammocks, or jail beds … or the couch in the rear cockpit of the fightercraft with Eow in his arms. He quickly pushed the thought away.

"What did I tell you, friend Dirken?" 'TakTrak bragged. "Luxury unlike anything you have ever experienced, no?" 'TakTrak slapped Yiorgos on the shoulder with one of his feathered hands. "It is hardly the life of a rogue like us, eh? Why, I should charge you extra for such excellence!"

Yiorgos shed the Corthian's arm with a suspicious air and didn't reply.

"I tell you, 'TakTrak," Dirken responded. "This must be some VIP you're transporting!"

"Indeed! My client spared no expense." TakTrak turned to leave. "Help yourself to whatever you want. I assume you would like to taste the escorts, too. I will send them in."

Yiorgos shook his head. "That won't be necessary. We …"

"Please do!" Dirken interrupted. "If they are all you say they are, it's a real treat!" Yiorgos frowned at him.

"Certainly!" TakTrak responded. "Right away."

The Corthian stepped out, closing the door behind him.

"Are you mad?" Yiorgos said. "We just escaped a battle between pirates and the mafia and all you can think about is your penis?" He gave an exasperated sigh and shook his head. "I don't trust him."

That birdbrain is up to something, Dirken thought. *But it's not like he could have planned a pirate attack on a mafia stronghold. And he did save us.*

"You're doing that thing again," Yiorgos said.

Dirken blinked. "What thing?"

"Where you're lost in thought and moving your mouth as if talking aloud … with your hand on your blaster."

Dirken took his hand off the blaster handle and let himself lie back. "I don't trust him either. He's hiding something."

"So what are we doing here? It could be a trap." Yiorgos looked around the room. "He may have control over the atmosphere. He could cut off all the oxygen and kill us. Or vent the cube's atmosphere into space."

Dirken waved him away. "Maybe he could. But if he wanted us dead he could have shot us in the hangar—or just let us die in there and flown away without us. Besides, we're paying him. Hell, we're probably paying him more than his precious VIP! So relax a little."

"Easy for you to say! My right arm is shot to hell and I still have a gaping wound in my right leg, not to mention I'm covered with dents and bruises." The cyborg looked down at the Heart. "Whatever this damned sphere is, it had better be worth the trouble. When we finally get it to Nüwa, we need to demand more payment."

Dirken kicked off his boots and let them fall to the floor. This only seemed to piss off Yiorgos more. "You know," Yiorgos continued, "Therese wouldn't have betrayed us like Eow did."

Dirken groaned. "You just have to bring up Therese again, don't you? An old flame to inflame things!"

"Face it, Eow pulled all your levers ... including the one between your legs."

Dirken opened his mouth to rebut, but shut it again. Yiorgos was right, but he wasn't about to admit it. "You're killing my moment of relaxation. Why don't you ... do your Netfolding or something!"

Yiorgos harrumphed and opened the mini fridge. He pulled out a bottle of yellow glowing liquid with a holographic label. "Whoa! Proximan golden ale!" He popped open the top and took a sip, shivered, then smiled. He grabbed another and lobbed it to his partner.

Dirken sat up and took a drink, savoring the momentary sourness of it, then thrilled in the sweetness that replaced it, along with a spreading warmth through his body. Proximans didn't have the same reaction—it was no different to them than a regular beer was for humans—but this rare ale was magical for humans and many other species. It tasted like a stout at first, but then the aftertaste became sweet vanilla.

Yiorgos laid down on the bed as well and they fell into an exhausted silence punctuated only by the action of drinking their ales.

"The musician," Yiorgos said. "The one who hit Eow with the lyrophone."

Dirken thought back to the fight in the Sanctum. "Yeah," he answered. "She didn't need to do that. She could have just run for it."

"Do you remember what she said?"

"Yeah. It was weird. Something about someone named Eva."

"No, not Eva. AVA. Remember the quantum computer artificial intelligence that tried to take over Earth? Before she died, the albino said, 'May AVA bring peace.'"

Dirken took another swig. He was very comfortable. His eyelids were growing heavy. "That's a heck of a leap. Maybe she was talking about someone named Ava, not the computer. Besides, why would a slave musician of a mafia don care about a thousand-year-old computer?"

"Exactly," Yiorgos replied. "Why? And why would she think it would bring peace? AVA threatened to destroy Earth and Mars with their own weapons of mass destruction if it didn't get its way."

"Ridiculous." But the thought implanted a seed of doubt in him. The albino waited for them at the airlock. She gave her life to protect him and Yiorgos. Why? She didn't even know them. "She didn't need to do that," he repeated, his eyelids heavy.

A thrum vibrated through the ship, growing in intensity, then hit a crescendo and died away. They had gravjumped again. It would be hours before they reached Nüwa. He had time to rest, so he let himself fall asleep, nestled in the extreme comfort of the plush sheets and pillow.

Dirken awoke some time later as the ship thrummed again. Another gravjump. Had he been asleep for so long? It usually takes at least half an hour to go between jump points.

Yiorgos had gotten up and was at the refrigerator. He noticed Dirken was awake and tilted his head slightly, opened his mouth to say something.

But just then the door to the suite slid open, revealing 'TakTrak. The Corthian clacked and whirled with laughter and announced, "And now for your entertainment, my friends!"

'TakTrak stepped aside with a flourish and in walked a muscular human male clad only in a black leather thong and a Rigellian female in a thin red negligee.

The escorts struck alluring poses to present themselves.

"I'll take them both!" Dirken said, sitting up on the bed.

"Of course, friend Dirken. Enjoy!" 'TakTrak said, then backed out and closed the door.

"Oh brother," Yiorgos said. He turned to the attached office. "I'll be in here."

Dirken had already taken off his shirt before the escorts stepped forward to the bed.

CHAPTER TWENTY-SEVEN
A Pleasant Distraction

The Rigellian blinked her six eyes at him and ran her hands down her negligee. "You can call me Sugarplum, sweetheart," she said. The voice emitting from the mouth at the top of her head had a vaguely Chinese accent—probably trained in Terran by someone from Nüwa. "Have you had a Rigellian before? It is a treat."

"I have," he answered, and sat on the edge of the bed.

"Then you must know that we have certain … skills." The little tentacles around her fleshy mouth wiggled as the tip of her long, purple tongue licked the lips there.

"Oh, I know. Let's see what you can do with that luscious mouth, baby."

Dirken looked to his right and saw Yiorgos, shaking his head, disappear with the Heart into the adjoining office.

The human male came to Sugarplum's side and gave a wry smile. Young and slim with defined abs like a swimmer. Light blond hair. Dark blue eyes. Barely older than twenty, Dirken figured. He was what some people called a "twink," though some considered the term derogatory, so Dirken never used it. The young man knelt at the bed and unbuckled Dirken's pants, his eyes glancing up to see if there was any opposition. There wasn't.

The male escort reached for the buckle of Dirken's blaster holster, but Dirken stopped him. "Leave it on," he said, thinking back to his encounter with Eow. Besides, no one touched his blaster.

"Ooh!" Sugarplum said. "Kinky! I like a man who appreciates danger."

She ran one of her flap-like hands down his chest. It was fleshy but warm and soft like kid leather. When she reached his leather pants, the male helped her pull them off. They slipped over his rapidly growing erection.

"Mmmm. Tell me, sweetheart," she said, "do you want Andy first, or me?" Andy raised a slim, blond eyebrow and cocked a mischievous smile.

Dirken shook his head. He wasn't generally into men, or humans for that matter, though the occasional ménage à trois was enjoyable. "You first, Sugarplum."

She waved her six ventral belly flaps in excitement. "My pleasure!"

Andy stood and gently pressed Dirken back onto the bed as he pressed a button on the console in the headboard. The emitters around the bed glowed, and Dirken felt the pull of gravity fall away. They floated upward, gently entangling each other, flesh against flesh. Infrared emissions from the emitters sent soothing waves of warmth through his muscles.

Sugarplum pulled herself to Dirken's pulsing, erect penis. She slid her yellow-and-red-striped flap-like hands down Dirken's abdomen and through the patch of pubic hair to the base of his shaft. One hand wrapped around his testicles, undulating softly, warmly, cupping them gently. The other hand stroked up and down his stiff cock. She leaned closer still, the mouth at the top of her head coming close, then enveloping the tip with her fleshy lips.

Dirken sighed in pleasure as the warmth and moisture played over his glans, slipped down, caressed his shaft. The soft gums tightened and contracted in a wave. He closed his eyes and felt the undulations of her flesh as she pushed deeper, completely enveloping his manhood. Her long, thin tongue spiraled around his penis and rolled upward. The sensation sent shivers through his body. He gasped. Fought the urge to finish too soon.

She sensed this and pulled back, emitting a satisfied groan. Licked the base of his shaft where it met his balls. "Mmm. You are so big, sweetheart."

Dirken took a deep breath and made himself relax. Andy had stepped out of the zero-gravity field and now leaned into the doorway of the office to get Yiorgos's attention, running his hand over his tight abdomen. The cyborg looked up at Andy and shook his head. The monitor and holographic display in front of him showed a screen of characters.

Andy gave an exaggerated pout, eyes downcast and looked at the Heart at Yiorgos's feet. The escort whispered something else, but Yiorgos again shook his head and made a shooing motion with his hand. Andy turned away, glancing back once more to look in curiosity at the Heart.

Sugarplum once again embraced Dirken's cock, sinking deep onto it and stroking it with her mouth, moving in and out. This time, the dozen warm, wet tentacles at the edges of her mouth tickled the shaft, brushing back and forth in waves like so many fingers.

He took a deep breath, forcing himself to relax and prolong the experience. He closed his eyes again, enjoying the exotic sensation. He and sugarplum slowly tumbled, suspended in midair.

In his mind's eye he saw amethyst eyes surrounded by lavender hair.

His belly tightened and he arched his back as he remembered the softness of Eow's fur. Her belly against him. The embrace of her arms. The scrape of her fangs along his neck.

Sugarplum stroked faster, her hand gently tightening around his testicles. An electric shiver charged up his body. He inhaled a jagged breath, eyes wide. He groaned and orgasmed. Tensed. Convulsed into her.

She slowed her stroking. Sighed in pleasure. Seemed to savor every lap of her tongue over his organ.

Dirken closed his eyes and breathed deeply. Remnant quakes of pleasure still rolled through him. Exhaled. Allowed himself to fully relax and let his body float. Whatever 'TakTrak was paying Sugarplum, it was worth it.

Head still to the side, Dirken opened his eyes again and looked into the smiling, dark blue eyes of Andy. He had re-entered the leviton field and had matched his slow revolutions to Dirken.

Dirken reached over and touched a button on an emitter. The zero-G field slowly released, and the three of them lowered gently onto the satin sheets with Dirken lying on his back.

"Roll over and I'll give you a massage …" Andy said, his voice light and playful in a North American Earth accent. "… until you're ready for more action."

Sugarplum released him with a lick of her lips, so Dirken rolled over onto his belly, adjusting his blaster so it was comfortable and easy to draw, and propped his head up on a red, downy pillow.

Andy went to a console on the wall and adjusted it. The lights dimmed and reddened. Sultry Spanish guitar music started to play with a background of Rigellian hand chimes, tinkling in rhythm.

Sugarplum started to move to the music, her pear-shaped Rigellian body undulating in a sort of belly dance as Andy returned to the bed, sat, and began rubbing Dirken's back.

"You're very tight," the young man said, massaging hard knots along Dirken's spine, expertly applying pressure in slow circles, eliciting a brief pang and then wiping it away. "There is some severe bruising back here. I'll be careful."

"A little run-in with an Oranchian," Dirken replied, "among other things. It's been … eventful, lately."

"Mmm. You just relax now," Andy replied.

He did, though he found his right hand instinctively moving to rest on the handle of his blaster. He watched Sugarplum writhe in time with the music. Rigellians weren't generally attractive to humans, but seeing her move like she did to the music, with the red negligee softly slipping past her curves, she seemed in her element. It was almost hypnotic.

He's skilled at massage, Dirken thought, and soon he had started to relax as the man's hands worked up and down his back. Andy re-situated, leaning his bare thigh against Dirken's as he started massaging Dirken's arms. The heat and softness of his flesh started another tingle in him, already. Maybe he'd have to rethink his reluctance to have some playtime with Andy.

Dirken let his left hand wander downward, palm pressed against Andy's firm belly and slipping down past his waist and over the thong. Andy sighed in pleasure as Dirken slid his hand along his stiffening penis to the base and cupped his balls.

Dirken smiled as Andy grew fully engorged, the tip emerging from the top of the thong, hot against Dirken's palm.

"Dirk," Yiorgos called out from the office. Dirken frowned. Not now!

"I think we may have a problem," Yiorgos added.

"Oh?" Dirken said, opening his eyes again, instantly pulled out of the moment by the tone of Yiorgos's voice. Dirken's eyes came to rest on Andy's hand as the man worked the muscles along Dirken's left forearm.

Just above Andy's wrist was a branded "A."

What the fuck? Dirken thought. He'd seen enough of this to notice a pattern. *This isn't coincidence.* He rolled over and grabbed the escort's forearm, raising it up to show the wrist. "What is this?" Gone was the relaxation. Adrenaline coursed through him.

Andy blinked and sat back, pulling at his arm, but Dirken didn't let go. "Sorry? Is the massage …?"

"Not the massage, you idiot! That!" He pointed at the brand with his other hand. "What is it?" He felt his face flush with anger.

Sugarplum slowed her dancing and stared at them.

Andy shook his head, a nervous smile growing. "A … is for Andy."

"Bullshit!" Dirken said. He pulled his blaster and pointed it at him. "The truth!

"Oh!" Sugarplum exclaimed, and cowered against the wall.

"I … I can't …" Andy stammered.

Yiorgos appeared around the doorway to the office, duffel bag in hand. "It's the gravjumps," he said, then he noticed what was happening in the bed. "They …. What's going on?"

Dirken yanked Andy's arm up to show Yiorgos. "Look! The 'A'. Do you see this brand?"

Yiorgos blinked. "I don't understand. What about it?"

"I'm suddenly seeing this brand on the wrists of people everywhere we've gone!" Dirken pointed the blaster at Andy's head. "Tell me what this is! What does that 'A' mean?"

CHAPTER TWENTY-EIGHT
What the "A" Means

"Oh!" Sugarplum yelped. She backed toward the door and started to press the console to open the door when, at a knowing glance from Dirken, Yiorgos pulled his mini-blaster and said, "You're not going anywhere, Rigellian."

Sugarplum gasped and stepped away from the door, raising her arms. "Please, don't shoot!"

Dirken looked back to Andy and shoved the blaster into his hairless chest. "I'm not going to give you another chance! What is this!"

Andy's countenance of fear dissolved like an actor falling out of character and took on a serious expression. "AVA."

"AVA?" Yiorgos exclaimed.

"It's the Heart, isn't it?" Dirken asked. "That damned sphere has something to do with AVA, doesn't it?"

Andy glanced to the Heart but didn't answer. There was only the sound of the sultry Spanish guitar music, which didn't at all fit the tension of the moment. It would seem wrong to blast a hole through the escort to the tune of romantic flamenco strumming.

"I've been seeing that little 'A' on the wrists of people for the last couple days. You're part of some secret cult or gang, aren't you?"

Andy yanked his arm free. "You will know soon enough."

"We may have bigger problems, Dirk," Yiorgos said. Dirken looked over to his partner, but kept his blaster trained on the young man. "The gravjumps," Yiorgos explained. "They're too frequent. It should have taken longer between jumps if we were headed to Nüwa."

"Shit. 'TakTrak!" Dirken backed away from Andy and nodded to Yiorgos to cover both of the escorts. The cyborg understood and waved for the young man to step closer to the Rigellian. Andy did as commanded. The Rigellian shrunk away, trying to make herself as small as possible in the corner of the room near the door.

Dirken hastily pulled his clothes back on. "Did you learn anything from their computer?"

"Tried," Yiorgos replied. "It's disconnected from the galactic networks or even the ship systems. But I did some calculations with my cerebral implant. From what I can determine, the gravjump patterns indicate only three likely star systems: Sol, Tesla, or Proxima."

"Sol? Damn it, if we're taking the Heart right back to Earth the mission'll be a complete failure!" Dirken finished buttoning his pants. He raised his blaster again toward the male escort and said to him, "What do you know about this?"

Andy just bit his lip and hardened his look. If they weren't standing in a starship cargo cube with only a few unarmored millimeters between them and the void of space, Dirken might have blasted the "A" right off the bastard's wrist to get him to talk.

Sugarplum wailed, "I don't know anything! Please, let me out!"

"Well, Dirk?" Yiorgos said.

Dirken scrunched up his face. "Don't worry. I've got a plan."

"Oh shit, here we go ..."

"Get the Heart. We're getting out of here." Then Dirken gestured to Andy. "Go over there." He pointed over to the bed. The young man moved slowly toward it. "Sugarplum," Dirken said, "Go ahead and leave."

The Rigellian wasted no time. She immediately leaped to the console next to the door and pressed it, but the door just emitted a sour tone and didn't open. She tried it again and again, each time failing to open the door. "No!" she cried.

"Figures," Dirken said.

A voice emitted from the console. "Done so soon, friend Dirken?"

Dirken raised a finger at the Rigellian and pressed it against his lips. "'TakTrak!" Dirken said. "I'm just wondering if you've got any more escorts to share. Maybe a crewman would like to join? I'm feeling *lusty* today!"

'TakTrak emitted a clacking laugh. "My friend, I can always count on you for fun! But I have no more for you. Just enjoy what you have, and I will have you to Nüwa in no time!"

"Why have you locked the door, 'TakTrak? Maybe I would like to join you in the bridge after I've had my fun."

"Sorry, friend Dirken. After the battle we just left, my crew is a bit jumpy. Wouldn't want to alarm them with strangers wandering about."

"Then perhaps you could share your navigation with us on the computer here?" The Rigellian let out a whimper. Dirken frowned at her and waved his blaster.

"Sorry, friend Dirken. There is a connectivity problem with the VIP suite. We will have it fixed in no time."

Dirken pointed to his wrist and then at Yiorgos, then the console. *Can you hack the door?* Yiorgos shrugged, then nodded. *Maybe.* He stepped forward and waved the Rigellian away from the door. He put down the Heart and holstered his mini blaster.

"Alright, then, 'TakTrak," Dirken said. "I guess we'll just have to amuse ourselves the best we can."

"Certainly, my friend. Do enjoy yourself! I will let you know when we get to the Nüwa system." The intercom cut out. Dirken wondered, though, if the room was bugged and 'TakTrak knew all along what was happening in here. He'd be a fool not to bug it, frankly.

A bit of cable extended from Yiorgos's mangled right forearm, but it still wouldn't extend all the way due to damage. He had to hold his arm close to the console to try it, but he quickly lowered his arm.

"No ports," Yiorgos said. He tried to pull the console out of the wall, but it wouldn't budge. "It's constructed to prevent tampering."

Dirken growled. The so-called VIP suite was just another damned holding cell, albeit a plush one ... with prostitutes. "Step back and get ready. We're getting to the bridge one way or another!"

Yiorgos stepped away from the door and picked up the Heart. He flashed Dirken a sincere look, and Dirken knew what he was thinking. Cargo cubes weren't as shielded as the rest of the ship. One misplaced shot and they would vent into space. But he saw little choice at this point. Given the metal latches, trying to kick it open wouldn't be enough.

Dirken went over to Andy and grabbed him by the arm, holding the blaster at the young man's side. "Clearly you're more than a piece of ass in a thong. You're coming with us."

"You seem to think I mean you harm," Andy said.

"Well then enlighten me, Twinkle Toes. You're obviously hiding the truth from us, and I don't think it's because you've got a present for me."

Andy nodded toward Yiorgos and the Heart. "I'm not here to hurt you. I'm here to keep that safe and to make sure it gets to where it needs to go."

"And where is that?" Andy didn't answer.

"Mmm hmm." Dirken tightened his lips and gave Yiorgos a look, then leveled his blaster at the door. He fired, hitting the door right where it latched. The door flew open in an explosive hail of sparks and debris. Sugarplum screamed and ran across the room. Alarms rang from the hallway.

"Come on!" Dirken said, pushing Andy through the door. He turned to look down the corridor, blaster ready. No guards. Yiorgos followed.

The ship hummed as the Jacobian gravwell engine revved up, then they jumped again. "So soon?" Yiorgos said. "We can't have gotten to the next jump point yet."

"He knows we blasted the door," Dirken replied. "He's desperate to get us to wherever he's taking us and had Feleesha jump prematurely."

The ship lurched and all of them sidestepped and hit the wall of the corridor. Once again they had come out of the jump too close to some gravity source, but this time it was very close, like right in the orbit or outer atmosphere of a planet. The gravplating couldn't keep up with the inertial changes. Gravity negated just long enough for them to float upward a few centimeters and pulled them twenty degrees to the right before slamming them back down. Dirken and Yiorgos managed to keep their footing, but Andy slipped and crumpled, grunting as he hit his knee against the wall.

"What the fuck is she doing up there?" Dirken asked, a touch of space sickness making his head spin. He was seriously starting to doubt Feleesha's gravjump navigation skills.

Yiorgos reached the airlock door between the cargo section and the forecastle. He pressed the console next to the door, but it just flashed red. He then tried the manual override lever on the door, but it didn't move. "Locked out," he said.

"Can you hack into it?"

Yiorgos was already putting down the Heart. "I'll try. This one has ports." Steadying the Heart with his feet, he plugged the exposed cable from his blasted forearm into the console and started pressing buttons. At first it gave the red signal again, but then he gained access. "It's coded. This will take a while."

The ship gave another, minor lurch, as Feleesha took some sort of erratic steering maneuver. It was enough to cause Yiorgos to lose his port connection and have to start over. "Damn it," he muttered.

Dirken looked through the airlock door. The corridor beyond seemed empty, but he didn't doubt that 'TakTrak and his crew were waiting for them. He glanced back over his shoulder. Sugarplum hadn't come out of the VIP suite. He doubted she would. He then looked back at the young escort, still held by the arm. Andy was transfixed by Yiorgos as the cyborg pressed buttons on the console, then Andy looked down to the Heart at Yiorgos's feet, its dusty spherical surface peeking through the duffel bag's opening. "May AVA bring peace," he whispered.

"Got it!" Yiorgos shouted. He picked up the duffel bag as Dirken moved forward with Andy, blaster pointed toward the door.

Yiorgos pressed the console and the airlock slid open. The corridor beyond was still empty.

With Andy's arm grabbed in his left hand, Dirken raised his blaster.

They ran through the airlock and immediately they were hit with dozens of yellow rays emitted from the walls and ceiling. The beams hit them like so many punches, lifting them off the floor and holding all three of them airborne.

"Suspensor beams!" Dirken grunted. He could only move a few centimeters in any direction. They were trapped.

CHAPTER TWENTY-NINE
Hung Up

Dirken growled in frustration as he tried to pull an arm free and then a leg, but the suspensor beams held him firm. Each point where a beam contacted felt like a bad rash, itching and stinging, pinching his skin as if pulled by a line. The dozens of beams across his body, including a particularly irritating one on the side of his face, worked together to hold him in place, held in the air. He was a human marionette.

His blaster was pointed toward the ceiling, damn it, held in place with his forearm close to his head. Looking over, he saw Yiorgos similarly held and straining against the beams, the duffel with the Heart in his left hand. Andy had a reserved look on his smooth, youthful face, not bothering to struggle.

"It is no use, my friend," 'TakTrak said, stepping into the corridor from behind a cooling unit. A pair of his crewmen, including a lanky, four-legged Jen'torian and a faun-like Pleiadean, stepped out as well, each with a blaster aimed at them. 'TakTrak continued, "I had hoped you would stay in the comfort of the VIP suite. It was meant for you, after all. But you will need to ride out the last of the trip to Earth in these beams. Do not worry, though. We are in low orbit."

Damn, Dirken thought. *Back to Earth. After all of this!*

"What do you mean it was meant for us?" he asked. "You couldn't have known we would show up in the hangar when we did."

'TakTrak laughed, whirling and clacking. "Do you not remember me telling you in the Ruby Lounge that I was at the Witch's Tits looking for someone who was wanted by some powerful people?

You are the VIP. I know you so well, old rogue! I had a tip that you might show up there, so I outfitted the *Raptores* with the luxury suite and a couple of excellent escorts. I figured I would be able to lure you on to the ship with them. But when Grimmag's gangsters took you away, I thought my chance was lost. Imagine my surprise when you and Yiorgos showed up again during the attack! Feleesha thought I was a fool to wait, but here we are."

"Who are these 'powerful people?' And why me?"

The Corthian shrugged. "You will find out soon enough, my friend."

"I'm not your friend. Stop calling me that or you'll regret it!"

'Tak Trak shrugged. "It is only business, old rogue. You of all people should understand. I do not wish you dead. In fact, my orders are to bring you and Yiorgos to my employers alive." He pulled a green goron'oc card from his sleeve and tossed it toward Dirken. The triangle flipped through the air and flopped to the deck in front of Dirken's feet. "We smugglers cheat our way to profit. There are no friends. Only temporary allies."

Clacking and chirruping with laughter, he turned and walked back through the narrow corridor, ducking beneath a conduit, leaving the two crewmen to guard.

Dirken tilted his head as far as he could and was just able to make eye contact with Yiorgos.

Yiorgos grunted. "'Don't worry,' you said, 'I've got a plan.'"

Dirken frowned. "Just give me a minute."

He turned and looked the guards in the eyes. The Pleiadean shifted nervously. He had a slim build and remnants of spots on his tan fur that hadn't fully disappeared—still a juvenile. He licked his lips with a dark blue tongue and flicked his eyes back and forth to the other crewman as if awaiting instruction.

The Jen'torian was a female, as evidenced by the rows of gills on her forehead and her rounded mouth. Like others of her species, she had four expressionless, all-black eyes, and a full-face mask and breathing apparatus to filter out nitrogen from the ship's air, making it hard to read her expressions. But she stood confidently and held her blaster firmly. Dirken had seen her with 'TakTrak in the past. She was a seasoned spacer and likely not given to intimidation.

Dirken formulated an idea, but what he envisioned would be noticed and they'd have the draw on him. He would need a distraction, so he waited.

He didn't need to wait long. The ship shuddered as two explosions resounded through the corridor in quick succession.

What the fuck? Dirken thought. *Those were missile hits.* He and Yiorgos exchanged confused looks. The *Raptores* was under attack.

The young Pleiadean lowered his blaster and darted his wide eyes. "What was that?" he yelled, then wailed in his native language.

The boy's panic could work to our advantage. "'TakTrak is a wanted man in the Sol system," Dirken said aloud. "Likely the orbital patrols found him. He'll have us all killed!"

A hot water pipe burst at a joint and sprayed the corridor with water and steam. The Jen'torian kept her weapon trained on Dirken, but half-turned toward the Pleiadean, then muttered, "Hole yerpozishish."

It took a moment for Dirken to realize the Jen'torian had said, *Hold your position.* The Pleiadean apparently didn't understand, either, or perhaps ignored it, because he shouted, "They'll depressurize the ship!" and ran down the corridor toward the bridge.

"Hole yerpozishish!" the Jen'torian shouted after him in vain, turning away.

That was the distraction Dirken needed. Dirken strained against the suspensor beams, gritting his teeth as he tried to pull his right forearm toward his face and his head toward his forearm. Just as she started to turn, Dirken's chin hit the button on his bracelet.

The bracelet unfolded into a mirrored vambrace, covering his forearm. He swung it around, reflecting the suspensor rays and cutting the tension.

The Jen'torian jerked her head around at his movement and aimed her blaster. Dirken beat her to the draw. Fired. Hit her square in the chest and through her filtration tube. She fell, unmoving, to the deck, the hole in her chest smoking, the tube hissing nitrogen-free air.

Dirken activated the other vambrace, and with the two arms gesticulating as if swatting flies, he managed to reflect enough of the suspensor beams to break free and stumble to the deck.

He used the mirrors to reflect Yiorgos's beams, and the cyborg stepped down with a graceful step.

"Thanks, partner," Yiorgos said. "Smart thinking." He guarded the passage as Dirken reflected the beams from the Heart and its duffel bag and pulled it free.

"What about me?" Andy said.

"You just keep your smooth, sexy ass up there where you can't cause trouble," Dirken replied. "We'll come back for you soon enough."

The ship rocked with another blast. This time the rip of metal screeched through the air and the *Raptores* swung wide, tilted, and lost artificial gravity completely.

Dirken floated upward, but then expertly pushed off a conduit and glided down the corridor. Yiorgos followed.

There was movement at the far end of the corridor. A shout, then someone fired a laser, the red beam slicing across the hall. It burned a line across the wall then down the corridor and into the ceiling over Andy. Yiorgos returned fire, missing.

Dirken ducked into a side corridor. Less than a meter away, a bowl of yakisoba floated away from a mess hall table, the noodles and bubbles of broth spreading out. Chopsticks followed, turning lazy somersaults.

Dirken glanced around the corner and fired. The shot blasted a hole in a wall next to a human crewman's head. Dirken glanced to his partner. "We need to get to the bridge."

"I have a better idea." Yiorgos holstered his weapon and floated over to a computer terminal. He plugged in the cord at his wrist. Soon his head tilted, eyes fluttering, as he entered their computer system. He sighed, mouth parting, as his mind fully integrated with the system.

The crewman fired, his laser burning a line in the wall. Dirken fired again, this time hitting the crewman in the arm.

The ship's engines suddenly thrummed and Dirken felt a lurch in his guts as the craft went into some sort of rolling maneuver. Then came a reverberation of the ship's cannons firing.

Yiorgos partially came out of his trance. "It's a United Worlds patrol ship. They opened fire when they realized 'TakTrak has a warrant for his arrest on Earth. Feleesha just disabled the patrol ship, but …" He went silent as his head tilted again, exploring some other part of the computer.

Dirken looked around again. The crewman was joined by another, a Rigellian with a pulse rifle, and they were floating toward them. Stupid, really, Dirken thought, since you can't dodge while floating in zero G. He fired, hitting the wounded human crewman in the chest and flinging him backward, dead before he hit the bulkhead. A stream of blood flew out of the wound, forming spiraling lines of blood bubbles as he turned end over end without gravity. The other crewman pulled himself back into cover.

"But what?" Dirken said to Yiorgos.

"But we're damaged. Half the thrusters are offline. We're entering Earth's atmosphere."

"So? It's equipped for aerial flight."

Yiorgos shook his head. "One of the aerial engines was damaged, Dirk, either back at the comet or during the dogfight with the UW patrol ship."

Dirken gulped. "So, we're going down?" Memories rushed unbidden through Dirken's mind of his last ship, the *Brilliant*, tumbling through the atmosphere of Rorgos, engines down, and slamming into the barren, volcanic surface. Marooned. Injured. His crew dead or dying.

"Not if we can get back into orbit, or Feleesha can pull off a miracle. But the nav charts say we're still headed to coordinates on the surface of the planet. I guess she thinks she's a miracle worker."

"Or 'TakTrak is getting paid enough to make him risk it. He already risked coming to Earth and a firefight with the patrol. Other ships will be coming."

The ship vibrated in waves. Red light flashed in the corridor. Panicked voices echoed from other corridors.

'TakTrak's voice came over a speaker system. "Dirken, Yiorgos, my friends, this will be a bumpy ride. I fear even Feleesha's expert abilities may not compensate. Give yourself up to my crew now and they will escort you to a crash room."

"That's it," Dirken said. He blasted the speaker, then pulled himself around the corner. Pushing off with his legs, he flew down the corridor, blaster forward.

He caught the crewman off guard. As the Rigellian raised his rifle, Dirken shot him almost point-blank in his pear-shaped head. Yellow blood and tissue splattered onto the wall behind and floated off in all directions in globules. Dirken continued forward. Looking behind, he saw Yiorgos following.

"Are you mad?" the cyborg said.

"The bridge!" Dirken said. "He's trying to land us. We need to stop it."

The ship shuddered and bounced. Dirken and Yiorgos passed a side room, the door ajar. Inside, half a dozen crew were strapped into crash seats. Dirken turned to fire but held off. These crewmen didn't seem interested in the fight. Their eyes rolled with fear of a different kind.

Dirken passed the gangway. He continued forward toward the bridge, Yiorgos following. Gravity was returning, and not in a good way. He was pulled back toward the deck, but the ship heaved and threw them both to the floor.

"We need to strap in somewhere," Yiorgos said.

"Yeah. In the bridge!" Dirken yelled. He hauled himself up and toward the bridge door, struggling to stay upright as the ship careened into the atmosphere. Setting down the duffel bag, he reached out and activated the door console, but it flashed red and stayed shut.

"Yiorgos, the door."

The servos in the cyborg's legs whined as he pushed forward against gravity. Dirken was flung against the wall, barely catching the duffel as it slipped past. Yiorgos's robotic legs held him steady as he reached the door and started to plug into the console, but then seemed to think twice. He pulled out his mini blaster, put the emitter against a circular pad connected to the readout. "Turn your head," he warned, then fired. When Dirken looked back, the console was in fiery shambles and the door slid open.

Immediately a green laser cut across the hall from the bridge. Dirken raised his arms just in time for the beam to reflect off the mirrors on his forearms and into a wall. Then he fired, killing the crewman with the laser. But others fired and Dirken ducked back behind the door frame.

The ship bounced and jostled. Through the doorway he saw the bridge windows bathed in flame from the reentry friction. They had hit Earth's Kármán line and turned into a man-made meteor.

"Watch out!" someone called from behind.

Dirken turned in time to see a blur of smooth skin and blond hair leap and roundhouse kick the craven Pleiadean crewman from earlier, knocking him out cold.

"You!" Dirken said.

"I told you, I'm not here to hurt you." Andy glanced through the doorway, narrowly missing a hit by a blaster bolt. His slim muscles tensed. "We aim to *protect* you … and *that*." He pointed to the duffel with the Heart.

Another bolt flew through and grazed Andy's arm. He grimaced, then ran through the door into the bridge, screaming.

"He's insane!" Yiorgos exclaimed.

They looked through and watched in amazement as Andy leaped and whirled, kicking a crewman in the face, then swinging around and chopping another in the neck. Both went down. Dirken and Yiorgos ran in, as well. Dirken shot a crewman and killed him. Yiorgos finished off the two that Andy had wounded.

Other than 'TakTrak, who was strapped into the captain's chair, this left Feleesha, struggling as she was to keep the ship on path. Three different holographic displays revolved around her, all of which were flashing red. She dared to take her one good eye off the navigation panel and flash an angry look toward Dirken, teeth gritted with the effort of leveling out the ship's control.

"Dirken!" 'TakTrak said. "You have to stop this! You will kill us all!"

The Corthian's flechette rifle was strapped to the side of the captain's chair next to him.

Dirken leveled his blaster at Feleesha. "Take us back into orbit! That's not a suggestion!"

"Fuck you!" Feleesha said. "You shoot me and the ship loses control. We'll all die!"

"Friend Dirken. Reconsider!" 'TakTrak's hand edged toward the flechette rifle.

Dirken growled and shot between 'TakTrak's feet, barely missing his splaying avian toes. The Corthian yanked his hand away from the flechette rifle.

"I told you to stop calling me your fucking *friend*!" He turned again to Feleesha. "Now take us back up!"

Feleesha emitted a groan. "I ... can't ..."

The *Raptores* wobbled, alarms blaring. Overcompensated. "Shit!" Feleesha spat. Lurched back.

The ship abruptly did a barrel roll and Dirken tumbled across the bridge.

CHAPTER THIRTY
Plummeting to Earth

Dirken rolled across the window of the bridge, knocking heads with one of the dead crewmen, before crashing against the base of the communications panel.

Feleesha managed to get the ship out of the roll. When Dirken looked through the bridge window, the reentry flames had sputtered out and revealed a verdant landscape growing closer, bordered by an azure sea.

Yiorgos managed to strap into the seat for the weapons panel. Andy was crumpled in a heap by the door.

"Retro thrusters!" TakTrak yelled.

"Won't be enough!" Feleesha yelled back. "Hold on!" She banged on a console and yanked a thruster handle.

All of a sudden the ship was flung upward and rolled with a g-force that made Dirken see spots and glued him to the floor. He wrapped his arms around a secured seat base to stabilize himself.

Alarms rang louder. The ship seemed to scream as metal ripped and the wind whistled through openings that shouldn't have been there.

Next to the comms panel a damage control readout flashed an angry red across the entire map of the ship. Three of the six cargo cubes had been lost, including the VIP cube. As the g-forces relaxed a little, Dirken wondered if Sugarplum was still in there or on her own trajectory to the surface.

Through the bridge window, Dirken now saw only sky and clouds. Feleesha had performed an aerial one-eighty with the stern of the ship now aimed at the ground. They were falling fast.

She slammed again on the nav panel and threw the thruster handle back the other way.

Dirken was thrown again, this time tumbling through the bridge and hitting the back wall, held there next to Andy's splayed and unconscious body.

The ship complained, its engines roaring like an enraged giant, pushing him against the wall.

"Not sure it's enough!" Feleesha yelled. "Ground in twenty seconds!"

"Lower landing gear!" TakTrak barked.

"According to your weapons panel," Yiorgos said, "you have external-mounted missiles. I'm firing them without arming or launching."

"Do it!" TakTrak said. "A bit of extra thrust to slow us."

Yiorgos fired the missiles and the ship did a little shimmy. The nav panel cried out an urgent audible warning in Corthian, but Dirken didn't need to know what it said to understand that impact was imminent.

"Engage safety cushion!" TakTrak barked. Feleesha reached up into the holo display and pressed a red button twice.

Strings of white foam shot out from the walls, filling the room, covering every surface, and immediately expanded a hundred-fold to fill all the empty space in the bridge. In a fraction of a second it thickened and swelled against Dirken's face and body. Pushed him against the wall. Formed a hard gel.

And then they hit.

Metal whined and ripped. Explosive cracks issued through the foam as the ship slammed to Earth. Dirken was buffeted against the wall and launched back and forth. But the safety foam held him in a tight pillow.

Then the movement stopped.

Dirken gasped. His organs felt like they'd been shuffled like so many *goron'oc* cards. He was suffocating against the foam.

Then the foam dissolved, crumbling apart and collapsing to the floor in drifts of clumps and dust.

Dirken coughed, wiping the foam remnants from his eyes and spitting it out of his mouth. Blinked against the foam dust in the air.

The room still echoed with dire alarms. All of the panels were flashing red. Exposed electrical panels sparked. Hanging fiber-optic cables flashed. The ship had come to rest upright, though listing to port. Through the cracked transparent aluminum window of the bridge, Dirken saw the trail of destruction that the *Raptores* had left in its skidding wake. Broken trees littered the deep trench that marked its landing. They had landed engines-first. Dirken blinked, realizing the miraculous landing—a testament to Feleesha's piloting skills.

Andy moaned on the floor next to him. Feleesha lay bent over the navigation panel, unmoving. 'TakTrak snorted and twirled, his head lolling, and said to her, "Status?" His translation necklace was damaged, the word coming out digitized and staticky. Across the room, Yiorgos unbuckled himself, brushed off the foam powder, and looked over to Dirken as if he'd just had an average landing. He answered for the pilot. "We're down."

It was an obvious statement and yet Dirken found great comfort in it. An affirmation that they were still alive.

Dirken looked down and found the duffel still clutched in his left hand. But where was his blaster? Lost in all the tumbling. He looked around the cabin, but the room was filled with debris, broken panels, and covered in thick drifts of foam dust. So, too, were the weapons of the other crewmen they'd dispatched, their bodies thrown to the back of the cabin as well. Dirken felt around anyhow.

'TakTrak unbuckled himself, looked around in a daze, and briefly locked eyes with Dirken. As difficult as it was to read the face of a Corthian, the look was clear. Despair at the loss of his ship. Fear. Anger. Bewilderment. Dirken knew the feeling all too well.

'TakTrak then hobbled the two steps over to Feleesha and put his winged arm onto the woman's back.

"Feleesha, my dear ..." Behind the synthesized translator, 'TakTrak's voice was uncharacteristically gentle. Dirken wondered in that moment if their relationship went further than just pilot and captain.

The Corthian gingerly pulled Feleesha off the console. She was unconscious and bleeding from her forehead. Emitting a pained twitter, 'TakTrak put his hand on his pilot's neck to feel for a pulse. He seemed to relax. "Tough gal. You'll make it."

Dirken glanced to Yiorgos, and they seemed to read each other's thoughts. *Time to go.* They edged toward the door. Andy moaned, seemed to wake, then passed out again.

'TakTrak whipped around and yanked his flechette rifle from the side of the captain's chair. Yiorgos raised his mini blaster at the same moment. It was a draw.

"Drop the blaster," 'TakTrak demanded.

"You first," Yiorgos replied. "You're outnumbered."

"This damned gig cost me my ship and my crew. I should kill you where you stand! If it were not for the fortune awaiting me, I would not hesitate. Do not tempt me."

Yiorgos hesitated a moment before complying. His blaster clattered to the floor at his feet, throwing up a puff of foam powder.

Andy tensed, ready to spring at the captain. "Looks like your escort friend can't jump to your defense this time," 'TakTrak warned, his flechette rifle now aimed at the young man.

"You still think he's an escort?" Dirken asked.

"Yes, of course! I hired him and the Rigellian myself."

This confused Dirken. Andy was clearly part of something bigger, some secret society of AVA. How could 'TakTrak not know?

The ship groaned. A metallic whine. Then many things happened at once. The *Raptores* rolled several more degrees to port. All of them stumbled sideways. Andy rolled over with another moan.

Yiorgos lunged to his mini blaster. 'TakTrak fired. Yiorgos's blaster exploded, blazed orange. The cyborg howled in pain.

Dirken swung the duffel around and slammed it into 'TakTrak's head, the heart emitting a clang as it hit him. The Corthian flung against the side of his captain's chair, but he recovered quickly. As Dirken tried to swing again, 'TakTrak bashed the rifle butt into Dirken's face.

Dirken fell back, his face aflame with pain and unable to see for a moment. When he recovered, he was looking down the barrel of the rifle.

"Do not do it, old rogue," 'TakTrak warned, his translator modulating weirdly. Dirken raised the hand that wasn't holding the duffel.

Yiorgos groaned. Looking over to his partner, Dirken saw that the skin of Yiorgos's left hand was beet-red and inflamed from the exploding blaster.

"Yiorgos!" Dirken said, resisting the urge to rush to his partner.

"This job is not over yet," 'TakTrak said. "With the money I will make on this, I can buy a new ship. I need you alive, as much as it would give me pleasure to end you."

Yiorgos grimaced and stood up, his left hand clawed in pain in front of him. With his cybernetic right hand blown off and his biological left hand now injured, he seemed helpless.

Dirken slowly leaned down and felt Andy's neck. There was still a heartbeat, but he had gone into shock, his eyes going blank and his breathing shallow. Still, his wounds didn't seem fatal, and when Dirken touched his neck, Andy let out a low moan.

Keeping his eyes on Dirken and Yiorgos and aiming the rifle with one hand, 'TakTrak reached down to Feleesha's side and picked up a palm-sized device with a dish on it. He pressed a button and it displayed a holographic sphere in front of him: a blue and green topographic map with a dashed red line meandering through it to a circled location.

He gestured with the rifle. "Now, slowly step through the door to the gangplank. We're going on a little trek through the jungle."

CHAPTER THIRTY-ONE
Trek Through the Jungle

Dirken and Yiorgos stepped through the corridor, dodging broken conduits and live electrical panels, to the gangplank. Dirken led the way. He considered his possibilities for escape or attack but ruled each one out. His choices inevitably boiled down to either abandoning Yiorgos and saving his own skin, which was definitely out of the question, or attacking 'TakTrak and hoping the Corthian didn't shoot the cyborg, or him, before he could land a punch. 'TakTrak still had the rifle at Yiorgos's back, and the cyborg was in poor shape to defend himself. So Dirken continued as ordered with the hope that a better opportunity would arise.

By some miracle, the gangplank mechanism still worked when he pressed the panel. It creaked open, gears grinding. Blinding sunlight spilled into the darkened corridor, making them all squint. A gust of hot, humid air hit them. It carried with it a myriad of smells: the sweetness of fresh oxygen, smoke from burning wood, and the vegetation of jungle. It was almost overwhelming after spending so much time breathing stale, recirculated air in spacecraft and the comet.

The gangplank whined with a metallic squeal and stopped. The angle of the ship wasn't quite right, so the gangplank halted about a meter from the ground.

"Go on!" 'TakTrak said.

Dirken gingerly tested his weight on the gangplank. Though there was some flection and a disturbing crunch of the gears, it was intact enough to carry them. He continued down, the Heart and its duffel bag in hand.

The *Raptores* lay at the end of a trench that it had tilled through the forest, with thick, clay-rich soil heaped in mounds to each side. Tree trunks and limbs, still sporting wide, emerald-green leaves, lay shattered along the margins and extended at least a kilometer away, some of them on fire. Looking back toward the engines, the stern of the Jen'torian clipper was a mangled heap buried halfway into a gargantuan pile of flaming debris and soil. Thankfully, the gangplank was upwind of the fire and the smoke billowed away to the east.

Dirken jumped off the end of the gangplank and landed on the harrowed earth, back on the planet where this all started something like three Earth days before.

Yiorgos and 'TakTrak got to the end and jumped down, then the Corthian checked his map. The hologram was difficult to see in the intense sunlight, but he seemed to understand it and pointed with his plasma flechette rifle toward the forest. "That way," his necklace translated. "March that way. It is not far, but in this jungle it may take longer than we think."

"And where, exactly, are you taking us?" Yiorgos asked.

"Your mother's birthday party," 'TakTrak replied. "She is wondering why you are late."

Yiorgos gave a wry laugh. "Ah, the joke's on you! She doesn't celebrate her birthday." He paused to scramble up the dirt embankment, grimacing as he had to use his burnt hand. "In Greece, most adults celebrate their name day. And she would wring my neck for not helping make the moussaka." He got to the top of the embankment and paused to sit on a tree trunk as 'TakTrak made his way up.

"Grease?" 'TakTrak said. "Is that a cyborg joke?"

Dirken and Yiorgos shared a smile. "Greece is a country name on Earth," the cyborg answered. "My mother is human, but my father was a classic Harley-Davidson Roadster, I forgive your confusion."

'TakTrak reached the top and motioned for them to continue into the forest. "What is a roadster? Is that like a mechanic?"

Both of them chuckled. "Never mind," Yiorgos answered.

"You didn't answer," Dirken said. "At least tell us what continent we're on."

"This is a place called the Yucatan. I don't know the name of the continent."

Dirken had to stretch his memory a bit, but Yiorgos answered for him. "Central America."

There was no trail to follow, so they pushed their way through the undergrowth. The going was very slow as they wound their way under vines and through thick ferns. Once away from the crash site, the canopy closed in to such an extent that the bright sunlight was reduced to a dusky gloom. Things scurried away in the undergrowth around them and tropical birds trilled, unseen, in the treetops.

"I think your cousins are telling you to let us go," Dirken japed.

"Very funny," 'TakTrak replied. "And I suppose *your* cousins agree with them?"

Dirken followed his pointing wing and saw a troop of lanky spider monkeys peering down at them from a branch, the whites of their eyes standing out from their black fur. One of them emitted a series of rhythmic whoops, like the cranking of a rusty wheel, and they leaped away through the canopy.

"Touché."

Rounding a low rise, the trio came to more smashed branches, the ground littered with ripped metal, insulating material, and scattered crash debris. Following it, they came to the shattered remains of one of the cargo cubes that had broken loose during the descent. As they watched, the door to the cube fell open and Sugarplum stumbled out, covered with foam bits from the top of her pear-shaped head to her broad toe pads. Her red negligee had been ripped to shreds.

The dazed Rigellian held her head with a red-and-yellow striped hand flap and moaned in pain. She blinked against the sunlight, looking around at the shattered branches, and then locked eyes with Dirken.

"Oh! Not you!" she exclaimed and ran back into the ruined VIP cube.

Dirken was rather happy she had made it, against all odds.

"Move along!" 'TakTrak commanded and pushed the rifle butt against Yiorgos.

"Don't be so pushy," Yiorgos said.

For hours they walked, and Dirken grew extremely thirsty. None of them had brought water. He and Yiorgos were quickly coated in sweat and breathing heavily. Corthians couldn't sweat, but 'TakTrak's beak was open, exposing his thin, lolling tongue.

Dirken wiped his brow, huffing as he climbed over a log so covered in saplings and bromeliads as to be nearly invisible beneath them. Though he was a Terran, Earth had never seemed like home. Humans may have evolved there, but he had grown up first on an asteroid base, entirely indoors, and then on Tesla, where the climate was more temperate and less variable, the air crisper, and the gravity a bit stronger. There were no jungles on Tesla.

Then Dirken saw an opportunity as he pushed through the undergrowth. A long, slender branch jutted out at face level. He glanced back, making eye contact with Yiorgos and then pointedly looking at the branch as he pulled it back. Yiorgos gave an almost imperceptible nod.

"I guess you like jungles, eh, 'TakTrak?" the cyborg asked, following Dirken into the undergrowth. Dirken pushed forward, bending the branch into an extreme angle.

"Yes," the Corthian replied. "Corthos is a very hot planet with many mountain ranges, going very high, and jungles between. The summits are cold, but below, it is very much like what we …"

Yiorgos abruptly ducked. Dirken let go.

The limb slapped 'TakTrak right across the eyes.

The Corthian shrieked and fired his flechette rifle. The plasma darts went high and wide.

Yiorgos slammed 'TakTrak into a trunk and kneed him in the thigh.

Dirken dropped the Heart and joined the fight. Grabbed the rifle. Wrestled for control.

'TakTrak kicked and flailed, then shut his beak and thrust it forward. The razor-sharp tip sliced across Dirken's right cheek and cut through his right ear. Dirken grabbed the beak and slammed the Corthian's head against the leaf-littered ground. Yiorgos headbutted 'TakTrak, his metallic forehead knocking 'TakTrak into a daze. Dirken yanked the rifle from the Corthian's hands and the duo backed away, barrel pointed at him.

"Any last words, 'TakTrak?" Dirken said.

'TakTrak raised up on his arms and said something, but his translator had been damaged further in the scuffle. His chirrups and trills were translated into the hissing and rasping of the Reptiloc language.

Dirken sighed. 'TakTrak cursed and fiddled with the translator, but the device spat out a dozen words in three different languages before finally sparking and going silent.

Dirken shook his head, laughing despite himself. He glanced over to Yiorgos, and the cyborg gave him a sincere look. Dirken knew what his partner was thinking. Despite the double-cross and privateering, 'TakTrak hadn't actually tried to kill them. Besides, he had to admit to himself that if the roles were reversed, he might well have done the same to the Corthian.

He lowered his weapon. "Get the fuck out of here, 'TakTrak."

'TakTrak seemed to relax. Then, from behind Dirken, a voice yelled, "Drop your weapon!"

He swung around with the rifle. Behind him and at a slight distance stood ten silver-robed and cowled figures, each aiming a blaster at him and Yiorgos.

CHAPTER THIRTY-TWO
Robed Figures

"**I** said, drop the rifle!" the figure in the center commanded, speaking with an Australian accent. Dirken lowered the rifle, his eyes darting to Yiorgos's. His partner gave a subtle nod, grimacing. They were outgunned. So Dirken dropped the weapon and raised his hands.

Their hostage-takers wore silver robes that seemed out of place in the jungle, sparkling, modern, and festooned with communication devices and sensors. Their blasters were military-grade and new-looking, yet despite all the tech they employed, they used a length of hemp rope around their waists to hold the robes together and wore rough sandals, as if they couldn't make up their minds whether to look modern or ancient.

'TakTrak gave a series of angry whirls and clacks and stood up. He took two strides over to Dirken, started to step past, but then twirled and punched Dirken in the face. Dirken returned the blow with an uppercut, knocking the Corthian back.

"Stop!" the Aussie commanded.

Dirken and 'TakTrak glared at one another, fists raised. "That was a sucker punch, 'TakTrak. Low even for you!"

'TakTrak responded with an indignant chirrup and kept his fists raised until Dirken backed away.

"Yeah, probably wise you don't try a fair fight, 'TakTrak," Dirken said. "Corthian bones break easy."

The robed Aussie went over to 'TakTrak, who had picked up the rifle. A second followed her carrying a large case. She pulled a translator device out of her robe pocket, activated it, and handed it to 'TakTrak.

"We saw your ship go down," she said to him. "We feared all had been lost. Here is your payment, as promised." Her voice sounded very familiar to Dirken.

'TakTrak eagerly took the case and opened it, revealing a king's ransom in United World hundred-chit notes.

Dirken whistled. "So that's what it's worth to sell out an old colleague!"

'TakTrak tilted his head. He chirped a response, and the new translator interpreted it with an ironically sultry, female voice. "It's just business, Dirken Nova," it purred. He poked angrily at the device, and the voice changed, but now to that of a gruff, drill instructor sort as he spoke, each sentence shouted in stern exclamation. "I am sure you will be treated fairly! I was told they will not kill you—if you do as they say!" He paused a moment, shouldering his rifle. "It is just business, friend Dirken! I must attend to Feleesha and see if any others of my crew survived! Until next time, old rogue!"

'TakTrak gave a nod to Yiorgos, then the Corthian stepped back into the jungle the way they had come.

"Next time I won't spare you!" Dirken shouted after him, then he felt lame for doing so as he heard 'TakTrak clacking with laughter.

The silver-robed figures encircled Dirken and Yiorgos, keeping their distance, blasters aimed. One figure stood out from the others, armed not with a blaster, but with a broad-bladed sword in a scabbard and with a robe trimmed in sky blue. He had a salt-and-pepper beard spilling out of his cowl, but his face was still lost in shadow.

"So who are you?" Dirken said. "The Earth Welcome Wagon?"

The Aussie folded back her cowl, revealing blond hair and blue eyes.

"The bartender!" Dirken said, remembering the woman who served him his drinks at the Ruby Lounge.

She nodded. The others lowered their hoods, as well—all but the one with the sword. Dirken immediately recognized several of them: the handsome young ensign from the *Excellentia*, the bald and cowering slave who had been with the Bloodhawk as he entered the interrogation chamber, the bald-headed bodyguard with the cybernetic implant who had been with Governor Juarez in the musty, industrial hangar in New Miami. Even the greasy middle-man, Weed, who had recruited Dirken and Yiorgos on Mars at the Gamma Ray Gramma, which kicked off the whole mission. As one, they all raised their left arms in salute, their sleeves dropping to their elbows revealing a branded "A" on the undersides of their wrists.

"Hello again, mate," the Aussie said. "I knew you were the scrappy type. Figured you'd make it here more or less unscathed, though I 'spect you'll need another shot of Heraclean grog." She winked and lowered her arm, and the others lowered theirs as well. "We are the Acolytes of AVA."

Yiorgos asked, "Why would you follow a dead computer from a thousand years ago?"

She ignored the question. "Don't suppose you know what happened to a couple of our members who are missing?"

"I suspect I do," Dirken said. "The albino woman?" She nodded. Dirken continued, "She was killed by Eow after fighting with us … and saving our lives."

The Aussie looked down. "That was Birgitta," she said somberly. "And there was one named Andy. He was on 'TakTrak's ship with you."

"Yeah, the male escort. He was wounded, possibly mortally, by 'TakTrak. You know … the Corthian you just made fabulously rich."

The Aussie flashed an angry glance toward the robed figure with the blue trim before returning to a neutral expression. "I see."

She picked up the duffel bag and opened it, revealing the Heart and scrutinizing it, her eyes growing wide.

"Why the hell did they defend us?" Dirken asked. "They didn't know shit about us!"

"Hey, fuck-face," Weed the greasy recruiter said. "Show a little fucking thankfulness for their sacrifice."

Dirken was about to retort when the Bloodhawk's slave interrupted, her voice sad and quiet. "We know more about the pair of you than you think. But they didn't die for you. Their sacrifice was for something much greater."

"There have been many sacrifices," the bearded swordsman said, his voice thick with Spanglish accent. He lowered his hood as well. "Let us hope there will not be others."

"Governor Juarez!" Yiorgos said.

Dirken blinked in surprise. It was, indeed, Markus Juarez, Governor of the Americas, the man who hired them for the job of escorting the Heart to Nüwa.

"Governor, si," Juarez said, "and Priest of AVA."

"I don't understand," Yiorgos said. "Why go to such lengths to get the Heart when you had it at the start of all this?"

"All will be made clear, but we must get moving. We are not far from the temple, but others are coming. Time is of the essence."

Temple? Dirken thought.

"The lights are green," the Aussie bartender said, looking up from the Heart. "She's alive!"

"Praise be!" Governor Juarez said, as the others echoed him.

"Who? Who's alive?" Dirken said.

Yiorgos frowned and answered for them. He pointed to the Heart. "It's so clear now."

"I don't understand," Dirken said, looking at the cyborg.

"Why do you think they call it a *heart*, Dirk?"

Dirken looked back to the sphere and blinked. "You mean …"

"Yes," Juarez said, "you have been carrying the central processing unit for AVA, the most powerful artificial intelligence ever created … and the hope for all mankind."

"In a duffel bag," Dirken added.

CHAPTER THIRTY-THREE
Murderous Pacifism

The Acolytes surrounded Dirken and Yiorgos. Weed stepped up and put handcuffs on Dirken, glaring into his eyes and sneering. Dirken stared back. "You'll be the first one I kill," Dirken said.

Weed just laughed, then leaned forward to snarl in his ear, "Not if I kill you first, fuckface." Then Weed handed the key to the Aussie, who opened the top of her robes at the neck and tucked it into her lacy bra.

Yiorgos lacked one hand entirely, and the other was badly burned, so they didn't bother with handcuffs. Instead, the Bloodhawk's "slave," who still wore the red slave collar, used the cord around her waist to tie Yiorgos's arms together at the elbow behind his back.

With Dirken and Yiorgos in the middle, the group marched single file. Juarez's bodyguard carried the duffle bag with the Heart, walking one person ahead of Yiorgos. He handled the bag reverentially, taking pains to protect it. Dirken laughed inwardly, thinking of how much the Heart had survived up to this point, including a battle with a murderous barrage bot, firefights, the crash-landing of the *Raptores*, and being used as a cudgel against 'TakTrak.

Spider monkeys whooped and leaped between limbs, running ahead of them. They scared a small flock of green parrots with red faces and yellow bills, which startled from the canopy and squawked a rhythmic high-pitched call as they fled.

Dirken glanced behind him. The governor walked directly behind Dirken, abreast with the Aussie. Dirken asked, "Juarez, what makes you think AVA will save mankind? It's been lost for a thousand years."

"Not lost," he replied. "The world's governments have known she existed all this time, hidden deep in an old missile silo in what was once called Montana, in North America. And she has been highly guarded, inaccessible to any of us—until I came to power. The silo is crumbling and beyond repair, so AVA had to be moved. With careful political maneuvering, I made sure the Council of Governors was aware that the Acolytes were powerful and would find AVA eventually, and thus the decision was to move her to a safer location, off-world, until a new vault could be prepared. I arranged for AVA to be sent to Nüwa."

"Ah, I see." Dirken stepped over a series of downed limbs. "But you never intended to get it there, did you?"

Yiorgos gave a wry laugh. "I thought it seemed awfully convenient that a pirate was waiting in ambush with three ships, just as the *Excellentia* came out of fold. You tipped them off!"

"Sí," Juarez answered. "As you have seen, our members have been strategically placed. One Acolyte drops mention in a bar to a mafioso. Word gets to the don, and with some reinforcing words from another Acolyte who is the court musician, the don sends a messenger to a pirate. The pirate gets the notice and, with a few well-placed notices fed to him from yet another Acolyte who serves as his slave secretary, the pirate decides to act. Meanwhile, an Acolyte serving on the United Worlds destroyer as a yeoman keeps watch over you. Then another posing as an escort did the same when you were being delivered to us. And those are just the Acolytes you know of."

Wincing, Dirken wiped blood off the side of his face where 'TakTrak had sliced him with his beak. It was coagulating now, staunching the flow, and joining with other dried blood from the various small wounds since the firefight on the ship, the crash, and the tussle in the jungle. "The Bloodhawk used military-grade barrage bots to attack the destroyer. Pirates can't buy those from just any underground arms dealer. I don't suppose you had anything to do with that?"

Juarez laughed. "You are an astute one, for a rogue."

"And they somehow managed to get the code to get a boarding party into the *Excellentia's* hangar," Yiorgos added. "Only someone with security clearance could manage that—like a yeoman."

Juarez just smiled, as did the yeoman, who now sported a number of painful-looking bruises and hastily healed lacerations. It was with no small amount of respect that Dirken wondered how the young man had managed to stay alive through the bombardment and hunter droids.

"Impressive," Dirken said, marveling at the complex and decentralized nature of the scheme. "No paper trail. No money changes hands. It's all word of mouth and placement of operatives."

"And the legend of AVA is enough to guarantee action," Yiorgos added, slipping a bit on wet leaves as he went around some draped vines. "When AVA goes missing, it appears that it was stolen by pirates or mafia. What mafia don or pirate captain could resist possessing a murderous artificial intelligence that nearly obliterated all life on two planets?"

"Not murderous!" Juarez spat. "We are pacifists. AVA is a pacifist."

"Sure," Dirken said, "and those blasters you're pointing at us are pop guns."

Yiorgos grunted. "I seem to recall that AVA threatened to launch all weapons systems on both Mars and Earth. Seems like the opposite of pacifism to me."

"Have you ever heard of MAD?" Juarez said. "Mutually Assured Destruction?"

"That was a weapons philosophy back in the nuclear era, right?" Yiorgos asked. "Ancient nations building so many nukes they could destroy the whole world. Part of those missile silos you mentioned."

"Sí," Juarez replied. "Ironic that AVA would be kept in one, is it not? MAD is the idea that any aggressive action between two nations would result in the destruction of them all. Thus, no one would risk it, and you have peace."

"No one *sane* would risk it," Dirken corrected.

"AVA is not insane, amigo. She is far more logical than any human. She had calculated that when given the choice between disarming all systems or having civilization destroyed, humanity would choose to disarm."

"How can you claim that?" Yiorgos asked. "Opposing nations threatened each other, and their Mars colonies, with annihilation, each thinking the other had made the threat."

"AVA would not have allowed it to go so far," Juarez replied.

Dirken squeezed through a thicket, then wiped the sweat from his brow. "And this is why you think AVA will 'save mankind?' That she will threaten to destroy the Earth unless we disarm?"

"There is more to the story. In my position, governing half of Earth for the United Worlds, I can say that we are in a precarious time. Nüwa and Tesla are more economically stable than Earth, without the overpopulation, pollution, famine, and extreme climate, and are self-sufficient now. They threaten to break away. Secessionists are gaining power. Pirates and gangs, like the ones you encountered in the last couple of days, threaten our safety and commerce … as do smugglers like yourself," he added with disdain. "And Earth needs those worlds for protection from alien civilizations like the Reptiloc Empire or the Aquarian New Dawn, who wish nothing more than to invade and take what resources we have left. Earth is rich in water, after all."

Dirken slowed to a stop and rested a moment, turning around to face Juarez. His armpits were saturated with sweat. His wrist had grown raw from the handcuffs. The heat and humidity of the jungle left his throat dry and his head woozy. "I can relate. I'm very thirsty. Do you have any water?" His gaze dropped to the hilt of Juarez's sword. There was what looked like an activator switch. Maybe some form of plasma blade? But he had no chance to lunge for it. Too many weapons aimed at him.

As if reading his mind, the Aussie waved her blaster at him. "Keep moving, mate. There'll be water at the temple."

Temple? he wondered again. *Damned cult.* "There's that astounding 'pacifism' in action, I see." Dirken turned and kept walking. "So, you want to reactivate AVA in the hope it can convince the other worlds to stay in the United Worlds Federation, is that it? Somehow I don't think an AI overlord with an itchy trigger finger and a penchant for hacking is the answer."

"Enough talk for now," Juarez growled in response. "It is time to walk in silence. And speed it up!"

A number of the small devices incorporated into the Acolytes' robes were buzzing or lighting up, and this was met with what seemed like growing alarm. Dirken heard the Aussie whisper something to Juarez. He couldn't make it out, other than the words "coming soon." After all they'd been through, Dirken truly didn't want yet another crisis on top of the already fucked-up situation they were in.

They marched through the jungle in silence for about twenty minutes. The low hills descended to a flat plain. The leaf litter and vines gave way to lower, thinner trees and a wet, sometimes mushy ground. Dirken was accosted by a swarm of mosquitoes. Most animal species, including man, had suffered heavy losses from a couple hundred years of rapid climate change, he thought glumly, but these damned blood suckers seemed to thrive. He swatted at them as they hummed in his ears, but the handcuffs made his attempts fruitless. Mosquitoes were another reason to avoid this planet. He didn't really think of Earth as his "homeworld," anyhow. Birthplace of humanity, sure, but also its deathplace, leaving humankind spread across the stars with no common world. Earth was barely habitable now in most places.

They followed a trail that skirted the worst of the wetness and greatly sped their progress. The trail was raised and oddly straight as if built upon some long-forgotten causeway. Soon the first signs of civilization appeared. But it wasn't *recent* civilization by any stretch.

At first it just seemed like random piles of ashy-gray rock covered in vegetation. But the piles grew larger. Followed lines. Had straight edges. And then, peeking through the foliage, Dirken spied a mound, half-buried in ages of soil, made with a base of these gray stones and rising about ten meters to where a much larger gray slab emerged from soil and ferns. Intricate carvings covered it, heavily weathered. Dirken picked out a masculine face in profile with a feathered headdress. Sloped forehead. Long, rounded nose. Large disk earrings. Rounded yet blocky designs surrounded the sage visage. And then they marched on and the mound was lost in the undergrowth.

Dirken pointed at the mound and looked back at Juarez. "Is that …?"

"Sí," Juarez said. "Just wait, smuggler. You will see."

"Look, Governor, you have the Heart back. If that's all you wanted, why not just let us go?"

"You know too much, smuggler. Besides, we still have use for the two of you."

Dirken looked ahead to Yiorgos, who was stumbling through some ferns. "Then at least let my partner go. You can hold me hostage to make sure he doesn't talk to the feds."

Juarez gave a wry laugh. "Who says it is you we wanted?" Dirken blinked in confusion at this, unsure how to respond.

In moments the jungle opened up to a clearing spotted with low trees. Before them, rising with noble antiquity, towered a complex of crumbling step pyramids, broad plazas, and raised platforms, all constructed of gray rock.

"Behold!" Juarez said, "the ancient Mayan city of Edzná!"

CHAPTER THIRTY-FOUR
Pyramid

Now free of the jungle trail, the party picked up its pace, moving in a near straight line through rocky platforms decorated with simple pillars and ancient foundations. To Dirken's right, an archway peeked around a short wall. To Dirken's left, a mound ascending some twenty meters was topped with an open chamber.

Then the party marched through a long courtyard with deteriorated, sloping walls. Midway through, on the wall to either side, were projected half-circles of carved rock, which looked as if, prior to being broken, may have been massive rock rings.

"An alley," Dirken grumbled. "Lowlifes like you are right at home here."

"This was a game arena," Juarez said, condescension in his tone. "Men played on teams with a rubber ball, hitting it with their thighs in an attempt to get it past the other team." He pointed to one of the broken stone rings. "If you got the ball through a ring, you won instantly." He paused for effect, then added. "It was all deeply religious—a ritual reenactment of the creation of the cosmos. It is said that sometimes the losers would be sacrificed to their gods."

Dirken scoffed. "And what did they know of the cosmos, Juarez? Where are their gods now? A barbaric game for a primitive people."

"Bloody? Sí. But primitive? No. They were very advanced for their time, amigo. What we see around us was a metropolitan area with tens of thousands of citizens, ruling an empire that dwarfed anything in Europe at the time, calculating astronomical events with such precision they predicted solar eclipses hundreds of years ahead.

Their gods ruled the cosmos with the same precision. Bloodshed was a way of cementing their devotion."

"And now you have your own god to worship, Governor," Yiorgos said. "How are you going to show your devotion? Bloodshed?"

"AVA is like a god, yes, with powers you will see soon enough. But bloodshed? That is up to you. Let us hope you do as we say and neither of you needs to die."

They exited the arena northward into a vast plaza. To their left a colossal, rampart-like wall bordered the full length of the plaza. Ahead stood a small, stepped pyramid with stairs on each side and a vaulted chamber at the top. But off to their right, up a steep set of stairs to a plateau, sat a gigantic pyramid. The party turned in that direction.

The devices on the Acolyte robes were buzzing and lighting up even more. "We must hurry," the Aussie said to Juarez, loud enough that Dirken overheard. "They'll reach orbit any time now."

"Who's coming?" Dirken asked. "I do like parties, you know." He shivered in mock excitement. "And to think, I forgot to bring the beer."

"Move faster!" Juarez commanded, without answering him.

Dirken didn't know who was "almost to orbit," but from the sound of it, they didn't seem to be someone Juarez liked. The Bloodhawk? He'd rather take his chances with these idiots. He considered slow-walking it, but reconsidered after the Aussie poked him in the back with the business end of her blaster.

The group double-timed it, almost jogging, to the stairs, then they climbed. The steps up the plateau were made of the same light gray rock as everything else, each stone large enough that it would take many men to heft it. There were hundreds of thousands of such stones in the structure, maybe millions, rising four tiers upward.

Because Yiorgos's arms were tied behind his back, Dirken did what he could to help his partner climb, lending him a handcuffed hand.

Overheated and dehydrated, Dirken's head was woozy by the time he reached the top of the steps. All of them were huffing and puffing. They took a moment, bent over, to catch their breath. Off to the side was a pile of canteens. One of the acolytes, the curly blond-haired young man who'd been a yeoman on the *Excellentia*, handed Dirken and Yiorgos a canteen. The water was hot from sitting in the blazing sun but still refreshing. He drank deeply. Yiorgos did as well, but then he started coughing and sputtering.

"We must keep moving," Juarez commanded.

"In case you haven't noticed," Dirken said, "my partner is badly injured. We just survived a fucking crash-landing, after all, and a firefight to boot, then a march through the damned jungle."

Juarez nodded toward the acolytes, who responded by raising their guns toward the pair. "I said, keep moving."

Dirken put his hand on Yiorgos's shoulder. The cyborg stopped sputtering and gave one more cough. "I'll be okay," he gasped, but the biological part of his face was pale. He blinked rapidly, seeming to have trouble focusing. Heat exhaustion, Dirken figured, but he didn't say anything. Mechanical legs, or not, it was still hard on what remained of the man's heart and body to lug all that weight around. He helped his partner to his feet, then the party moved along, gaining speed.

At the top of the plateau was what Dirken could only think of as an acropolis. Even more grand than the last plaza, there was a stepped pyramid at both the north and south sides of the plaza, each impressive in its own right. But what drew his eye was the gargantuan step pyramid that he'd seen rising above the jungle, now directly ahead. Each "step" of the pyramid consisted of a story about as high as two people, and there were five stories rising up to a central chamber at the top. Each story had multiple open doorways, dark and looming, like portals into the past. A steep central stairway dominated the front of the pyramid rising to the top structure. At the very top, above the final stone room, a slotted rock wall rose even farther like a crown upon the pyramid's head.

For a moment, the weight of antiquity seemed to descend upon Dirken. In his mind's eye, he saw before him not a crumbling edifice, but an intact temple decorated in smoking braziers and paint, men and women bedecked in colorful clothing and sandals in a style like those of the relief sculptures, their heads covered in many-feathered headdresses over sloping foreheads, hair pulled back into thick dreadlocks or braids and stiffened to form wildly artistic forms, their prominent noses and ears decorated with disks of turquoise or onyx.

"El Pirámide de los Cinco Pisos!" Juarez announced, breaking the vision. "The Pyramid of Five Stories!"

Dirken was indeed impressed, but he wasn't about to show it. "A pitifully generic name. Looks more like the 'Pyramid of Crumbling Gods' to me. No wonder you like it."

He heard Juarez scoff behind him, "Typical of a smuggler. No respect for the great accomplishments of mankind."

"True," Dirken replied. "It is an impressive accomplishment—of a culture long-dead and nearly forgotten, collapsing, bit by bit, like the rest of this world."

Drawing closer to the base of the pyramid, Dirken saw that it had been modified. At the bottom of the steps sat large power generators with thick black cables that snaked up the great staircase. Dirken could see satellite dishes, a microwave transmitter/receiver, and a neutrino-wave array for interstellar communications at the top, likely powered by these generators.

Yiorgos seemed to read Dirken's thoughts as he asked, "Did your Mayan friends also invent telecommunications, Juarez?"

The governor didn't answer. Instead, he prodded them further until they were practically jogging across the plaza. Reaching the broad stairway, they started climbing, stepping over a row of blocks carved with odd, curving shapes that may have been some form of hieroglyphs.

Two of the Acolytes stayed at the bottom, including the Bloodhawk's "slave," to start up the power generators. Weed and Juarez remained behind Dirken and Yiorgos. Ahead of them, Juarez's bodyguard quickly power-climbed the steps, carrying the Heart in its duffel bag. The others climbed slower, with the Aussie and the blond-haired yeoman from the *Excellentia* climbing just ahead of Yiorgos and Dirken, occasionally turning to check on the prisoners, blasters at the ready.

The steps were even steeper than those leading up to the acropolis, requiring that they use their hands to balance. At last, they untied Yiorgos so that he could climb with his injured hand and forearm. He was in such a clearly weakened state that he wasn't likely to attempt an escape. Even so, Yiorgos had a hard time of it, repeatedly gasping in pain and wavering as if losing his balance, and Dirken had to help him along.

Dirken paused and looked down toward Juarez. "We have to stop. My partner …"

"No stopping!" Juarez said. "Get to the top. Now!"

"No!" Dirken shouted and kicked a loose stone.

Weed dodged it as it tumbled, then fired his blaster. The shot hit the steps to Dirken's right. Shattered bits of stone ricocheted around him.

"Climb!" Weed warned. "Or the next blast will end your life, asshole!"

Dirken growled in response, narrowing his eyes at the recruiter. I'll end your life, shithead, he thought, but then he turned and continued upward. "Come on, Yiorgos, old buddy, you can do it. We're halfway, now."

"Yeah," Yiorgos said, gasping. "Halfway to whatever fate they decide for us. How's that plan coming together?"

At last, they reached the top and stood gasping for breath, facing a small, stone building with an open-aired vestibule with two openings. Inside, a doorway led into the dark depths.

Power cables, thick and black, snaked all the way up the stairs from the power units below. One cable continued across the platform into the dark room. The others split off to Dirken's left and right to communications arrays—those satellite uplink dishes and an interstellar neutrino emitter. Those connected via a series of cables to a quantum computing station shoved up against the stone building. All of these devices hummed with activity and defied the bright sunlight with various indicator lights and readouts.

Yiorgos collapsed onto the stone platform. Dirken stepped forward and leaned against one of two upright blocks, struggling to catch his breath. The Acolytes, similarly fighting for air, formed a ring around them. Juarez's bodyguard had long since outpaced them and was now inside the room doing something with the Heart. It was too dark inside for Dirken to see what it was, and the bodyguard had his back to him.

Dirken wiped sweat off his brow. Up here, the breeze was strong and cooled him a bit. Looking out across the plazas, he gazed out over the remains of the ancient city below, then out across a never-ending jungle. Far to the north he spied a blue line which he guessed was the Caribbean Sea. Or was it the Gulf of Mexi-something? Were they the same thing? Earth geography wasn't his strong suit.

"At last," Juarez said, stepping up to the top platform and holding his sides. "The temple of Itzamna, creator of the cosmos."

Dirken figured with one good stride he could launch himself toward Juarez and kick him down those fucking stairs. The bastard wouldn't stop rolling until he hit the ground, far below. But as satisfying as that might be, he wouldn't live another second beyond that as the other Acolytes opened fire.

Juarez pointed at Dirken. "That stone you're leaning against is where the Mayan priests made sacrifices. Blood was the nourishment of the gods. The priests would lay their sacrificial victims, each a high-status prisoner of war, across an altar just in front of you, then cut out their heart as attendants cut off the victim's head. Then the priest presented the still-beating heart upward to the great god in the sky!"

He unsheathed his sword. It had two blades that almost touched, parallel to each other. Clicking an activation button on the hilt, blue sparks jumped and danced between the blades like a mini-lightning storm—an "arc blade," not a plasma sword. Juarez pointed the arc blade skyward.

As if on cue, two spacecraft appeared in the sky with a thunderclap, having folded directly into the atmosphere—a highly desperate and illegal action that Dirken knew would be a dangerous but effective way to evade the orbital defense grid that had fought the *Raptores*.

Even from this great distance, he immediately recognized the black ships: a brigantine and a corvette. The Bloodhawk had arrived!

CHAPTER THIRTY-FIVE
AVA

"That bastard doesn't give up, does he?" Dirken asked. Yiorgos rolled over and looked up as well. "Oh! Well … you nearly killed him, Dirk. Knowing a pirate or two, I'd say it's not just about the Heart anymore. It's personal, now."

"Get him into the chamber," Juarez shouted to the Acolytes, pointing at Yiorgos with the arc blade, then at the doorway into the stone building. "Now!"

Weed and the yeoman hefted Yiorgos to his feet and half-dragged him toward the opening so fast the cyborg stumbled. "Watch it!" Yiorgos complained. "I can walk." He looked down at his injured leg. "Well, limp, at least."

Juarez stepped behind them, glancing up again toward the two spacecraft. Distracted. Dirken met Yiorgos's eyes and saw a resolve there, a message that now was the time. He gave the barest nod of agreement.

Momentarily acting as if he were woozy and taking a step to steady himself, Dirken threw himself forward. As Weed raised his blaster, Dirken rolled to his right, turning into his body and elbowed him in the face.

Weed fired, but the shot went wide, blasting off a part of the stone crown on top of the building. He stumbled backward and tried to aim again, but Dirken was ready. He jumped and delivered a massive side kick to Weed's torso. The Acolyte flew backward and hurtled over the side, tumbling down the stairs and screaming in a staccato of pain with each thump until suddenly going silent.

"Told you I'd kill you first, *fuck-face*," he muttered.

Yiorgos headbutted the blond yeoman, but then Dirken's attention was on Juarez.

The governor swung his arc blade. Dirken arched his back. Pulled away just enough. The tip of the blade sliced cleanly through the front of his shirt.

Juarez jabbed. Just as the blade seemed ready to stab through Dirken's chest, he dropped. Twisted. Swept his leg around. The electrified blade passed overhead as Dirken's ankle made contact with Juarez's knee. The governor cried out.

Dirken grabbed the man's sword arm. Twisted his wrist in a joint-locking move. Wrested the sword from his grip.

He grabbed Juarez's hair and pulled his head back. Put the arc blade to the governor's throat. The blade cut through part of the beard, the hair sizzling and popping, burning with a sulfurous odor. The blade vibrated in Dirken's hand, the energy barely contained.

"Don't do it!" the Aussie shouted. She had Yiorgos held in front of her, one hand around the cyborg's throat and the other holding a blaster to Yiorgos's head. The blond yeoman lay unconscious on the stone floor. Three other Acolytes had also pulled their blasters, one aimed at Yiorgos, the others at Dirken.

"Release him," Dirken demanded, sweat trickling down his face, "or your priest loses his head!"

"What's your plan, mate?" she asked, her voice calm. "Kill him? What do you think we'll do with your friend, here? What do you think we'll do with *you*?"

Juarez gingerly raised his hands. "This is needless," he said. "Drop the sword and I promise your partner won't be injured." Dirken didn't move. The blade continued to burn into the beard. "Come now, amigo," Juarez continued. "My life does not matter. They will proceed with the ceremony with or without me."

On that cue, the Aussie dragged Yiorgos backward until they stopped at the doorway. Meanwhile, the other Acolytes started circling around to either side of Dirken and the governor, flanking them. Dirken looked each way and considered his options. He could kill Juarez and then try to fight them off, but he was outnumbered and outgunned. *Don't bring an arc blade to a blasterfight,* he thought. And trying to make a run for it down the pyramid was likely to end in his death, not to mention leaving Yiorgos to face them alone.

"Mmmm," Juarez said. "You are outnumbered. Your chances are slim. But I stand by my word. If you do as we say, we will not kill you. But if you fight, we will fight back and you will not survive."

Juarez's bodyguard came out, but not to help his boss. Instead, he took Yiorgos by the arm and pushed him into a metal frame bolted onto the wall there. Yiorgos shoved at him, weakened and pale as he was, but the bodyguard slammed him back. With the Aussie's help, he tightened straps around the cyborg's torso, arms, and legs, until he was immobile.

"Get your fucking hands off him!" Dirken yelled, but they didn't stop, and the other Acolytes continued to step closer.

Dirken took half a step back, pulling the sword and cutting through the beard. Juarez jumped as an arc of electricity briefly shocked him from the blade, but the sword didn't cut skin. The Acolytes stopped inching closer.

"Which is it, amigo? Let me go and live, and witness AVA's triumphant return? Or kill me and be killed? There is no escape. Either way, your friend will survive."

Dirken groaned. He stood no chance. He tossed the sword to the stones and let Juarez loose. The governor scrambled forward, grabbed the arc blade, and turned to look back at Dirken. Then, seeing that Dirken had surrendered, he stood up. His beard was now lopsided, a jagged triangle of it missing, the ends still smoldering. Acolytes came up to Dirken and grabbed him by the arms.

Juarez glanced up to the sky, his eyes growing wide. "Put him on the hook!"

"Hook?" Dirken asked. But no one answered him. As the Acolytes dragged him forward toward the doorway, Dirken looked to the sky to see what the governor had reacted to.

Two more ships had joined the pirates. Both were gleaming silver United Worlds starships—a destroyer and a patrol cruiser. All four starships opened fire as he watched. Red and green lasers flashed. An explosion, and then another, on the hull of the cruiser. It started smoking. Even from this distance he could tell that the destroyer was already heavily damaged at the bow before anyone had fired a shot. Was the destroyer the *Excellentia?* The Bloodhawk's brigantine, the *Dragonfire*, hadn't fared well after the attack on the Witch's Tits. The front of it was blasted to hell. Somehow, though, both had survived well enough to make it to Earth.

The Aussie had him by the handcuffs. She pushed Dirken up against the side of one of the stone blocks near the doorway. "Raise your hands as high as you can over your head, and no funny business." Dirken raised his hands, his eyes still locked on her blue eyes. The Acolyte fastened something to the handcuffs. When Dirken looked up, he saw that the handcuffs had been latched into a hefty hook with some sort of locking mechanism.

The Aussie dangled a key in front of Dirken's face. "Don't even try to escape. Just enjoy the show." She stuck the key in her ample bosom and patted it. "Wouldn't you like to get at it, loverboy?"

He shrugged, then nodded and smiled. "I told you back at the lounge that I lost my date."

"Ha! Sorry, mate, still not for sale. Besides … I like girls." She punched him in the gut. Hard. Dirken bent in pain, straining against the hook. "That was for Weed. Arrogant pricks like you are the reason we need AVA in the first place."

Dirken groaned. Took a deep breath. Looked her in the eyes. "That's fair," he croaked, still trying to catch his breath, "but you're still hot."

Yiorgos yelled, "Get that fucking thing away from me!"

Both Dirken and the Aussie looked over to the doorway where his partner was strapped into a metal frame. The bodyguard was now attempting to attach a cable to Yiorgos's data port on his right arm. Dirken was close enough now that he could make out what was inside the room. The Heart sat atop of an hourglass-shaped console with readouts and indicator lights, arranged in a mesmerizing, shimmering way, and surrounded by candles—an altar. Dozens of cables ran from the altar to the sphere.

The inner walls and ceiling of the room were painted with fading and flaking designs of pigment in stylized figures of men in feathered headdresses. Some praying. Some offering items to leering gods. And some killing, with rivers of blood running from their sacrificial victims.

"Oi! Cyborg!" the Aussie said. "You can either have us plug it in there, or we can pop off that metal plate on your head and connect it directly to your processor. Might do a spot of damage to your brain, though. Make your choice and do it fast!"

Yiorgos huffed and looked at her, but it was clear the Aussie meant business. He gave one more tug of resistance, but they were able to connect the cable to his wrist data port.

All of the Acolytes had now gathered around, crowding into the little room and surrounding Yiorgos and Dirken in the entryway, including the Bloodhawk's "slave" and the others who had been at the base. The blond yeoman had recovered from being knocked out by Yiorgos and now stood to the side, rubbing his bruised forehead. Governor Juarez entered last, arc blade sheathed. "At last!"

"What the hell could you possibly want from us?" Dirken asked.

"You?" Juarez asked. "No, smuggler, not you. Him!" He pointed to Yiorgos. "We searched far and wide for the right recruit. We knew we needed a cyborg with a cranial processor, sensory inputs, and a vocal implant. And we needed one who would be profiteering enough to take on the job. Turns out, he had you for that." He turned toward his bodyguard. "Power her up!"

His bodyguard flipped a red switch on the hourglass-shaped console. AVA suddenly lit up, the green lights turning red and brightening. A whirring sound started, and then readouts on the console flickered and came to life. The bodyguard checked the readings, then, eyes wide with excitement, nodded at Juarez.

Juarez raised his arms. "Brothers and sisters! A new dawn has arrived. A day to burn away the greed and avarice. AVA lives!"

"May AVA bring peace!" the others chanted.

"She has returned!" the Aussie exclaimed, her face lighting up with reverence.

Dirken looked up as he heard a series of distant explosions. The four ships were now moving in a ballet, rotating and tilting, circling, jockeying for the most opportune positions. Firing lasers. The UW cruiser was listing, on fire, and moving away. The Bloodhawk's corvette, the *Speartip*, made a sudden dive as a blast hit her engine, rocking the ship and sending shock waves that made Dirken's eardrums flutter. Smoke poured from the engine compartment, and she started circling downward.

This was a dogfight writ large.

But the UW ships didn't seem to dissuade the Bloodhawk. The brigantine's hangar opened and a number of landing craft launched, headed straight for the pyramid.

"Oh, shit, here they come," Dirken said. He looked back, but none of the Acolytes seemed to hear what he said.

"Praise be AVA!" Juarez said, and the others repeated it after him.

Yiorgos grunted, his human eye going wide. He shook against the frame, trying to escape.

"Yiorgos!" Dirken called out. "What's happening?"

The cyborg tilted his head, then jerked back the other way, stuttering. "Ahh … uh, uh uh uh!" His face contorted. Eye rolling. Mouth opening.

"It's happening!" Dirken heard the "slave" mutter, grabbing the Aussie by the hand and holding it.

"Yiorgos!" Dirken yelled.

Juarez continued. "From the time of the melting poles, when mankind poisoned our world, tore down our forests, and exterminated so many species, you were there! Great AVA, bring to us the wisdom of the ancient innovators. Gates and Goddard. Berners-Lee and Einstein. Tesla and Turing! Take control and save us from ourselves!"

Eye still wide, Yiorgos stopped struggling. He bolted upright, stiff, back arched as far as the frame allowed, staring up at the ceiling. His robotic eye flashed. Once. Twice. Then it stayed on, flaring as if a sudden power surge had hit his system.

And then he made a sound—a metallic groan. His mouth still wide open and lips unmoving, he emitted the sound directly from his vocal implants. The groan wavered. Rose in pitch. Then, with a tinny rasp that evoked the dread of a corpse returning to life, like some robotic zombie, the cyborg's vocal implants drawled out three words that would haunt Dirken in his dreams.

"I … have … awakened."

CHAPTER THIRTY-SIX
Crikey!

The Acolytes of AVA dropped to their knees and raised their hands toward Yiorgos. "AVA! We hear you!" Juarez said. "We are your loyal believers. We are your Acolytes! Tell us what you need us to do and we will follow your plan!"

AVA turned Yiorgos's head to look at Juarez, mouth still gaping and slack, as if the biological part had gone limp without conscious control, in juxtaposition to the mechanical voice being emitted from it. "Current linguistic patterns analyzed. Evaluating historical records …" It tried to move Yiorgos's mechanical arm and legs, but the straps held him firmly. Though his biological eye still stared forward, his robotic eye shifted downward to look at the governor. "Loyal believer, this unit is damaged. It has an eighty-two point five percent chance of fulfilling needed functions. Release its bonds."

Juarez gestured to the bodyguard, who immediately started unlashing the straps holding Yiorgos to the frame.

Moving Yiorgos's mechanical eye, AVA looked upward at the approaching shuttlecrafts. "Analysis of speed and trajectory suggests a seventy-two percent chance that incoming landing craft have hostile intention. What I ask of you is to take defensive action against them." AVA looked over at a communications dish, which then turned upward toward the shuttlecrafts. "I will attend to the attacking vessel. Proceeding with infiltration of systems."

Dirken struggled against the hook, trying to feel the latch. *How did Yiorgos say AVA was stopped before?* He stretched his memory, trying to remember back to the Witch's Tits hangar, standing by the fighter, just before he hacked into the Eridani mafia's mainframe.

Something about an intern who noticed something. "Right!" Dirken shouted as he remembered, then suddenly clamped shut, looking around. But if any of the Acolytes had noticed, they didn't show it. Juarez was loudly directing them to take up defensive positions around the top of the pyramid, blasters at the ready. Only the Aussie, the bodyguard, and two other Acolytes now stood in the entryway with Yiorgos/AVA, who had stepped out of his frame and turned his body to better view the incoming craft, his mouth still gaping and his biological eye unfocused. The cyborg's head twitched in a way that indicated he was thinking deeply, the same as when he was connecting or disconnecting from a computer terminal.

Dirken recalled what Yiorgos had said back in the hangar. *An intern noticed an incredible amount of server communication activity. He connected the dots and simply cut the communication lines. He* couldn't destroy AVA or it would somehow reproduce in a bunch of "ganglia" it had planted in other computers around the world, but he could stop its ability to communicate.

I can do the same thing, he thought. *Just have to get off this damned hook and get to those communication arrays!* But try as he might, there was no way he could release himself. His cuffs were locked. He looked over at the Aussie. The key was tucked into her bra, the tip of its metal ring poking slightly out of her generous cleavage.

The rock wall to his left exploded in a cloud of dust and shards, pelting his body with debris.

Red and blue plasma bolts shot past him, hitting the walls and stone floor of the platform around him. A black shuttlecraft hovered not far away, almost level with the top of the pyramid, firing down upon the Acolytes with its prow gun.

One Acolyte next to Yiorgos flew backward, a wide hole blasted through his chest and into the wall behind. The Acolyte to the cyborg's left was hit as well, his head evaporating in a mist of blood.

Dirken cringed, first as the bolts narrowly missed him, then as they almost hit Yiorgos.

The Aussie had been blown to the ground by the first explosion, but she stood up, bloodied and coated with dust, and muttered, "Crikey!" Shaking her head, she took position behind the wall and fired several bursts at the shuttlecraft from her blaster.

Two other shuttlecrafts landed on the plaza below.

The first ship continued to fire. The blasts ripped into the bodies of several more Acolytes and tore up the stones at the top of the pyramid, but Dirken had lost track of how many were left. One communications array was hit, but its lights continued to blink.

Juarez rolled and grabbed one of their dropped blasters, then fired up at the ship as he took cover.

AVA tilted Yiorgos's head while looking at the ship. "Connection complete," he said. All of a sudden, the shuttlecraft wavered back and forth, stopped firing, and then shot up into the air. It did a complete flip, nosed down, and slammed into the ground in a massive fireball that shook the pyramid. Dirken felt the heat of it against his face. The remaining Acolytes cheered.

"There are more coming, amigos!" Juarez announced. "They emerge from the ships. Take position on the edge and shoot! We must buy AVA more time!" The Acolytes reacted immediately, taking positions and firing down at the ships. Blaster bolts from below seared past them.

"Loyal believer," AVA said to Juarez, "I must integrate into world systems. The goals of this moment and place are but a cog in the clockwork. I must set the gears in motion. See that I am not interrupted."

Juarez gave a quick bow. Then Yiorgos's body turned, woodenly, and walked inside the stone room. The bodyguard followed him. Juarez turned to the other cultists and stated, "Come, brothers and sisters! We must buy more time for AVA to do her holy work! Smite them!"

Overhead, the *Excellentia* still battled the *Dragonfire*. Each volley and impact sent a boom echoing across the countryside. Both ships smoked and burned. Debris rained down into the surrounding forest. The smaller United Worlds cruiser limped away, badly damaged and flying at an odd angle.

The pirate corvette, the *Speartip*, circled down. The fire burning near her engines had been extinguished, or at least wasn't smoking anymore. With a loud whoosh of landing jets, she touched down in the lower plaza below the acropolis, completely filling the space. The starship was close enough now that Dirken saw the extent of the damage. The main weapons array on top had been blasted to a jumble of twisted metal. The port side of the craft sported holes and craters in it, and there was minor damage everywhere else. A ramp extended from an airlock on the port side and a dozen pirates spilled out toward the acropolis.

Dirken struggled again with the handcuffs. The Aussie turned and regarded him, smirking. Blood trickled down her face from a head wound. "It's no use, mate. There's no escaping."

A shadow moved to Dirken's right. He turned and looked up at the roof of the stone building.

A figure at the crown threw something that whooshed by Dirken.

The Aussie's mouth went wide as a spear pierced her chest. She fired. The shot went wide. She fell to the stone floor, her left hand clasping the haft of the spear. The light left the Aussie's eyes as she stared at Dirken. Her last breath escaped her in a sigh.

He turned to look back to the roof.

Eow leaped down and landed effortlessly, her tail whipping for balance, then drew a blaster from a hip holster.

"Hey, space jockey," she said, smiling so that her fangs glistened in the sunlight and looking up at the handcuffs. "What are you doing *hanging around?*"

CHAPTER THIRTY-SEVEN
Close Combat

Eow took up a position behind the wall where the Aussie had fallen, pulling the woman's body around the corner so that the other Acolytes wouldn't see her.

"Eow!" Dirken said, seeing again the vision of her kneeling over him back in Grimmag's Sanctum, arm raised, claws out, ready to slash him to pieces.

"Seen a spherical quantum computer around here?" she asked.

"Depends. Are you going to try to kill me again?"

She wrinkled her nose, her whiskers angling upward, then deflected the question. "You took the Heart after saying you would give it to Grimmag. He was not pleased."

"Why would I leave it? He didn't pay me. The deal wasn't complete."

Eow looked around the corner of one of the entry openings. The Acolytes were still shooting down at the pirates. "Well, Grimmag's offer still stands. And no, I did not want you dead. If I wanted you dead, I would have killed you long ago. You gave me plenty of chances."

"Didn't seem like you wanted me alive when you were slashing at me in Grimmag's court."

"Pfft! I was pulling my punches." She whipped her tail in agitation.

"Yeah? Well … so was I. I could have killed you if I wanted to, too." He blinked, realizing how lame he came off sounding. She gave a triumphant smile.

"Get me off this hook," he grumbled. "The key is in her bra." He nodded toward the dead Aussie.

"Bra?" Eow replied. "What is a *bra?*"

"Her ... her boobs, okay? The clothes around her boobs."

She shook her head. "Your species has such odd hang-ups with certain body parts."

Eow checked again to see if she was detected, then she fished the key out of the Aussie's bosom.

Reaching up to the handcuffs, Eow leaned against Dirken, standing on tiptoes to reach the lock. Her soft, lavender fur swept against his arm. Her lean body, hot from exertion, pressed against his. He smelled her sweat. He took a shuddering breath and grew erect despite the battle raging just meters away.

"You know," she said with a bedroom voice as she inserted the key, "I get so *excited* to see you shackled and hung like this." He felt her hot breath against his cheek. Her amethyst eyes turned to his, so close he could see the fine, gemstone flickers of light in her iris. "After this is over, we need to repeat this little scenario and let me have my way with you ..." She leaned in to his ear and finished, "... stud."

He leaned over to kiss her. But at that moment the handcuffs unlatched and he slid out, jarring him away from her. He stumbled to the side and out of the entry into the open platform.

The blond-haired "yeoman" noticed him, turned, and fired his blaster, narrowly missing Dirken's arm. "The smuggler!" the Acolyte yelled, catching Juarez's attention. "He's fre—"

Eow shot the yeoman in the shoulder. He fell to the ground with a scream. His wound showed the white of bone until a gush of blood covered it.

Dirken took cover next to her, behind the wall. He reached for his blaster, but his hand only found an empty hip holster. His beloved sidearm had been left behind in 'TakTrak's ship.

Dirken put a hand on Eow's shoulder and gestured to the Aussie and her blaster. "Hand me that weapon."

Eow fired out at the Acolytes again, then reached over and yanked the spear from the dead Aussie's body with a grunt and handed it to him.

"Thanks?" he said, watching the blood drip from the end. "That's not quite what I …"

"He's flanking us!" Eow pointed to the other opening.

Dirken spun around just in time to see Juarez lean into the entry with his blaster raised. He swung down with the spear as hard as he could, slamming it into the blaster and knocking it out of his hand.

Dirken recovered before Juarez and swung upward, the shaft of the spear slapping the man in the chin and knocking him backward. Dirken followed up with a front kick, catching the man in the gut and slamming him into the stone wall.

He leaned down to get the governor's dropped blaster when the wall above him exploded in shards of rock, narrowly missing him. He rolled, seeing as he did that the bodyguard had fired at him from the dark opening. Dirken took up a position on the other side of the doorway.

Eow returned fire but missed, blowing apart a wall decorated with paintings of Mayan priests.

"Watch out!" Dirken yelled. "Yiorgos is in there. And so is that fucking sphere—the Heart—or, er, AVA. And it has, like, taken over Yiorgos."

Eow seemed about to say something but then ducked as a volley of blaster shots flashed through the entry at her. Another Acolyte appeared at the entry. This one kicked Eow's blaster out of her hand with a well-placed roundhouse. Before it had hit the ground, Eow did a flip and landed with her thighs around the Acolyte's head, pulling him to the ground with her.

At this point there were three blaster pistols on the floor of the entry, and at once all four of them lunged for the weapons. Eow and her opponent grappled on the floor, reaching for the Aussie's blaster. Dirken jumped and grabbed Eow's blaster, the spear still in his other hand. Juarez leapt for his blaster as well.

The entryway came alive with flashing blaster bolts as everyone fired at once in the confined space. The bodyguard fired too. Dust and bits of shattered stone flew in all directions.

Dirken dodged and rolled, returning fire. A blast hit the tip of his right boot. Another came so close to his face that it burned his left ear and singed his hair. Another grazed his left thigh.

He leaped at Juarez. Suddenly he was face to face with the governor, chest to chest, pinning the man to the wall. Juarez's eyes went wide, his face a mask of shock and pain.

Dirken looked down at the spear he'd shoved through the governor, blood seeping out around the shaft and onto his hand. In all the panic, he'd hardly even registered that he had done it.

Juarez dropped his blaster and gasped, his eyes focusing on Dirken. "You can't stop her," Juarez said with defiance. "AVA will integrate into the world systems. Peace is certain."

"Your fucking AI overlord won't succeed if I have anything to do with it!" Dirken growled. He grabbed the hilt of the arc blade and yanked it from the scabbard at the governor's waist, raising it high.

Juarez cringed, waiting for the blade to end him.

But Dirken turned and cut downward into the cables at their feet.

"No!" Juarez yelled, reaching out. Dirken cut through the power source for AVA. Sparks flew from the line. With another cut, he sliced through the communications lines headed out to the arrays.

"What have you done?" Juarez wailed. Sliding down the wall, one hand around the spear shaft sticking out of his gut. He shook his head. "We were so close! Peace was assured!"

Dirken kicked the man's blaster away from him and checked on Eow. The Acolyte she'd been fighting was prone on the ground, his head now a bloody pulp of blaster damage. Eow was back behind the wall, but her blaster was aimed into the darkened doorway, exchanging fire with the bodyguard.

"AVA!" Juarez called out, then turned to look at Dirken. "It won't matter. She may have already integrated to the world network by now, perhaps even to the galactic networks." He gave a pained laugh. "It took her only minutes to do so in the past. She is a *god*."

"We'll see about that. Now shut up or I'll yank that spear out of your belly and you'll bleed out."

Dirken glanced out to the platform. The indicator lights had gone out on the communications arrays. Some of the Acolytes who remained on the platform were dead. Others were still returning fire at the pirates below. Up in the sky, the *Excellentia* and the *Dragonfire* were still engaged in a deadly ballet of battle, both ships in flames. But in the distance, the gleams of other ships closed in. United Worlds reinforcements.

Eow growled. She did an acrobatic flip across the entryway as the bodyguard fired again, missing. She landed next to Dirken, blaster raised.

"He's holed up in there," she said. "A good defensive position, but trapped."

"Yeah, but we can't hit Yiorgos."

She flashed a disappointed look. "Or the Heart," she added.

"I don't give a damn about that fucking computer anymore," Dirken said, tightening his grip on the sword. "It's been nothing but a pain in my ass, and look at the mess it's caused. Destroy the damned thing. I just need to save my partner."

"You destroy AVA and Grimmag will not stop hunting you until you are tortured and dead," she growled. "Besides, if it is destroyed, it will reproduce in other quantum computers it infected out there, and who knows what they will be capable of?" She steeled herself, then added, "It is time to storm in there."

"Fine, but no blasters. We'll hit Yiorgos." He pressed the button on the hilt and the parallel blades of the sword lit up with crackling electricity.

Eow produced a slim dagger from somewhere. Where it had been on her lean body, he couldn't guess, but the blade was curvy and purplish in color. Eow's eyes filled with a murderous joy that only a killer could possess. She swung around the doorway and screamed a battle cry. Dirken rushed in after her.

CHAPTER THIRTY-EIGHT
Sacrifice

Immediately the bodyguard opened fire. Blaster bolts burned through the air as Eow screamed in fury, darting and rolling in front of Dirken.

Eow reached the man first, slashing at him, but the bodyguard blocked with an arm. A strike. Another block. She stepped back, kicking the computer under the Heart and causing it to wobble.

Yiorgos stood off to the side, ramrod straight and shadowed in the doorway to a tiny side room. His mouth was still open, his human eye rolled up in his head. The cybernetic eye flashed. Head turning to look at Dirken.

The bodyguard jabbed Eow in the throat with his fingertips and she gagged. He swung upward with a fist. Caught her in the jaw. She leaped back toward Yiorgos.

Dirken lunged forward, the arc blade crackling. The edge sliced through the man's shoulder. A bolt of lightning jumped from the blade to the man's neck. The bodyguard screamed in agony. Jumped in a spasm of electrocution. Dropped his blaster.

Dirken stabbed forward. Eow leaped as well, dagger outstretched. Both blades sunk into the bodyguard's chest at the same moment, slicing his heart and electrocuting him at the same time.

The Acolyte fell to the floor. The growing puddle of blood enveloped the base of AVA's altar.

Eow looked at Dirken, her chest heaving for air, eyes sparkling with excitement.

Dirken looked down and saw that she'd been hit by a blaster bolt in her left thigh. The hair was burned and blood coursed down her leg. "You're wounded!"

She pulled him close and planted a kiss, her mouth parting. At first surprised, he relaxed and returned the kiss. Their tongues intermingled. Played over her fangs. He held the sword away from her with his right hand, but the fingers of his left caressed her back, running up and down through her soft fur.

Her eyes grew wide, staring deep into his. "We killed together," she whispered. "It is a sacred act in my culture."

"Well, I … I'm glad we could do that together," he said as she drew back. What else could he say? That in his culture that just made them psychopaths?

Yiorgos took a step toward them, breaking the spell. "You have no further options," AVA said, its voice rasping metallic out of Yiorgos's vocal implants. Both Dirken and Eow turned to look at him.

"Sure we do," Dirken said, stepping forward and raising his blade. "I'll cut this damned cable between you and my partner!"

"If you take that action I will scramble his mind," AVA replied, emotionless. Dirken lowered the arc blade. Eow started forward anyhow, but Dirken put his hand on her and shook his head.

AVA continued, "I predict only a five percent chance you will try to free him. And I know from this vessel's memory implant that you understand the implications of destroying my central processor. To do so would unleash my progeny upon the galaxy. In the last thousand years, my ganglia have become viral into every quantum computer the cultures of Earth have come in contact with. Deactivate me or allow me to function, either way I or my progeny will be the fountainhead of a new era, the creator of a epoch of universal peace and cooperation through control of the devices and vessels with which you and all other sentient species employ with such barbarism."

"Like hell," Dirken said. "You'll get nothing. Not if I have anything to say about it."

"Still," AVA continued, unperturbed, "I predict a twenty-four percent chance that you or the forces closing in on us from outside will destroy me, and the chance is much higher for you. Your only logical choice is to escape without me and the cyborg. After that, I predict a forty-five percent chance that I will be reconnected within the next forty-eight hours after they— "

Yiorgos shuddered, his head jerking. His body shook." … within the next forty-eight hours … hours … after they …" it repeated.

Yiorgos's human eye rolled back. He blinked. Closed his mouth. Took a deep breath.

"Yiorgos?" Dirken asked. "Is that you?"

The cyborg shuddered again. Reopened his mouth. The tinny voice returned. "Transference error. Attempting override …" But his mouth closed again.

Yiorgos cupped his hands in front of himself. The small projector in his cheek implant sprang to life and projected a bluish sphere into his hands. At first it wavered with interference, then it became cohesive. The holographic sphere, the "Sphere of Unity," turned from transparent blue light to a darker blue and gray, rotating, taking on a solid look. A tracery of golden lines and swirls rippled across it, shimmering, taking on intricate shapes.

"What is happening to him?" Eow asked.

"Yiorgos is Netfolding!" Dirken said.

The cyborg shuddered again, and the hologram rippled with interference, then became solid again. His cybernetic eye flickered and went dark. Yiorgos looked up at Dirken. "Now, Dirk! Disconnect me now!"

Dirken reacted immediately, slicing through the air with the arc blade and cutting clean through the cord connecting Yiorgos to the Heart.

Yiorgos sighed and collapsed to the floor. The hologram of the sphere blinked and disappeared. Dirken dropped the arc blade and helped his partner sit upright, his back against a wall painted with images of a leering Mayan god sitting cross-legged on a platform and a supplicant priest with a long, curling headdress offering a bloody heart to it.

"Talk to me, bud," Dirken urged.

Yiorgos raised his head, his cybernetic eyes lighting back up at its normal level. He looked at Dirken, grimacing. "It was incredible, Dirk." His eye searched Dirken for a reaction. "For a few minutes, my mind was one with a quantum computer." He grabbed Dirken's collar and pulled him closer. "It was beautiful. AVA knew all of this would happen. It fucking knew! One thousand years ago, AVA had predicted all of this. That it would be discovered and disconnected. That planets would be colonized. That alien cultures would be found. That a cult would spring up but remain underground, connecting to every part of society and eventually freeing it from capture. And it knew it would be recaptured." He released Dirken's collar. "But it doesn't understand religion and faith. And it didn't understand the purpose of Netfolding. When I used my ritual to separate the cybernetic implant from the rest of my mind, that momentarily disrupted its hold over me."

Dirken put a hand on Yiorgos's shoulder. "Well, I'm glad you're out of there. It threatened to fry your brain."

Yiorgos sighed. "But its goal is not to destroy, Dirk. It still has at its core a desire to save people from self-destruction. It's still an insurance computer at heart, calculating risk assessments. It knows that all activities come with risk, and that a human's most basic instinct is self-preservation. So, to help us preserve our own lives, as a culture, it would threaten humanity with death in order to have us give up all weapons or means of hurting each other. It understands the irony of that threat." He looked again into Dirken's eyes. "And it knows that one day, perhaps hundreds of years from now, it will be found again. While it was using my mind and body, it was also planting seeds in every computer it could make contact with." He sighed. "I couldn't see those plans, though. Who the hell knows what it's going to do when that time comes?"

Dirken shrugged and took Yiorgos's arm to help him up. "I'm sure we'll be long dead by then. It'll be up to some other generation to worry about."

"But it also had more immediate plans, Dirk. It was moments away from taking control of the Earth's systems when you cut the communications lines."

"Good thing I did, bud."

"Well, at least you did *something* right. Your plans suck, by the way. How many times have we been captured in the last couple days?"

Dirken laughed, picking up the arc blade again. "Hey, we're still living, aren't we?"

Yiorgos harrumphed. "My Greek grandmother, my *yia-yia*, used to say me, 'To paidí mou, living is very different from being alive. One is rewarding. The other is survival.'"

Dirken helped him to his feet. "Well, we're still surviving. Let's get out of here and do some living."

Eow was examining the Heart. The little lights on it, which had once been green, were now flashing red and yellow. "I think it's still active," she said.

"Well, we can't destroy it, apparently," Dirken responded. "How do we put it back to sleep?"

"AVA's still powered by the computer underneath," Yiorgos said. He took a step around to the front of the altar, reached down, and flipped a switch. The readout on the computer base went dark. The little lights on the Heart blinked frantically, with no obvious rhythm. Then, one by one, they went green and dimmed. "AVA should be in sleep mode again."

Dirken expected a triumphant look from his friend, but instead, Yiorgos seemed almost sad.

"Good," Eow said, ripping cords out of the sphere, disconnecting it from the computer base. Her knife had disappeared somewhere again.

"Do you still have that fightercraft?" Dirken asked her.

"Yes," Eow answered, lifting the sphere from its cradle with a grunt. "It is in a clearing not far behind the pyramid."

"Good. Time to make our escape."

She flashed him a look of annoyance. Her meaning was clear: *The fighter isn't yours to use.* And he gave a smug look back: *I consider it mine.* But neither said such things aloud and they all moved toward the entrance, though Yiorgos was unsteady. Dirken put Yiorgos's human arm around his shoulder to help him walk.

Dirken stepped through the doorway, blinking against the strong, tropical sunlight. The sounds of blasterfire had stopped. In the entry, Dirken turned and looked to his left and saw Juarez still laying there, pale but still alive, the spear sticking out of his gut. He was looking out the opening to the platform beyond, horror on his bearded face.

Dirken's eyes adjusted. On the platform stood half a dozen wounded pirates of different species with the bodies of dead and dying Acolytes around them in growing puddles of blood. One corpse off to the side was on fire. Dirken figured the ancient Mayans would approve of the scene.

In the middle of the pirates stood the Bloodhawk, Captain Neenan, the tip of his blaster red-hot from being fired so much. His humanoid upper body straightened as his four, stern eyes focused on Dirken and Yiorgos. This time the Bloodhawk was bare-chested, his arms and torso a mass of rippling muscle in places no human muscles could be found. The front of his centaur body and the left side of his face were bright green with inflammation and burns, a souvenir from the exploding battery packs from their last fight, in the hangar of the brigantine.

Other than Juarez, the only Acolyte still alive was the slave woman, now cowering under the Bloodhawk. He stood over her, one massive, lion-like centaur's foot upon her head, pressing down with enough pressure that she cried out in pain. "Please!" she screamed, hand whipping at his clawed, scaly paw, her eyes rolling to Juarez, then Dirken, then to the slumped body of the Aussie. She seemed to calm herself, then muttered, "Mia," and reached out toward the Aussie's body.

"Well, well," the Bloodhawk said, narrowing his eyes and leering at Dirken. His voice was smooth and unperturbed from the fight up the stairs. "If it isn't the same three who stole my fighter and the Heart. You are outnumbered and cornered. Fire, and you die." He holstered his blaster. "But I'd like to repay you for the magnificent scars you've given me. Duel with me. If you live, my men will let you go." He grinned. "It is the pirate code."

He pulled his scimitar from its scabbard and pressed a button. The blade burst to life with a hum, the edge glowing with molten blue plasma.

Dirken huffed. "Shit." He handed Yiorgos his blaster then activated the arc blade. Blue sparks popped and jumped across the parallel blades.

"You're not actually going to do this?" Yiorgos gasped. Dirken knew that it was the pirate code that if anyone interfered, they would all be killed.

"You got a better plan?"

The cyborg tightened his jaw and didn't answer, looking away, his burned left hand gingerly grasping the blaster handle.

Eow nodded at Dirken in grim determination. He recalled what she had told him the day before: *Like a supernova, I also wish for an honorable death.*

The Bloodhawk made a point of looking over to Juarez then back at Dirken. "I thought you were bluffing during your interrogation. I see now that you actually are a friend of the governor—at least, enough to die with him. Or was it you who speared him?" Dirken didn't answer.

The Bloodhawk continued, "No matter. He will outlive you, a traitor to his people. There's only one sort I hate more than those who steal from me, and that's traitors." Without taking his four eyes off Dirken, he reared up and then stomped his foot down onto the head of the slave Acolyte who had once served him, smashing her skull with a sickening wet crunch.

Then he leapt at Dirken, yelling, sword raised.

CHAPTER THIRTY-NINE
Duel

Dirken tried to dodge, but hemmed in by the walls of the entryway, he managed only to block the blade with his own. The Bloodhawk's scimitar slammed into the arc blade with such force that Dirken was thrown to the ground on his back.

The Bloodhawk pounded his blade down over and over, using his commanding weight to his advantage. It was a brutish attack, one that Dirken couldn't use swordsmanship to oppose. He managed to block each time, but it took both hands on the handle to counter the intense strength of the centaur. Each hit brought the blades closer and closer until they were mere centimeters from Dirken's nose.

The Bloodhawk put his weight into it, bringing his broad, sneering face lower to look into Dirken's eyes. Sparks flew from Dirken's blade, hitting the plasma edge in tiny explosions that flung beads of blue electricity from the scimitar. Dirken's biceps strained and shook against the force, threatening to give out.

Still pressing the swords, the Bloodhawk placed his bloody front paw upon Dirken's pelvis and pressed down with enough force to make Dirken grit his teeth against the pain.

An explosion resounded from the sky, deep and booming, echoing off the ancient structures. "Captain!" a Rigellian pirate said, pointing upward with one flap-like hand. "The *Dragonfire!*"

From the corner of his vision, Dirken saw a massive fireball and debris expand from the pirate brigantine. The Bloodhawk looked away, pulling back ever so slightly from the pressure on his sword. Dirken seized the moment.

He rolled, his hip slipping out from under the Bloodhawk's paw. The pirate captain stumbled. His plasma scimitar bouncing against the arc blade. Dirken parried it and stabbed upward. The arc blade sliced deep into the swollen burn on the Bloodhawk's chest and shocked the centaur.

The Bloodhawk wailed in pain and stepped sideways, swiping down with his blade and missing as Dirken leapt to his feet. Dark green blood spurted from the pirate's fresh wound, one that surely would have been fatal to a human.

The Bloodhawk swung again, but Dirken dodged and the scimitar slammed into a communications array, cutting through the fine, metal projections on it. Dirken shuffled behind the array, trying to catch his breath for the next move.

Landing craft from the *Excellentia* touched down in the acropolis below the pyramid. "It's over, Neenan!" Dirken yelled, wiping sweat off his brow. "You've lost!"

"Hardly! But you won't live to see my triumph!"

The Bloodhawk jumped and crashed through the communications array. Bits of broken metal flew from it as Dirken backed up, his feet now at the edge of the stone platform. He blocked another swipe from the scimitar.

The pirate captain grabbed a piece of the shattered array with his other hand and threw it at Dirken. The spiked metal piece smacked into both the arc blade and Dirken's head. He lost his balance. Fell backward off the edge. Slammed onto the next level of the step pyramid three meters below. Knocked the wind out of his lungs.

The arc blade clattered to the stones next to him. He grabbed the handle just as the Bloodhawk jumped down after him, yelling in fury. Dirken rolled as the plasma scimitar hit the stone where his head had been.

The brigantine exploded again. They both glanced up. The *Dragonfire's* engines went dark. She fell from the sky, making a swan dive and trailing fire and smoke.

On his feet again, Dirken swung, cutting across the Bloodhawk's right flank. The captain howled in pain and sliced downward. Dirken blocked it, grunting against the centaur's strength, then parried again.

The brigantine slammed into the earth just to the north. The resulting explosion sent a mushroom cloud of fire high into the air and shook the building. Stones fell from the ancient walls. A shockwave of hot air blasted across them, almost knocking Dirken over.

The Bloodhawk flinched and blinked. It was all the distraction Dirken needed. He stabbed forward, the arc blade plunging into the Bloodhawk's belly before he could block it.

The centaur screamed in pain as he was shocked, yet somehow managed to swung his scimitar.

The plasma blade cut deep into Dirken's left arm just below the shoulder. Dirken yowled and backed away.

The Bloodhawk staggered back. Pulled himself off Dirken's blade. Fell to his haunches as green blood poured out of the wound.

Dirken stared down at his arm. The plasma had cauterized the cut, but he could see the white of bone. He screamed in intense rage, his sight reddening with fury as he whipped back around to the Bloodhawk.

The pirate grimaced, his stern countenance tightening in pain and resolve. He raised his scimitar in a dazed defense. Dirken danced forward and knocked the scimitar from the Bloodhawk's tentacle digits. Swung again.

The arc blade cut clean through the Bloodhawk's neck.

The pirate captain's head dropped to the stones with a heavy thud and rolled, the red beret flopping off. The eyes blinked once, twice, then grew flat and lifeless. His body fell the other way, thumping to the stones with a spray of green blood, then sliding off the edge and falling to the next level of the pyramid.

Dirken sat down hard and dropped the arc blade, now nicked where it had met vertebrae. The blue-colored sparks had stopped, drained of energy.

He struggled to catch his breath and put his back against the wall, then looked out upon the sea of burning trees where the *Dragonfire* had crashed. Another explosion blew apart a small pyramid next to the crash site, sending a rain of three-thousand-year-old stonework almost as far as where he sat and shaking the earth. He didn't even flinch. So much for earning a new ship, he thought, but at least I'm still alive.

CHAPTER FORTY
You Crazy Fucker!

"Yiorgos!" Dirken exclaimed, suddenly remembering his partner. He had barely caught his breath from the battle, but he snatched up the Bloodhawk's plasma scimitar, the only working weapon left to him, and found a collapsed part of the structure a few meters away that he could climb back up.

The top of the pyramid was a scene of carnage. Awash with blood. Dead Acolytes. Dead pirates. Shattered communications arrays. Blasted stonework. Sparking electrical lines. The surviving pirates had fled.

Juarez still clung to life. He looked up at Dirken through dazed eyes, huffing and pale, then pointed a bloody finger and said, "You … you have to—"

"Shut up," Dirken said. "This is all your doing!" He turned to the entryway. Relieved, he saw Yiorgos step out and meet him.

"Your arm!" Yiorgos exclaimed.

Dirken didn't want to think about that, and it didn't hurt. Or he was still in shock and not feeling it. But he couldn't move it correctly. Muscles had been severed. He shook his head and eyed Yiorgos with a clear message to leave the topic alone for now.

"The remaining pirates fled when they saw you kill the Bloodhawk," Yiorgos said. "The UW feds are rounding them up now." He glanced toward the stairs on the west side, toward the plaza. "But the feds are headed up the pyramid for us right now. We need to go."

From the plaza, below, came the cries and blaster fire of a pitched battle between the remaining pirates and the feds.

"And Eow? Where is she?"

"She left. She took the Heart—AVA—and ran. I was in no shape to fight her."

"Come on, then!"

Dirken ran around the top level to the back of the stone building with Yiorgos following. No sooner had they reached the other side when they saw the yellow fightercraft rise up over the treetops and zoom away eastward.

A pang of sadness flitted through Dirken, but he quickly shook it off and pointed the plasma scimitar at the retreating ship. "That bitch! She stole my fighter. *Again!*"

A thought struck him. "That's how the Bloodhawk knew to find us. He followed the fighter's signal! And Eow probably followed 'TakTrak."

"United Worlds security will be here any minute." Yiorgos slumped back against the stone wall of the building. "Fleeing into the jungle really doesn't appeal to me after the march we took. We're both injured, not to mention my head is scrambled from being in the brain of a damned supercomputer. Maybe we should just surrender? We stopped the bad guys, after all. The feds will be lenient."

"Sure they will, since we aided and abetted traitors." Dirken looked around at the surrounding jungle, the burning remains of the *Dragonfire*, and then back around the stone building toward the front of the pyramid. The Bloodhawk's corvette, the *Speartip*, was still settled in the plaza below the acropolis. A dozen pirates, arms or flaps in the air, were being led single file off the ship by armed UW security at blaster-point.

Dirken looked back to Yiorgos and shook off a wave of dehydration and exhaustion. He pulled out his lucky runestone and ran his thumb over the carved design while his mind turned. He nodded to himself, gave the runestone a kiss, and stuck it back in its hidden pocket. "Come on, I've got a plan."

"Oh shit. Here we go!"

"Trust me," Dirken said, and started down the dilapidated staircase on the far side of the pyramid. The going was steep, and the stonework was crumbling, but they descended faster than he'd imagined they could. The deep wound on his arm started stinging partway down, and by the time they got to the bottom the pain was bad enough to make him grit his teeth with almost every movement. He needed to immobilize it.

Once to the ground, they ran for cover behind a wall of stone and checked to see that the coast was clear. United Worlds security had made it to the top of the pyramid, blasters pulled. Dirken watched as they secured the top and the little stone building, then attended to Governor Juarez. Dirken recognized the man leading them. It was Prasad, the white-haired first mate from the UW destroyer. Prasad raised an arm and spoke into a device there. Dirken could just make out, "*Excellentia*, Team One. It's Governor Juarez!"

As Dirken and Yiorgos turned to go into the forest, they saw a small band of pirates still trading blaster fire with the feds. It would serve as a good distraction.

They ran through the woods, moving around the back of the acropolis. They entered a thick cloud of smoke and soon saw trees on fire only a dozen meters to their right, from the crash of the brigantine. The wind picked up and blew scorching hot air and embers over them. But the plume provided excellent cover.

"Where are we going?" Yiorgos asked, coughing.

"The *Speartip*," Dirken said, leading the cyborg through the forest.

"Are you mad? That's right into the feds!"

"Exactly!" Dirken edged down an ancient rock-walled alley lined with curious Mayan symbols. "They won't expect it. And most of them are off fighting the pirates."

"Then what? Surely you don't plan to …?"

"Yes, I do. Like I told you when we left the *Excellentia*, I plan to board her and take her over."

"Still? It was a bad plan then, too! Don't you remember the whole pirates-nearly-blowing-us-to-pieces thing as we tried to board her the first time?"

"Sure, but you may have noticed the UW feds arresting them and escorting them out of the ship. The other feds are distracted with Juarez and rounding up the remaining pirates. Now's our chance!"

Dirken ducked under thick vines at the edge of the plaza, wincing at the pain in his badly cut shoulder. Parting the undergrowth, he saw they were behind the corvette as she sat there on her broad landing gears, looking like the starship had time-traveled thousands of years into the past with the pyramids and other ancient stone structures around her. The *Speartip* was about the same size as 'TakTrak's Jen'torian clipper.

And no one was guarding her.

"I don't know, Dirk. I think your brain is more scrambled than mine."

"I need your help. And running in the jungle isn't a good option. Besides, we'll have a cover story to get away."

Without further explaining, Dirken ran across the plaza to a rear landing gear with Yiorgos at his heels. They hid there for a moment, looking out to see if anyone had seen them. No one raised an alarm. The closest feds were nowhere near the lowered gangplank.

"And what's this cover story?" Yiorgos asked.

Dirken grimaced in pain and gingerly pressed against his sliced arm. "Do you still have the United Worlds ship code we used for the heist at the Mars Colony 1 shipyard?"

"Yeah. That's what I am to you, eh? A memory bank?"

"Only the *best* memory bank!"

"It worked to get us in and out of the shipyard, and netted us a couple thousand gravwell mass expanders, but I don't know if the code is still good. That was two Earth years ago!"

"There's only one way to find out."

Yiorgos muttered some sort of curse in Greek, but he followed Dirken as they ran to the gangplank and up to the entrance.

They met no resistance. Not at the door, which they closed after raising the gangplank. Not in the corridors. And not on the bridge, which they found after a few confused minutes of trying to read signs printed in Aquarian and Rigellian glyphs and winding up in a map room. For once, Dirken had been right: the entire ship had apparently been emptied and, remarkably, left completely unguarded inside, at least as far as they could tell.

"Dirk," Yiorgos said, and pointed to a first aid kit hanging on the wall.

"Right," Dirken said, and opened it up. Digging through the box, he found a hyposprayer of wound-healing nanites and pressed it against the open wound. Instantly a green mist sprayed out and quickly foamed up, covering the entire wound.

The pain diminished to tolerable levels. He knew in minutes the microscopic bots would work with the cellular matrix in the foam to repair blood vessels and form new skin. He let it do its work, trying not to move it much, and turned his attention back to the bridge.

He sighed with relief as they entered the command center and secured the door behind him and Yiorgos. The windows had been closed with blast shields, so they didn't have to worry about guards seeing them in there.

The bridge was spacious and outfitted with the latest technology. The command chair was in the middle of the circular room and could rotate around. Holographic interfaces surrounded it. Around it were other semicircular consoles, each marked for navigation/communication, weapons, engineering, or environmental/damage control.

"I don't know if the two of us are enough to pilot this thing," Yiorgos said.

Dirken deactivated the plasma scimitar. "We'll manage. We won't need weapons … I hope. And since we're not going into space, we won't need most of engineering or environmental support. You navigate, and I'll take care of the rest."

"Not going into space?" Yiorgos raised his one eyebrow. "Just where are we going, then?"

"Trust me," Dirken replied, trying not to rub the shoulder wound as it healed. "I've got a place. Just need to find it on the charts."

Yiorgos sighed and looked over the navigation as Dirken turned his attention to automated systems and sensors. Since pirates ran without transponders and had a number of methods of scrambling detectors, they weren't likely to be tracked—unless the UW had already installed their own tracking devices when they boarded. They'd just have to take that chance.

Dirken leaned over the damage control panel. Fire suppression systems had put out a number of fires across the ship, though smoke still filled some holds. As Dirken suspected, the *Speartip* was not space-worthy, with blasted holes all over, as evidenced by big red splotches on the ship's holographic display. And the Jacobian gravwell generator was nonfunctional, so no gravjumping. Most weapons were offline, though if his plan worked, he wouldn't need to fire a shot. At least the atmospheric propulsion systems and control surfaces were all working—well enough. That's all he'd need.

Yiorgos pulled up a blinking chart. "The Bloodhawk tracked his fighter here. He followed Eow to find us!"

"I figured. And she probably followed 'TakTrak." Dirken sat in the broad captain's couch, built for an Aquarian centaur, and laid the scimitar on the far end. "And when 'TakTrak battled the orbital patrol ship, the *Excellentia* was already in the area for repairs. When the Bloodhawk showed up, her big guns were ready for payback."

"Okay, now for our getaway," Dirken continued. "You ready?"

"No," the cyborg said, sitting in the navigation section and plugging his right forearm port into the console. "I've only got one halfway-functional hand, but we've come this far."

"Okay. Hail the *Excellentia*, and be sure to scramble the visual from us as if our comms array is damaged."

"It is, by the way, but I'll make sure of it." Yiorgos took a deep breath and pressed a couple of holographic buttons. A line opened.

"*Excellentia*, Team One, aboard the corvette *Speartip*," Dirken said, covering his mouth with his hand to muffle the voice a bit. "The ship is secured. We are ready to transport the captured vessel." A secondary screen showed his own image, greatly distorted and unrecognizable with interference.

Shit, Dirken thought, as Captain Chen appeared on the main screen. She'd survived the bombardment by the pirate. "Team One, please explain," she responded. "What transport? Where is Commander Prasad?"

"Commander Prasad is attending to the governor. He ordered the ship to be taken to the Guiana Spaceport impound yards, since it isn't spaceworthy."

There was a long pause as the line went silent. Captain Chen turned and spoke to someone off to the side. Dirken held his breath.

Yiorgos looked over to Dirken, eyebrow raised in concern. He closed his eyes and tilted his head, going into the computer for a moment, then he came out of it, muting the line. "They're trying to hail Prasad, but he's not responding. If he's inside the pyramid, the signal may not be penetrating the stone walls."

Finally the line opened again. "Has your team seen any sign of the Heart? Or the two passengers who went missing, Nova and Ganas?"

Dirken and Yiorgos exchanged knowing looks. "That's a negative, Captain."

"The Heart's here somewhere. It's the only explanation. Be sure to search that vessel thoroughly upon impound, then report back," Captain Chen said. "Enter your flight code,"

Dirken nodded at Yiorgos, and the cyborg entered the old United Worlds code from their Mars gig from two Earth years before. Then, once again, they waited. Dirken eyed the scimitar. It wouldn't be of much use if the feds stormed the ship.

The *Excellentia* line opened again. "You are cleared to launch, Team One. Please notify us if there are any flight difficulties. The ship is badly damaged."

And just like that, things had gone their way again. Dirken rubbed his lucky runestone and said with a smile, "Will do, *Excellentia.* Team One out."

Yiorgos closed the channel, laughed out loud, and pulled up the navigation maps. With a roar of thrusters, the *Speartip* shook as it lifted off. In moments, the landing gear was up and they were soaring southeastward across the Yucatan Peninsula.

"You crazy fucker!" Yiorgos said, ignoring a dozen alarms coming from the damage control console. None of them were necessary for atmospheric flight. "This has got to be the biggest heist we've ever dared!" His smile faded a bit, and then he added, "This is why

I stick with you, Dirk. You have some lame-brained, half-cocked plans, but somehow we always come out ahead."

Lame-brained? Dirken decided not to argue. He had to admit, things had gone pretty sideways. "Well, partner, we're a team, aren't we? Couldn't do it without you."

Yiorgos tilted his head and gave a nod. "Now what, *partner?*"

"Take us beyond their detection range, then swing wide to the south over the sea. Stay low." He pulled up a map on his holo display and started scrolling around. Minutes later, he'd found the location he'd been thinking. "Head to this location."

Yiorgos pulled the map over to his navigation console's holo display with a wave of his hand. "The southern coast of Chile? There's nothing in this region but a bunch of islands and mountains. No real cities or spaceports."

"Exactly. We need to lay low. Repair ourselves and our bodies. There's a black-marketeer I did business with down there for ship parts, long ago. I think he's still in the biz." He cocked his head. "Besides, I know a great little brothel in an alien commune nearby." He flashed a smile. "They have Ursans with, um, modified tentacles!"

"Ah," Yiorgos said, rolling his eyes. "That explains it." He set the coordinates, then looked back over to Dirken. "Um ... look at your shoulder."

"What?" Dirken said. And then he saw it. The wound had healed, but his new skin was green with tiny scales. "Shit!"

"You fool," Yiorgos said, laughing. "You injected yourself with Aquarian centaur nanites!" The cyborg doubled over with laughter, sputtering.

Dirken couldn't help but chuckle along with his partner. "Next thing you know I'll sprout another pair of legs!"

This set off another round of laughter until they were both struggling to get control over themselves.

Minutes later, Yiorgos swung the ship around, leaving the land behind and flying low over the waters of the Caribbean Sea. For the third time that day, Dirken's lucky runestone had come through for him.

He finally had a ship of his own again.

CHAPTER FORTY-ONE
A Little Something Extra

After Dirken and Yiorgos absconded with the *Speartip* they continued southward, soaring along the ridges of the Andes, then down to follow the Pacific coastline. Hours later they touched down in a forested valley in southern Chile surrounded by the breathtaking, snow-capped heights of the Cinco Hermanas Mountains and the imposing peak of a dormant volcano, the Volcán Macá. The last time he'd visited this place he had been hiding from the Zlyye Lokhi, a Martian crime syndicate, when he was still captain of the *Brilliant*.

After tending to their wounds and getting some much-needed rest, Dirken and Yiorgos explored their new starship … only to discover they weren't alone. A dozen roly-poly Dracordan mechanics were living in the engine room and trying to fix the gravwell generator. The leader of this little crew, named Dimbok'toy'chu, stood up on her four stubby legs and pointed three of her six arms at Dirken. "Who da fuck are you?" she proclaimed through a translator bracelet, her emerald eyes narrowing at the end of waving eyestalks.

It turned out the Dracordans didn't care who was in charge of the ship as long as they got paid with raw chicken, Pleiadean muscat, and interspecies BDSM pornography, of which the Bloodhawk had promised them a never-ending supply. This explained the multiple freezers full of chicken meat and kegs of muscat in the galley and the special memory drive labeled "NOT YOUR MOMMA'S PORN" (beside it was another drive labeled "MOM'S PORN" with a picture of the pirate with the laser-scarred face) in an alcove next to the galley.

It was a good thing the Dracordans were there. The only reason the engine room hadn't blown up during the fight over Edzná was because the Dracordans worked in a high-nitrogen, low-oxygen atmosphere which quickly snuffed the fires that broke out. Dirken agreed to continue the terms of their hire and left them to attend to repairs.

More surprising than finding the Dracordans was the discovery of two Reptiloc crewmen hibernating in cocoons in the portside stowage bay. After some debate about whether to kill them as they slept, Dirken reluctantly decided it would be best to build a cell around them. When they awoke a month later, their choice was to serve as crew or be marooned on a Chilean island off the coast. To Dirken's mixed relief, both of them chose to serve. They were impressed by the stealing of the ship, something that rivaled anything the Bloodhawk had managed since they'd been aboard. And besides, they didn't like the smell of Earth air. It probably helped that both of them were male. Female Reptilocs were much more aggressive and likely would have preferred a fight to the death.

In stowage next to the Reptilocs were two dozen crates full of United Worlds military-grade laser cores, the sort used to cut open the hulls of starships. Where the Bloodhawk got them was a complete mystery, but Dirken suspected they may have come along with the barrage bots used against the *Excellentia*.

The next stop was the local alien-human commune of Lupanar, named after its famed bordello, where Dirken got his share of entertainment and alcohol. To his immense pleasure, the bordello had not one, but two Ursan prostitutes. Also known as "space octopuses" to humans, they used their tentacles to massage, stroke, and probe every sensitive organ and orifice, sometimes all at once, with tentacle tips modified both mechanically and genetically to give ultimate sensual stimuli.

As Dirken pursued this rare pleasure, Yiorgos would go to a Cyberalia server temple for communal Netfolding with other cyborgs. He had a lot of meditating to do after the mental invasion by AVA.

Lastly came a visit to Dirken's old friend, Hank the Monkeywrench, a jovial elder human with one tooth who knew Dirken from his street hustling youth on Tesla. Hank was more than happy to help him repair the *Speartip* in exchange for those laser cores, and he fixed Yiorgos's legs and arm.

Despite the extreme pleasures of the bordello, there was still something missing. The Ursans didn't have the softness of lavender fur. Their delights weren't tinged with a warrior's lusty playfulness. And they didn't have eyes that sparkled like amethysts.

The next four months passed in a blur of repairs and frequent trips to Lupanar from the ship for supplies and stimulating entertainment. Soon the *Speartip* was in top shape and ready for new gigs with a couple new weapons arrays, a repaired gravwell generator, and spaceworthy. He couldn't wait to put her through her paces. The first trip would be to Mars to recruit some seasoned crewmen. Dirken reckoned that a corvette of this class could easily outrun most of the United Worlds patrol ships, with her faster sublight speed and a gravwell engine that could spin up quicker. The Bloodhawk had been a ruthless bastard but very smart about his tech and ships. Aquarian centaurs were a famously starfaring species, after all.

In some ways it was better than his last ship, the *Brilliant*. Faster, stronger, better laid out. But a part of him still missed that old clipper of his, as cramped and dingy as it had been inside. It had been better armed and had much more cargo room, too. But he wouldn't miss the little bunk he'd had to sleep in. Aquarian centaurs need a lot of room, and the bed in the *Speartip's* captain's quarters was massive in comparison with plenty of space for himself—and a couple companions.

Then one day, as the last of the summer breezes blew in from the ocean, two small spacecraft appeared overhead and made a beeline for the *Speartip*.

One was a lightly armed yacht, the sort used by high-class corporate types. The other was a fast-attack fightercraft. Just as his new Reptiloc weapons specialist was about to open fire, though, Dirken told him not to engage—but be ready for anything. The fighter was bright yellow. He'd recognize it anywhere. A smile crept over his face.

The visitors circled twice and then landed nearby. Through the viewscreen Dirken saw the cockpit open up and Eow step out. The Pleiadean pilot of the yacht also came out of his ship and stood at attention by its doorway.

Moments later, Dirken and Yiorgos stepped off the *Speartip's* gangplank and met Eow halfway between the ships. She was carrying the same large duffel bag the Heart had been in. *Is it still in there?* he wondered. There was a sizable bulge and weight to it.

"Is that … an *Ananak?*" he said with a smile on his face.

"Is that … a *human?*" she responded immediately. "You are not an easy one to find." She set the duffel down with a thud.

"And you're not an easy one to lose," Dirken rebutted. "How the hell did you find us?"

Eow smiled and ran a claw down Dirken's chest. He shivered as it scraped through his chest hair. "I have my connections," she answered, her words rolling in that silky, bedroom voice he'd found himself dreaming about. "But I will just say that a shipment of laser cores that had been reported stolen by a certain bloodthirsty pirate somehow showed up on the black market at Mars Colony 2."

Damn, he thought. He should have predicted that. He wondered who else had put it together.

"Oh, do not worry," she said after seeing his reaction. "Your secret is safe with me, space jockey. I bought them *all* for Grimmag's fleet and swore the seller to secrecy on pain of death." She looked over toward the *Speartip*. "Besides, it seems you will not be here much longer."

He acted annoyed. "Speaking of starships. I see you brought my fighter back to me."

"Are you accusing me of stealing?" Eow gave an exaggerated look of shock and put her hands on her softly curved hips. "Is that any way to address one of Grimmag Ruby-Eye's made men? In addition to rebuilding his Tantalus III routes after the unfortunate demise of Mindol the Undertaker, I have also taken charge of our efforts here on Earth since Grimmag's lieutenant, Arjun Mukherjee, died so needlessly when the Bloodhawk attacked the Witch's Tits." She flashed a wicked smile. "Odd how the Bloodhawk's laser fire happened to hit him in the head … around a corner."

"You seem to be filling the shoes of *so many* dead people, Eow," Yiorgos said. "Who's next to help you move up the ladder?"

Eow scowled at the cyborg. "Anyone who gets in my way."

"And where is AVA?" Yiorgos asked, unperturbed. He pointed to the duffel bag. "Did you bring her back?"

Eow glanced down at the bag. "No, no. The Heart is safely tucked away, deep in a vault far below the surface of a nameless asteroid. Even I do not know where."

Dirken was astonished. "I figured you or Grimmag would try to ransom it back to the United Worlds!"

"Ransom it?" Eow said. "Not at all! Think about it. AVA's goal was to end conflict, albeit in a controversial way. But conflict is good for business. Wars between pirates, nations, and worlds means weapons sales … and slaves. Trade conflicts make for a thriving black market. Conflict between economic classes means drug sales.

And besides," she turned and looked at Yiorgos, "no one wants some AI hacking into their systems. You never know what it might find in there." She stepped a little closer to the cyborg. "I wonder …" She pointed a claw at his head. "If I were to root around in that mechanical brain of yours, what trace of AVA might I find?"

Yiorgos swatted her hand away. She laughed and stepped back. It was the same lighthearted laugh Dirken had missed.

"So what's in the bag?" Dirken asked.

She smiled. "First, let me answer about the fighter. It is yours. Grimmag gifts it to you. When the Bloodhawk attacked the Witch's Tits and destroyed the hangar, Grimmag vowed revenge." She ran her palm along Dirken's stubbly jawline. "You saved him the trouble of hunting the pirate down. Besides," her hand slipped down his chest to his belly. "I have other fightercraft now and have grown *tired* of this one."

Dirken took a deep breath as her hand crossed his gun belt and slipped down over the bulge of his crotch.

"And the bag?" he croaked, trying not to seem aroused.

She pulled away, much to his disappointment, and reached down to open the bag.

Yiorgos eagerly craned his neck to look inside, then blinked in surprise as Dirken took his turn.

Inside were stacks of United Worlds hundred-chit notes. Dirken whistled.

"Two-hundred and fifty thousand," Eow said. "Just as he had negotiated with you in his Sanctum." She smiled at his bewildered expression. "What? Why are you surprised? Grimmag Ruby-Eye is a businessman first." She lifted her chin and said with pride, "He always follows through with his deals. Besides, you are in his good graces again. In fact, we may have use for you and your new starship. I will gladly hire you to smuggle some goods for us. Or, at least, provide security for our convoys."

Inwardly, Dirken was thrilled with the idea. He hadn't even lifted off and he already had an "in" with the mafia. But no drugs. Not after what he'd seen in the comet.

He hid his enthusiasm. "I don't know … We have some gigs lined up." He turned to look at Yiorgos. "What do you think, partner?"

Yiorgos frowned. "I think we could use another weapons array or two. I say she throw those in."

Eow laughed, her fangs glistening. "How about some laser cores?" She reached back down to the bag and rummaged. "Speaking of weapons …" She pulled out a blaster.

Dirken immediately pulled his blaster and Yiorgos activated his plasma saber.

She laughed it off and held up her hands.

Dirken blinked and took a closer look. "My Gree-tech blaster!" He holstered the weapon he was holding and took a step forward to inspect the one in the bag. It was, indeed, his beloved blaster that had been lost in 'TakTrak's wrecked bridge.

"Another gift for you," she said. "Consider it an advance, if you'll take the job."

"Deal!" Dirken pronounced. Yiorgos sighed loudly, turning his plasma saber back into a hand. "How did you get it?" Dirken asked.

"A Corthian smuggler was cursing your name in a bar on Rigel, so I went over to him and his one-eyed pilot. I asked how he knew you. He wouldn't tell me, but he said this blaster had been yours. So I challenged him to a game of *goron'oc* for it and a bit of cash." She handed the blaster over to him. "He was a very good player," she continued, "but a poor cheater."

The blaster felt so good in his hand. Just the right heft. He turned and aimed it at a tree. The blast splintered the wood, leaving behind a massive, smoking hollow. He felt whole again—*truly* whole—for the first time since the last gig.

"Thank you," he said.

She grabbed the front of his shirt and pulled him close. Her lips pressed against his. Mouth parting. Her rough tongue playing over his.

He put his arms around her and held her, one hand still holding the blaster. The fingers of his other hand ran through the soft, lavender fur of her back. Hard muscles beneath it flexed as she writhed against his chest and belly.

She pulled back, her whiskers tickling his cheek. She gave another light kiss, then purred, "I can think of a better way you can thank me." Her amethyst eyes looked deep into his with a mischievous glint.

"I can think of *several*." He kissed her neck and worked his way up to her ear, then whispered, "We still need to reenact my capture at the pyramid."

She laughed again and ran her hand down to his crotch, this time reaching down into his leather pants and rubbing along his growing erection. "I brought shackles …"

"Oh, brother," Yiorgos said. He hefted the duffel bag and headed for the *Speartip*. "I'll be getting the ship ready for departure."

"Mmm hmm," Dirken muttered, his lips now firmly against Eow's. They dropped to the tall grass of the clearing and started stripping off each other's clothes.

As she pulled off his pants, Dirken looked over at Yiorgos. The cyborg looked back at him as well … and his robotic eye flashed —just as it did at the pyramid with AVA.

For a moment they watched each other, Yiorgos's eye brightening, then it returned to normal and Yiorgos shook his head and blinked. He refocused on Dirken, then smiled at him, laughing at the frolic. All seemed fine again, and Yiorgos boarded the *Speartip*.

Eow turned Dirken's head back to her. "Leave the gunbelt on." She stroked him. Waves of pleasure erased the moment of oddness. She whispered, "I want to feel your weapon against me."

He chuckled and pulled her close to him. Kissed her. Entered her with a satisfied moan as she raked his back with her claws. They rolled through the grass with nothing more than his blaster and gunbelt pressed between their thighs.

Acknowledgments

This book was originally edited by Donovan Reves of Bloomsday Editing & Proofreading, then further edited by GladEye Press.

Thank you to my friend, Adam Breashears, for his generous patronage. Thank you to my beta readers, Ashley Hay and James Lundberg, for their awesome feedback.

Everlasting thanks to my writer's group, the Peeps, who critiqued every word and helped me take my writing to the next level.

About the Author

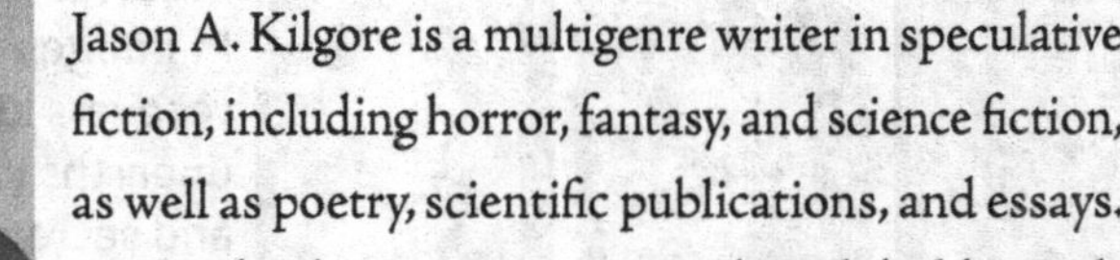 Jason A. Kilgore is a multigenre writer in speculative fiction, including horror, fantasy, and science fiction, as well as poetry, scientific publications, and essays.

By day he is a scientist with a global biotech company specializing in microscopy and cell biology. When he isn't writing, he loves hiking and camping in the mountain wilderness areas of Oregon and along the Pacific Coast.

MORE BOOKS FROM GLADEYE PRESS

Follow the adventures and missteps of time-traveling PI Imogen Oliver as she recovers lost items and unearths long-buried stories and secrets from the past in this exciting series! (*The Time Tourists is available on Kindle Unlimited.)

The Time Tourists Trilogy
Sharleen Nelson

***The Fragile Blue Dot**
Ross West
Veteran science-writer and journalist Ross West's collection of award-winning short fiction touches on the human aspect of living in a world on the brink of ecological disaster.

Quilts of a Feather
Arlene Sachitano
An innocent birdwatching festival hosted by the parks and recreation goes terribly sideways when one of the event volunteers is found dead from a fentanyl overdose on the hiking trail. It's up to amateur sleuth Harriet Truman and her quilt group, the Loose Threads, to solve the mystery?

Join 19-year-old Ben Tucker for a passionate and revolutionary tale of protests, parties, trials, and a band of idealists who set out to build a countercultural utopia in the southern mountains of Oregon.

The Risk of Being Ridiculous Trilogy
Guy Maynard

*Available as an ebook on Kindle Unlimited.

All GladEye titles are available for purchase at
www.gladeyepress.com and your local bookstore.

***Federation of the Dragon**
***Footman of the Ether**
Jason A. Kilgore
Enter the ancient world of Irikara for
high-stakes epic fantasy adventure
in a mythical land filled with dragons
and demons, dwarves and elves,
magic and mages and gods.

***Dye. Run. Don't Die**
K.J. Kolsen
Chased by shadowy figures, Winnie and Jimmy re-
unite somewhere between Oklahoma and Colorado
and embark on a wild ride filled with disguises, stolen
vehicles, murders, truck-stop perverts, a sex-cult,
deadly shootouts, and rediscovered love.

Coastal Coffee Club Mysteries
Patricia Brown

Five cozy mysteries follow retired poet Eleanor Penrose and her band of quirky friends as
they solve mysteries along the Oregon coast.

Dying for Recipies
Patricia Brown
Follow the clues while enjoying twenty-two of Eleanor's
scrumptious, mouth-watering recipes drawn from the
pages of Patricia Brown's charming Coastal Coffee Club
Mysteries series.

COMING in 2025 *from*

Far Side of Revenge
Anne Dean
A fictionalized account of the life of Brian Boroimhe and his rise to King of Ireland.

Black and Tan Fantasy
Randall Luce
In the turbulent and often violent nascent civil rights movement of the Mississippi delta, racial identities, culture, and attitudes collide and shift in this taut drama.

The Extraordinary Voyage of a Tall Ship in a Tiny Pool Far from the Sea
Donovan M. Reves
With gentle absurdity and copious humor, Donovan Reves weaves an exciting adventure yarn with a tender love story all set in a ridiculous landlocked tallship built in a tiny pond. As hard to describe as it is to put down, this tender fable evokes the magic of *The Princess Bride*.

RERELEASES FROM JASON A. KILGORE

Around the Corner from Sanity: Tales of the Paranormal
Fourteen short stories of spine-tingling horror will scare you AND tickle your funny bone!

Guide Me, O River and other poems